HEART

OF
THE

WEST

OTHER COVENANT BOOKS
BY CAROLYN TWEDE FRANK:

Trapped in East Germany

HEART

OF
THE

WEST

a novel

Covenant Communications, Inc.

Cover image: *Woman Wearing a Bonnet in Field* © Magdalena Russocka / Trevillion Images

Cover design copyright © 2018 by Covenant Communications, Inc.
Cover design by Christina Marcano

Published by Covenant Communications, Inc.
American Fork, Utah

Printed in the United States of America
First Printing: January 2018

24 23 22 21 20 19 18   10 9 8 7 6 5 4 3 2 1

ISBN-13: 978-1-52440-495-6

To my husband, Gregory. Thank you for booking a hotel in Craig, Colorado, as part of our 2015 vacation, where we stumbled across the town's cowboy museum and the idea for this series was born. And thanks for humoring me as I veered off on a tangent in my writing career and dipped my toe in the waters of romance writing, and then for taking me seriously when I discovered I loved this new genre and desired to continue writing romance novels.

CHAPTER 1

Western United States, 1895

KATE HADN'T HAD A BATH since the day before she'd fled Long Island. Tired and dirty, she stepped into the empty stagecoach at Baggs, Wyoming and settled into its worn leather seat, anxious for the last leg of this journey to be over. The train ride from New York to Rawlins had been comfortable enough because she'd paid extra for a private compartment. But stagecoaches had no such luxuries. And from what she'd read about the West, neither did anything else out here. It would be tough. She'd need to adjust. But she'd do it. Somehow.

Yesterday, a man and his wife had sat across from her in the coach, bickering constantly, bringing her into the conversation here and there. All the while she tried to maintain a courteous smile as if they were all chatting about the weather. To make matters more difficult, she'd had to turn her face toward the window, more than was polite, to catch a breath of fresh air. The alcohol-thick breath of the man who'd sat next to her had soured her stomach. Her nausea had mounted every time he had sidled closer, asking more times than she cared to count, "What's a pretty gal like you doin' way 'n the heck out here?"

What was she doing out west? Had her decision to leave home been a mistake?

Darwin crept into her thoughts, and she straightened up in her seat. *No! And I am not going back.*

The weathered but kind face of the coach driver glanced through the open door of the stage. "You ready to go, Miss Donahue?"

"Yes, thank you." Kate let out a sigh of relief as the driver shut the door. It looked as though she was going to have the coach to herself today. She peered out the window at the driver, hoping, wanting to confirm this bit of good fortune. "Mr. Mills, am I your only passenger?"

"It looks that way."

"Are there anymore stops before Craig? A chance of picking up more passengers?"

Though it wasn't ladylike, Kate longed to lie down across the bench seat and let the bumps rock her to sleep. She'd gotten very little sleep last night at that boardinghouse the brochure had called a hotel. The mice scurrying to and fro in the rafters had kept her awake much more than the hard mattress had. It had been a long three days—a long week, when she considered everything else that had happened.

"Not much chance of that." Mr. Mills scratched his beard. "You'd be lucky to see a jackrabbit along the road, let alone another human being. This next stretch of road is not exactly what I'd call easy on the eyes. And we're climbing considerably. You'll want to put that coat of yours on." He pointed to the fur wrap she'd kept out of her suitcase to use as a pillow for her journey. It being late August, she hadn't expected to use it for warmth.

"Thank you, I'll do that," Kate said, trying to imagine a landscape more stark than the Wyoming landscape between Rawlins and Baggs. Yet it had held its own unique beauty—miles upon miles of openness, rolling plains, and blue sky that reached on forever. It had lent her a sense of freedom, soaring into a vast wilderness where creatures, both man and beast, were free to spread their wings and do whatsoever their hearts desired.

Kate wrapped her mink stole around her shoulders and propped her handbag on one end of the bench for a pillow. She let down all the leather blinds to keep out the dust and wind, anxious to lie down.

The door to the coach swung open.

Kate sat upright and looked through the opening.

"It appears we will have another passenger to keep you company after all." Mr. Mills held out his hand toward a cowboy who approached the stagecoach.

Frustrated, and chiding herself for her selfish desire to have the coach to herself, Kate stared at the cowboy. He appeared cleaner than the others Kate had met so far. New leather boots, intricately tooled leather gun holster, and a lack of sweat stains on his hat told Kate this man was not the everyday, dirt-poor cowboy. This man had money—or at least came from a family who did. He looked to be in his early twenties like her. His handsome face, slicked-back dark hair, thick mustache with curled ends, and the way he walked toward the coach with head held high, reminded her of Darwin. Her skin prickled at the thought of her ex-fiancé.

Mr. Mills hoisted the cowboy's single bag onto the top of the stage and climbed back down. "Welcome aboard, young Mr. Jones," he said as he motioned for the man to climb inside. "Headed back home, I see."

"Yep."

"Well, enjoy your ride." Mr. Mills smiled as the cowboy stepped inside the coach and caught sight of Kate.

"Oh, now I will." The cowboy sat down across from her and opened the blinds on his side. His mustache covered most of his lips, but his eyes confirmed they were smiling. "Morning, miss." He tipped his hat up slightly and glanced around the coach. "Are you traveling alone?"

"Yes, I am."

"Well, pleased to make your acquaintance, Miss . . . ?"

"Katherine Donahue."

"Miss Donahue. My name is Stanley. Stanley Jones. My pa is Benedict Jones." He paused as if anticipating a reaction to the name.

Kate offered him a cool but polite glance, thinking about how much he looked like Darwin and sounded like Darwin with that better-than-thou annoying voice, hoping that the similarities stopped there. The world didn't have room for two such self-absorbed men.

"Benedict Jones, owner of the Circle J Ranch outside of Craig."

"Sorry, but I am not from around here."

"Ah, I reckon you're not." Mr. Jones held onto his hat as horses whinnied and the stagecoach started forward. "I would've met you before now." His eyes scanned her from head to toe. "That pretty brown hair and those green eyes would be hard to forget. What brings you to Craig, Colorado?"

"How do you know my destination is Craig?" Kate tightened the stole around her shoulders, thinking him a bit presumptuous.

"Because it's the end of the line. John Mills lives in Craig. Tomorrow he'll get up and drive his boss's stage back to Rawlins. And do it all over again in two days. The man is hard as nails to want to make a living like that. Fact is, we all gotta be tough—or crazy—to want to live out here on the high desert of Colorado." He straightened his hat, gazing at Kate. But this time he appeared to be focusing much deeper than on the burgundy traveling dress she wore—he appeared to be thinking.

From the puzzled expression he bore, Kate could guess his thoughts. *Why would an unchaperoned woman, with obvious wealth and upbringing, be traveling alone out here in the heart of the West?*

Because it's about as far away from New York as a girl could get! Kate responded to her own thoughts with more passion than she cared to admit to feeling, and she sat straighter in her seat, pulling her stole even tighter around her shoulders.

Mr. Jones raised his eyebrow. "So . . . are you just coming for a visit, or are you going to join us crazy folks and stay a spell?"

"I don't believe that's any of your business, Mr. Jones."

He laughed and glanced out the window. "If you ask me, I'd say you're running away from somethin'."

Oh, how she wished she could have continued in the coach alone. She wanted nothing to do with men anymore. She didn't want to make trivial conversation with them, act prim and proper, and feign interest in their passions while hers never held a chance of even being mentioned.

"Well, I am not asking you." Kate rolled the blinds up and tied them into place. "And you're quite incorrect, Mr. Jones." She stared out at the bleak landscape. Not a single tree or blade of green grass was out there to remind her that summer still lingered and fall lay around the corner. The last thing she was going to tell this man was her real reason for coming to Colorado. Darwin and her own father had already proven that men struggled with the idea of her being a doctor. She hoped that they would be different out here on the edge of civilization; she hoped the need for a good physician would outweigh their prejudice. But for some reason she feared this man would be no different.

"Really now?" Stanley leaned forward in his seat. "I'm mighty good at knowin' what women are thinkin', so I say I'm right." He leaned back again. "Well . . . if you ever need a man who's good with a gun to watch your back, you just let Stanley Jones here know." He pulled the gun from his holster and tipped the brim of his hat.

Kate startled at the sight of the gun. She composed herself quickly, telling herself again that many things would be different out here in the West; she'd need to get used to it. "Thank you for the offer." She folded her arms tight across her stomach. "But I won't need your help."

"Well, if you change your mind, you just let me know and I'll come runnin'. Everyone in town knows who I am, so you'll have no trouble findin' me." He latched on to the front of his tall cowboy hat. "It's been a long week; been doin' business for our ranch. I hope you don't mind if I catch a little shut-eye." He slouched back, resting his head against the wall of the coach, and pulled his hat over his eyes.

"Not at all," Kate responded in a quiet voice, grateful for the break.

She tried to get comfortable and relax, but every muscle in her body seemed to have stiffened with the arrival of Mr. Jones. The sound of the wheels rolling over the rough road became a welcome relief from the uncomfortable conversation.

Was she running away?

Maybe.

No. She was just pursuing her dream. It was one thing to remunerate her for the fact that her father had paid little attention to her as she'd grown up. His neglect had served her well as she'd attended college and then medical school. He had gladly paid the bill as long as she hadn't bored him with the details and had promised him it wouldn't get in her way of finding a husband. That was . . . until she had graduated. When she'd announced three weeks ago that she was officially a physician and anxious to begin helping people, he'd practically exploded. "That's men's work! You don't need to work; you're a Donahue!"

Her mother hadn't really sided with him, but she hadn't stuck up for Kate's desire either. "Oh, Kate, your place is at Darwin's side, being a dutiful wife and mother, entertaining guests. You're nearly twenty-five; you can hardly afford to lose him."

Kate's hands clenched tighter as she thought about Darwin—the man she had almost married, the man she'd given her heart to and who had sworn he'd felt the same about her, the man she'd assumed would want for her to meet her true potential and work at the things she loved. He'd taken her news worse than her parents.

"No! You can't! What will people think of me, having a wife who insists she's a doctor? Your place is at my side playing the role of a senator's wife—wearing that pretty smile of yours while you entertain dignitaries and assure them of my abilities to govern. In return, I'll play the role of a dutiful husband."

Is that all their marriage would have been, playing roles like actors on a stage? Is that what he'd been doing all through their courtship? She'd always known her strong will had bothered him. Had he been pretending it was merely an "endearing little quirk," while deep inside he was planning on suppressing it once they got married? The darkness in his already black-brown eyes told her that was the case as they had fought their last fight four days ago.

"Fine, you've got your diploma now, but that doesn't mean you have to use it," Darwin had said while standing stiff as a statue in Kate's drawing room, waiting to take her to the theatre. "I'll see to that."

"What is that supposed to mean?" Kate had said, but she'd feared she already knew.

"I have friends in the medical community. I'm sure they'll agree where your rightful place is—and it won't be in any of their hospitals."

"You wouldn't!"

"Oh, yes, I would. It will be my right as your husband. Any well-bred man would agree with me."

"Then I don't want a well-bred man. I'd rather have a destitute peasant, one who loves me for who I am. And that obviously is not you, Darwin. We're through—I'm calling off our engagement."

"You can't break it off," he'd said with panic widening his eyes and etching extra lines in his face. "I need your—you. My political career is just starting. With your beauty by my side, it will only help my chances for success." He'd meant it as a compliment, but it had backfired. She'd seen it for what it was: the truth. He wanted her for her money, her name, and her looks.

She glanced across the jostling coach at Mr. Stanley Jones. Would he—and every other man out west—be like Darwin and all her previous suitors: self-centered creatures that only saw women as a source to feed their stomachs, egos, and sexual desires? It had been the hardest thing she'd ever done, leaving her parents and her privileged lifestyle behind. She knew full well things would be a lot different for her out west, and she was prepared to face the lack of running water, steam heating, and regular bathing. She was prepared to learn how to hitch her own wagon and shovel manure if she had to. She was prepared to let go of her breeding and blend in with the townspeople. But . . . was she prepared for the men to be just like the ones back east?

CHAPTER 2

KATE AWOKE FROM HER LABORED nap, sensing the wheels on the stagecoach slowing down. The glow of a setting sun shone through the gaps where the blinds met the windows, illuminating Mr. Jones's face with a stripe of orange.

With his hat no longer pulled over his face, he was sitting up straight, his eyes locked on Kate's. His lips smiled underneath his mustache. "About time you woke up." He pulled the blinds up and peered out the window. "We're almost to Craig."

"Did you have a good nap, Mr. Jones?" Kate asked, trying to be polite. She'd be living in this town now. It would be best if she made friends right away.

"Please, call me Stanley."

"I prefer using Mr. Jones, thank you."

"Fine, Miss Donahue. And I had a right nice nap, thank you."

The coach slowed dramatically. The smooth roll of the wheels beneath told Kate they were on a groomed road. A whitewashed framed house passed by the window. And then a blacksmith shop. Kate stuck her head out the window slightly to get a better view of the town she was about to call home.

Just before she'd graduated, Kate had read about Craig in a magazine, how investors had drawn up plans for a whole city. They'd sectioned off blocks for homes and a business district in anticipation of an onslaught of homesteaders. Already people were flocking to this new corner of the country for the chance at a piece of the American dream: owning their own land for next to nothing. Accompanying the article had been an ad soliciting "businessmen of all kinds" to come "set up shop" and take advantage of "this migration of families."

The night she'd called off her engagement, that article had come to mind, offering her an avenue of escape. "Doctor" had been one of the professions listed they needed in Craig. Needed. They needed a doctor, and she longed for her skills to be needed. The next morning, when she'd told her parents of her decision to end her engagement, her father had demanded that she crawl back to Darwin, beg his forgiveness, and give up her silly notions once and for all. Her mother had wholeheartedly agreed. With emotions higher than ever, she'd packed her bags while they were away at a luncheon, hired a cab to the train station, and purchased a one-way ticket to Craig.

Looking out on her new home, she just hoped the term businessmen included business women too. Surely, if this town were in need of a physician, as the ad had said, a female doctor would suit them just fine. Shops of varying sizes lay sparsely on each side of the main street, which headed directly into the setting sun. Occasionally one of them rose up out of the dusty road with more than a single story and made from something other than poorly whitewashed wooden planks. Kate slunk back into her seat and pinched her eyes shut, tired of the dust, tired of traveling, and tired of disappointment—the town was smaller than she'd anticipated.

"Not what you expected, huh?" Stanley looked at her with that same hidden smile on his face.

"I thought there'd be more population."

"Oh, there's enough. Most live outside of town. This here's cattle country."

The stagecoach came to a stop. "Craig, Colorado!" Mr. Mills declared from atop the coach in a voice rich with enthusiasm.

Stanley Jones moved swiftly to the door, hopped out, and held out his hand toward Kate. "Allow me."

Kate gathered her mink stole and handbag. Nodding in appreciation, she accepted his hand. It felt cold. "Thank you, Mr. Jones." She let go as soon as she stepped onto the ground. Raising her hand to shield her eyes from the setting sun, she scanned the scant collection of buildings. The stagecoach sat in front of what she assumed to be the town hall by the sign above one of two doors. Apparently it shared the building with the land office. Fortunately, it was a fair-sized structure, though its wooden slates had turned brown from the sun, just as had the grass poking through the dirt at its foundation. "Is there a hotel?"

"Yep." Mr. Jones pointed down a long block to one of the few brick buildings dotting the street. Its red bricks had been laid in meticulous fashion, with arches over the windows of each of its two floors and a decorative border beneath a trim of whitewashed wood at the roofline. "The Craig Hotel is a right nice place for these parts. As soon as John here gets our bags down, I'll take 'em over for you."

As Kate gazed with a measure of relief at the hotel that would have to serve as her home until she could get set up in her own place, a wagon ambled by, blocking her view. It was driven by a mere boy. He looked too young for such a task, his legs dangling from his seat, not able to touch the foothold on the front of the wagon. But he maneuvered the team of horses with obvious skill, reining them into position in front of the stage and bringing it to a smooth stop.

"Good," Stanley said upon spotting the boy. "Logan, hurry and climb up there and fetch my bag." He motioned to the top of the stagecoach with a flick of his wrist. "I don't want to wait for John to quit yakkin' with that mutton-lover. We'll be here all evenin'." He pointed to Mr. Mills, who chatted with a man on the other side of the stage Kate couldn't see. "And while you're up there, toss me down Miss Donahue's things too. There's a steamer trunk, a big bag, and a little black one." He glanced at Kate as if to verify.

Kate nodded, dumbfounded that he'd asked that boy to do something he could easily do himself.

She watched the boy crawl from his perch on the wagon onto the ground with seeming difficulty. Her heart ached for this young boy as his left leg dragged through the top layer of the road's dust while his misshapen but obviously stronger right leg pulled him toward the stagecoach. Using mostly his arms, the boy climbed to the top of the coach quicker than Kate had expected he would.

Kate pointed as the boy grabbed ahold of the small leather bag that carried all of her medical tools. "Here, I'll take that one." She reached up for the bag the boy held over the edge of the coach, planning out in her mind how she'd loop it around her wrist like her handbag so she could drag her steamer trunk with one hand, carry the big bag with the other, and take them to the hotel by herself. There was no way she was going to let Stanley Jones make his crippled young servant carry her load.

"Oh, no, no." Stanley stepped in front of her and grabbed the bag from the boy's outstretched hands. "I'll get that for you, Miss Donahue."

As he lowered the small bag, Stanley bumped his elbow on the door of the coach, causing him to drop it. He hurried and grabbed it from the dirt, dusted it off, and handed it to Kate. "Here, you take this one. It's light. Hopefully, the fall didn't break anything. Then again, what would a lady like you carry other than her pretty clothes and a few pieces of jewelry?"

Kate snatched it from his hands. She hurried and opened it and made a quick survey of her tools. Her stethoscope rested atop a now disheveled stack of clamps and scalpels. Everything else appeared intact. Thank heavens she'd packed her vials of medicine in between the bed sheets in her trunk. She let out a quick breath of relief.

Kate felt Stanley at her back. He was staring over her shoulder and into her bag. She clasped it shut.

"Is that doctor stuff?" Stanley said as if he'd seen the bag filled with nefarious items unfitting for a lady.

"Yes, it is," Kate said, figuring she'd have to tell the men of this town sooner or later. She threaded her arm through its handles and reached up to Logan for her next bag. "And I can get this next bag myself, thank you."

Stanley held out his hand, palm up, motioning for Logan to hold on. "You're a doctor?" He stared at Kate, his single eyebrow—the one that ran across both eyes—furrowed.

"Yes. And if you don't mind, I'd like to get settled. It's been a long trip." She reached up.

Stanley pulled her arms down.

Kate resisted.

"Why would a pretty thing like you want to be a doctor? Especially on the Colorado Plateau? Around here women are as scarce as good grazin' land. You'll find yourself a husband before you can blink an eye."

"Did it ever occur to you that I want to be a doctor?" *And I don't want to find a husband.*

Stanley let out a laugh. "Why?"

"I want to help people."

Stanley's eyebrow furrowed again, but this time offering an expression that told Kate she'd presented a foreign concept.

Kate walked around Stanley to the other side of the stage. "Young man," she hollered up. "Could you please hand me my trunk and other bag over here?"

Logan was there in a second, scooting her trunk to the edge of the railing that held in the luggage. "Are you sure, miss?"

Kate set down her things and reached up. "I'm sure."

"Whoa, hold on there, Logan." Mr. Mills climbed up and moved to Logan's side, grappling for Kate's steamer trunk as Logan let it sail over the railing without tempering the effects of gravity by holding on.

The case dropped into Kate's outstretched arms, propelling her backward. The weight was too much, the angle of her arms too weak. She let it fall to her shoulders. All control vanished. Panic tore at her gut. I can't let it fall! Not with those vials inside.

"Hold on, lass," said a calm voice that seemed to come out of nowhere. "I've got it."

Kate felt the weight lift from her shoulders and her arms freed. She spun around, knowing that voice didn't belong to Stanley Jones. It had an Irish accent—and was too pleasant. The sun shone directly behind the man. All she could see was a silhouette of a man balancing her trunk on broad shoulders as if it were filled with feathers.

"Would ye like me to take yer bags to the hotel, lass?"

Kate didn't think twice. "Yes, thank you, that would be wonderful."

He walked around Kate, reached up, and bade Logan with his available arm to hand him her last bag. As he lowered the bag down, Stanley came around the back corner of the stage.

"You?" Stanley glared at the man. He hurried to Kate's side. "You don't want his help." He reached out and latched on to Kate's doctor bag. "Here," he said, pulling it from her grasp. "Let me and Logan help you with your things."

Kate resisted. "I do want his help. I've already agreed to it." She turned to the man carrying her bag and trunk. The case balancing on his shoulder blocked her view of his face. At the moment she didn't care that she was entrusting her sole belongings to a total stranger, a faceless man with a kind voice; she didn't want Stanley Jones's help. "Sir, would you take those things to the hotel lobby now? I'll meet you there shortly."

"Sure thing!" The man's voice raised slightly, taking on a pitch of elation, and then he headed off.

Kate yanked her doctor bag away from Mr. Jones. "I'll take this, thank you very much." She turned toward the hotel, staring at the gentleman carrying her bags. He appeared much shorter than she'd first thought, nearly a head shorter than Mr. Jones. But his broad shoulders and the seeming ease with which he carried her things communicated much more strength than Stanley's tall, slender frame. And the soft curls of strawberry-blond hair at the nape of his neck added a sense of softness to his muscled frame, leaving Kate with a pleasant impression.

Stanley stepped in front of Kate, blocking her view of the man and her things. "You don't want to waste your pretty eyes on him now." His lip curled up. He looked over his shoulder at the back side of the man. "He's a mutton-lover." He turned back to Kate. "And an ornery recluse that isn't man enough to accept it when his wife leaves him. I've got tick-infested bulls back at my ranch that'd be better company than McCurdy there."

"He's merely carrying my luggage for me, Mr. Jones." Kate turned on her heel to skirt around him and scurried toward the hotel, anxious to leave Stanley Jones behind her.

By the time she caught up to the man Mr. Jones had referred to as McCurdy and a mutton-lover—whatever that was supposed to mean—he was stepping onto the wooden sidewalk in front of the hotel. "Hold on, Mr. McCurdy," Kate called out. She wanted to see the face of the man who had been so kind but had been touted as an ornery recluse.

He turned around.

Kate gazed into his face and gulped. Though the sun had now set, leaving the main street of Craig in muted shades of browns and grays, his face touched her senses in full color. Strawberry-blond curls framed clean-shaven skin that had seen its share of days in the sun. A wisp of pink kissed his full lips and cheeks, making them stand out more than his small rounded nose. His deep tan accentuated his eyes—eyes that drew Kate in with their brilliant shade of blue. But there was something more than the color in those eyes that drew Kate in, a hint of something deep inside the man that endeared him to her: sadness.

"Yes, Miss Donahue," he spoke her name with seeming confidence.

"I'd like to pay you for your trouble," she said, wondering how he knew her name. He must have been listening to her and Mr. Jones back at the stagecoach. Or perhaps Mr. Mills had mentioned her name.

"'Tis no trouble at all, Miss Donahue." He set down the bag and, with the case still on his shoulder, opened the door and motioned for Kate to enter the hotel.

"But I insist." Kate had budgeted for such gratuity. In New York she had grown so accustomed to it. But how much was customary out here? What was customary out here? She felt awkward and out of place already.

Mr. McCurdy stepped into the hotel behind her and deposited her things by the front desk. "Campbell," he hollered into a back room. "Ye've got a customer waiting out here." He turned to Kate and gazed into her eyes, sending a flush of warmth to her face.

Kate tore her eyes away from his gaze and fumbled with her handbag, struggling to extract her coin purse.

He held out his large calloused hand, palm up. "Please, no. Allow me this privilege." He turned to leave.

"Yes, miss, can I help you?" A deep voice pulled Kate's attention behind the front desk. A middle-aged man with a thick crop of dull brown hair and a pencil-thin mustache held a pen in hand and an expression of anticipation on his face.

"I need a room for tonight," Kate said and then remembered this wasn't just a weekend getaway. The reality that she was on her own nearly two thousand miles from home with only her small savings to get her by until she could establish her practice hit her like a bolt of lightning from a summer storm. "Actually, I'm not sure how many nights."

"No problem, miss." The man Kate assumed to be Campbell pushed a ledger across the counter. "Just sign here by the X. It'll be a dollar a night. You're welcome to stay as long as you'd like." He placed a key on the countertop. "I'll put you upstairs in room three. Head on up, and I'll be up shortly with your things."

"Thank you so much, Mr. . . . uh?"

"Tucker. Campbell Tucker."

"Thank you, Mr. Tucker," Kate said. Wanting to be polite, she made a quick glance around the lobby that maybe would fit three or four other people then added, "This is a very nice place you have."

"Oh, it's not all mine." He scratched his mustache. "My brother owns most of it, and he pays me to manage it. He's the one that laid out the streets of this town and built his hotel. That was just three years ago."

"Well, it's very nice," Kate said, looking again at the cramped lobby, apprehensive at its size but appreciating the workmanship of the wooden staircase and railing. "Thank you again," she said, realizing there was someone else she should have thanked. She darted to the door. Outside on the wooden sidewalk, she planted her feet and scanned the dimming street for Mr. McCurdy.

He was nowhere to be seen. Kate felt like dropping down onto the rough wooden planks and crying but held fast to the doorframe. Why?

Her distress must have been caused by the long trip. It had to be. And all that had preceded it.

Leaving her family and inheritance behind so she could be free to live her own life was not going to be easy.

But she could stand on her own two feet without anyone's help—except for God's. She was strong. *I can do this.*

CHAPTER 3

PINK ROSES ADORNED THE PITCHER Mrs. Tucker had set on the dresser last night after Kate had retired to her hotel room. She poured water from another pitcher into a matching porcelain bowl and splashed her face with it. She was definitely awake now. Warm water would have been preferred, but such luxuries lay behind her now. She refused to let her thoughts dwell there. She wouldn't go back.

She couldn't go back.

Not after the scene with her parents when she'd announced her breakup with Darwin. The pain still jabbed at her heart as she remembered their words.

"You must marry Darwin," her father had said in that stern, grating voice she disliked so much.

Mother's voice had been softer but still hurt. "What will our friends think?"

"You don't want to be spinster, do you?"

"Darwin is correct; being a doctor is not acceptable."

"I refuse to let you do it!" Her father had been adamant. "If you insist on being a doctor, then I insist on withholding your inheritance. You'll be all on your own."

"Fine, I prefer it that way!" Kate had said before she'd stormed out of the spacious drawing room of their Long Island mansion.

That afternoon she had left her parents a note: *I am giving up my inheritance and leaving for a place where my skills as a physician are welcomed. Please don't come looking for me.* She had told the servants she was going shopping. That, in part, was true. She'd gone shopping for all her travel arrangements.

And now she was here, in the most remote corner of the United States she could ever imagine, without a penny of her inheritance, only one thousand dollars she'd withdrawn from the savings account her grandfather had set up for her years ago. She'd pulled it out of the bank as a mixture of coin and bills before she'd booked her train ticket.

Taking the key from the bed stand, she lowered onto her knees. She withdrew a jewelry box from beneath the bed and unlocked it. The thousand dollars looked like a lot of money, stuffed in a space the size of a big loaf of bread, filling every corner. But she knew it wouldn't last forever, especially after she ordered an exam table from back east and the remaining instruments she'd need to set up her practice. And then there would be rent. And a bathtub—that was a must. There would invariably be other expenses too, ones she wasn't aware of at the moment. She pulled out a five-dollar bill, locked the box, and slid it back beneath the bed.

For now she needed to live. When she had run into Mr. Tucker on her way back from the privy this morning, he had mentioned that his wife served their guests breakfast and supper for a nominal fee added to their bill. That left her on her own for lunch—or dinner, as she had found they called that meal here. She hoped Craig had a good, inexpensive place to dine. While she was out and about, she would buy some supplies she needed, maybe even see if they had a library in town. She grabbed her purse, stuffed the five dollars inside, and headed for the stairs determined to make her money last, determined to make the best of her new life.

At the top of the stairs, Kate let out a hiccup born of the ache deep inside her that refused to die. Everyone's attempts to control her life were one thing; she could push that pain to the side easily enough. But not the scar left on her heart from Darwin. She had loved him. But he had never really loved her, apparently. To him their marriage would have been one of convenience, position. The now-familiar pain tearing at her insides jabbed her again. When he had begged her to stay with him, the invitations had already been sent. He had sniveled through tears that had to have been formed by fear, claiming that he couldn't go on without her. Then he had switched tones and told of his "concern" that she would end up being nothing without him. But not once had he mentioned the reason she was waiting to hear, the reason that might have kept her in New York: Stay because I love you.

It was at that moment she'd known he didn't love her, only the position that came from marrying her. She could see no affection in his eyes as he'd begged, nor hear it in his voice. Love had never been part of his equation. How could she have been so blind?

It wouldn't happen again. She refused to have a loveless marriage like her parents.

What was she thinking? She was never getting married. Not now. Not ever. She didn't need a man.

Kate scurried down the stairs, anxious to start her day. She was going to pour her heart and soul into setting up a medical practice in this little town in the heart of the West. And she was going to do it alone. No more trying to please everyone else while her own dreams slipped away.

She passed through the lobby and into the dining room. A long table lined with ten chairs filled most of the room, but not a soul was to be seen. Seating herself at one end of the table, she scooted her chair in and looked around. The chatter of children filtered in from behind a set of swinging doors, along with the smell of frying bacon. Kate figured Mrs. Tucker must feed her children in the kitchen before she attended to her guests. She smiled at yet another difference here in Craig, but she liked this one.

The kitchen door swung open. Mrs. Tucker stuck her head into the room and looked at Kate. Blonde wisps of hair strayed from the bun atop her head and into her tired but kind-looking eyes. "Just let me finish feeding my brood and I'll have your breakfast right out." A few minutes later she came through the door backward, pushing it open with her hip. She swung around and placed a tray of flapjacks, scrambled eggs, and a strip of bacon in front of Kate. "If'n this isn't enough, just holler."

"This will be wonderful, thank you," Kate said, anxious to eat. She hadn't had a good meal since the train. When the woman turned to leave, Kate pointed to the empty table. "Are there no others?"

"Just you." The woman inched toward the kitchen.

"Please, could you stay a little longer? I'd love your company," Kate said with sincerity. It wasn't only because she needed to find out as much as possible about this town and its people so as to help her set up her practice—she felt alone.

Mrs. Tucker's cheeks flushed a light shade of pink. "Ah, I'm not good company. Just ask my husband." She hesitated and then slipped into the chair next to Kate's. "But I s'pose my legs do deserve a rest. My girls are all fed, and the dishes can wait."

Kate sighed with gladness. "Tell me about Craig," she asked as she lifted a fork of eggs to her mouth.

"Not much to tell. The winters are long and cold, and the summers are dusty. And it's a right poor spot for a hotel. And if'n my husband didn't have our little bit of savings invested in this blasted place, and we had somewhere else to go, I'd haul my four little ones out of here in a heartbeat. To a place with a school, and more fitting for girls."

"I'm sorry to hear that."

Mrs. Tucker raised an eyebrow. "Are you planning on staying here or something?"

"Yes, I am. I plan on opening a medical practice here in Craig." Kate wondered what the woman meant by a "poor spot for a hotel."

"A what?" Mrs. Tucker twisted her face.

"I'm a doctor, and I want to serve the people of Craig and the Yampa Valley." She hoped she'd said the name right, only having learned about the river valley in a magazine article. "I read that this community was in need of a doctor and decided this would be a good place to come and set up my practice."

"Well, Miss . . . Donahue, isn't it?"

"Yes, but please, just call me Kate." That seemed to be the way they did things out here—using one's first name.

"Well, Miss Kate, I hate to tell you this, but we've already a doctor in these parts."

Kate held back a gasp. "Craig already has a doctor?"

Mrs. Tucker gazed at the ceiling as if visualizing the doctor who had just put a road block in Kate's way. "Yep, Doc Greene. But then he's the sheriff too, and getting old, so most likely he could use the help. And from what I hear, he's got the bedside manner of a badger. But I wouldn't know, 'cause I keep to myself and doctor my girls with my own remedies. I don't need no horse doctor telling me how to make a poultice and use it." She reached out and patted Kate's hand. "Maybe you'll do okay here after all."

"Thank you." Kate took another bite of eggs. She had a hard time getting them down, and not because they weren't tasty.

"But then again, maybe you won't," Mrs. Tucker said. "I think I could take my girls to see you, if'n they needed more doctoring than I could give them. But I know Mr. Tucker would have a hard time with going to see you. In his mind, women have their places, and they should stick to them. He'll let me cook for our guests and clean their rooms, all right, but do you think he'd ever let me check a guest in, order in supplies, or give any input on how to improve the hotel? No, siree!"

Mrs. Tucker rose from the table, glancing at Kate with an I'm-so-sorry look. "Unfortunately, my guess is that most men in these parts think the same as my Campbell. Good luck, Miss Kate."

CHAPTER 4

THERE WAS A BIT OF a chill in the morning air. Kate rubbed her arms and stomped her way across the street from the hotel to the R. H. Hughes Mercantile. Men! Her chat with Mrs. Tucker a few minutes ago had dashed her hopes—momentarily. But now she was determined to push forward. What kind of doctor volunteers to be the sheriff? How could he possibly do both jobs well? He couldn't! She would set herself up a decent office, throw herself into her work, and prove to the people of Craig—and their bullheaded men—that she was just as good of a doctor as any man. Most likely better than this Dr. Greene who, according to Mrs. Tucker, had poor bedside manner and whom she'd referred to as a "horse doctor."

Had she meant that literally?

It didn't matter either way. But she would hold fast to hope—hope that at least a few men out here in the West could accept a woman doctor. After all, they were quite accepting of other things: no running water, sheriff–veterinarian–doctors, and sporadic mail service.

When Kate stepped into the store, she welcomed the heat radiating from the potbelly stove sitting in the middle of the room. Behind the counter on the right side of the store, a balding man with glasses and a long nose assisted a large man with dirty cowboy boots. On closer inspection, Kate noticed the large man's pants, shirt, and face were dirty as well.

Kate chewed her lip to stop from passing judgment, reminding herself she hadn't bathed since before she'd left home. With no running water in the hotel, taking a bath would be a chore—though Mrs. Tucker said there was a tub to be had and she'd haul the hot water up. Her mind called up scores of people she'd seen here in Craig or along her journey to get here, each going about their lives in dirty clothes. And what did it matter? It didn't—she was sure they were lovely people on the inside. Darwin, on the other hand, never wore a soiled shirt a day in his life—at least not longer than it took to remove it after spilling a spot of wine upon it, or a dribble of caviar. He had dozens more in his closet. These people . . . well, Kate had the feeling that some of them might be lucky to have one change of clothes. That thought made her heart ache for them. Yet they seemed happy.

She strolled past shelves lining the other side of the store, determined to be tight with her limited funds. If these people could make do with so very little and wear smiles on their faces, so could she. They were an inspiration to her.

Surveying bags of flour and boxes of baking powder, she knew these were the kinds of items she'd buy when she set up her household, which hopefully would be soon. Living in the hotel for an extended period of time would not be a good use of her funds. She needed her own place and to survive like everyone else did out here—by making her own food. A smile crossed her lips as she remembered with reassurance her constant visits to the kitchen against her mother's wishes, and how she'd insisted on learning the most basic of skills from their cook.

"Can I help you?" a pleasant female voice said.

Kate turned.

A short jolly-faced woman, who stood almost as wide as she was tall, gazed at Kate. "You're not from these parts, are you?"

"No, I arrived yesterday on the stagecoach."

"Really now? What brings a young lady like you to Craig? You come here with your husband—he got himself a job at one of the ranches?"

"No, I came alone. I'm not married."

The woman scanned Kate from her expensive trilby hat down to her patent leather shoes with pointed toes. "You don't look the type to be a mail-order bride."

"A mail-order—oh," Kate responded, a little rattled by the woman's assumption. She quickly suppressed the urge to be offended. The woman obviously meant no ill will. "No, that's not why I came."

"Then what? What brought you here?"

Though feeling a bit awkward, Kate thought she may as well let people know why she was here—put her shingle out, so to speak. "I read that the town was looking for a doctor, so I came with the hopes I could fill that need." Kate looked down at the heels on her shoes. *Much too fancy for this place. Buy yourself a more practical pair.* She brought her eyes up. "I'm looking for a place I could set up my office. If you happen to know of any, I'd very much appreciate any leads." Back in New York she would have hired an agent to find her a place, but she feared she'd have a harder time locating one of those than she would an office or an apartment.

"Well, don't that beat all?" The lady laughed. "A woman doctor. Old Doc Greene's got some competition. Good golly, ain't that wonderful!" She looked over to the bald man, now at the cash register. "Hey, Sam, this here single gal says she's a doctor and wants to set up shop here. Do you know if anyone's got a spot they'll rent out to her?"

Kate felt her face flush. She'd hoped to have the woman share some suggestions in a quiet corner of the store. "I only need a small space," Kate said as if to quell the awkward feeling filling the store. It didn't help.

The man with the long nose looked up from the cash register, peering through the glasses that rested halfway down his long nose. "Maybe check with Harlow Forbes over at the land office—he's got more space than he needs. Can't say if he'll sublet some of it or not, but I can give you a bit of advice. Doctorin's a man's job. You might want to try out East if you really want to undertake such a foolhardy task. But if you want to stay here, there's men aplenty from which to choose a husband. Pick one, settle down, and let him take care of you."

The big man with the dirty pants got his change from the shopkeeper and turned to face Kate. "Sure enough. I manage the Double Bar Ranch, down the road a piece on the way to Hayden. I know at least six of my ranch hands would gladly take on that task." He tipped his hat at Kate and exited the store.

If the big man's statement was meant to make Kate feel good, he'd missed his mark. "Thank you, anyway, uh, Mr. and Mrs. Hughes," Kate said.

"What?" The man with the glasses wrinkled his brow.

"I just . . ." Embarrassment tripped her words. "I mean, I assumed from the name on the front of your store that you two would be Mr. and Mrs. Hughes."

"Ah, R. H. Hughes Mercantile Inc. . . ." The jolly, round woman was at Kate's side now. "We're just one in the chain of stores he's got scattered through western Colorado. We're the Deckers. I'm Lavender." She motioned to her husband.

"M' name's Sam. We just manage the place; we don't own it."

Does anyone own their own business here? First there was Mr. Mills. He didn't own the stagecoach; he just drove it. Then there was Mr. Campbell, who managed the hotel for his brother, owning just a very tiny portion of the place. Now she found the R. H. Hughes Mercantile was run by Mr. and Mrs. Decker. More and more, Kate felt as though that magazine article had been luring people to Craig with false advertising. And she'd been pulled in. If these folks couldn't make it on their own, what hope did she have?

Kate bit on her lip to calm her jittering nerves. "Well, it's a very nice store you run." She handed Mr. Decker her list. "So . . . could you help me find these items?"

As Mr. Decker pulled items from the shelves, Mrs. Decker guided Kate by the elbow to the far end of the counter. She straightened a display of soap bars, bringing one of them to her nose and then holding it out for Kate to smell. "Right nice fragrance." She set the bar on top of the others on the display and patted Kate's arm. "Don't let our words discourage you none, miss."

"My name's Kate."

"Kate it is," Lavender said with a nod. "Like I was saying, Kate, don't let no one discourage you. I think it's a fine thing, you being a woman doctor. I'll come to you when my rheumatism acts up this winter."

"Thank you, ma'am." Kate felt a small thrill at the prospect of her first patient. She picked up a bar of soap. "Add this to my box too."

"Sure thing." Lavender took the soap again. "You need to meet our Roselund."

Mr. Decker turned an ear in their direction. "Now hold on there, Lavender, our girl don't need any more encouragement with her crazy ideas."

"Oh, hush." Mrs. Decker flicked her wrist at her husband. "Just get the lady's things. We're enjoying a little girl talk here. I get so very little of it in this town." She handed her husband the bar of soap and then wrapped an arm around Kate and ushered her to the farthest corner of the store. "Our Roselund could definitely use a bit of female companionship. Since we've moved to this town, she's seen fit to toss most of her dresses in exchange for men's trousers. I can't say I blame her, living way out here. But it really pains her pa that she's taken that even further and works as a ranch hand, breakin' broncos out at the Hoy Ranch. If you could maybe get to know her and have some of your fine manners rub off on her, we'd be beholden to you. I could maybe even talk Mr. Decker into coming to you next time he needs doctoring."

Kate and Mrs. Decker continued talking, moving from the new bolts of fabric that had just arrived to the harsh winters of the high desert. Kate enjoyed the woman's pleasant company. It infused her with a grain of hope that she could make herself at home with the people here in Craig.

Meanwhile, the store took on two new customers, each seeking Mr. Decker's assistance, thus delaying his filling her list. Kate didn't really mind. It was so nice to have a woman to talk to who actually showed interest in what Kate was saying.

A third customer walked through the door. His strawberry-blond curls and suntanned face caught Kate's eye. Mrs. Decker's words became noise in the background.

"So you know Lucas McCurdy?" Mrs. Decker leaned forward and looked Kate in the face to get her attention, blocking Kate's view of the man.

"Oh, no," Kate said, a little too fast. "He just helped me with my luggage yesterday when I arrived on the stage."

"That's interesting. Lucas usually keeps to himself. Only comes into town about once a month for supplies."

"So it's been about a month since you saw him last?" Kate asked, her curiosity piquing for some reason.

"Yep. I figured he'd be in here soon. Sure enough, he dropped in yesterday with a long list. Stocking up for winter, I daresay. Probably here to pick up his goods and then head out to his place."

"What about his wife?" Kate couldn't believe she'd just asked that. Was she really going to probe this woman to find out if what Stanley Jones had said was true?

"He don't have a wife. Leastways not one living with him. I met her a few times. Nasty woman, she was. Excuse me for gossiping, but sometimes a mean-spirited woman deserves it. She couldn't tolerate the winters out here. Up and left him two years ago this September. Took their little girl with her. Nearly broke the man's heart right in two. Hasn't said two words to me since—or anyone else, for that matter. Except to order his supplies, mind you."

Mr. Decker acknowledged Lucas's arrival with a slight raise of his fingers. "I'll be right with you, Lucas. Just let me finish up with these customers first."

Mr. McCurdy gave a nod, eyeing the merchandise. He strolled away from the counter in Kate's direction. His eyes moved from a display of lanterns to Kate. He hesitated for a moment as their eyes locked in recognition.

Mrs. Decker patted Kate's hand, pulling Kate's gaze from Lucas McCurdy. "It's been a delight talking to you, Kate. I'd better go help Sam." She winked as she slipped past Kate and Mr. McCurdy.

"Good mornin.' So . . . is Kate short for Katherine?" Mr. McCurdy's gentle Irish voice pulled Kate's attention back to him.

"Oh! Were you speaking to me?" Kate asked, amazed that this man of whom she knew so little—only that he was an ornery social recluse—was talking to her.

"Who else, lass?" He glanced from side to side at the shelves of flour and then grinned at her.

The way his lip curled up more on one side of his mouth than the other made her smile. She covered her mouth. "Yes, Kate is short for Katherine."

"Katherine." He said the name like it was a delicious chocolate on his tongue as he gazed at the ceiling. He brought his eyes back down to meet hers. "The name fits you. 'Tis a lovely name."

"Lucas," Mr. Decker called out. "I can help you load up your wagon now."

Mr. McCurdy tipped his hat to Kate. "Thank ye for letting me help ye yesterday. I do hope ye shall enjoy living here in Craig." He gave her another lopsided grin and followed Mr. Decker toward the back door.

"Kate," Mrs. Decker said, motioning for her to step over to the counter. "We've got your things ready."

Kate walked slowly over to the counter, her eyes refusing to move away from the back door. As she reached the counter, Mrs. Decker practically had to stuff her box filled with crackers and sundries into Kate's hands.

"Well, I declare, young Lucas McCurdy has changed since the last time I laid eyes on him. I'm glad for him." She punched some buttons on the cash register, causing a ding and the drawer to pop open. "That'll be fifty cents." As Mrs. Decker reached for the five-dollar bill Kate offered, she leaned over the counter close to Kate's ear. "I can see it in your eyes, girl, and the way you look at him. The Lord knows he deserves a good girl like you. But remember, he's still a married man. Unless, of course, he got himself a divorce. You might want to check with Mr. Smith here in town. He's an attorney. Set up shop two years ago like you're fixin' to do. You might want to talk to him; see if Lucas has talked to him."

"Thank you, Mrs. Decker," Kate said, to be gracious. She had no intention of pursuing Lucas McCurdy. Whether he was unmarried or otherwise.

CHAPTER 5

AFTER SPEAKING WITH MR. FORBES at the land office about subletting the back room of his building and receiving an "I'll think about it," Kate walked toward Ronald Smith's office. It had be three days since she'd learned of Mr. Smith from Lavender Decker. Was it a good idea to see this attorney?

Kate assured herself it was. Today's visit had nothing to do with Lavender's suggestion concerning Mr. McCurdy. She was simply going to ask him about how he went about setting up his office and establishing his business. If Lavender was correct, he'd seen a similar ad, and most likely had been lured here to Craig like her. He certainly wasn't from around here—at least his wing-tipped shoes and well-tailored suit weren't.

The Smith Law Office was a narrow building sandwiched between a gun-smith shop and a saloon. Ironic. Before she stepped inside, she peered through the window, checking out the man she assumed was Ronald Smith. He sat behind a desk, writing furiously on a paper tablet. He wore a dark suit with a white shirt and gray tie and appeared to be in his mid-twenties. His brown hair was as drab as the expressionless look in his brown eyes, and his face held no features that would make him stand out in a crowd. All in all, his appearance was as plain as his name. And he didn't look the least bit intimidating. A cowboy emerged from around a partition that separated the office from the entry. He sauntered toward the attorney and sat down in a chair at the front of his desk. Kate opened the door anyway, hoping she wouldn't have to wait long.

She could hear them talking as she walked in, the partition being thin and barely five feet tall, if that. She'd know that voice anywhere. Stanley Jones. She paused in the entry, not letting her presence be known.

"I'll tell you again, Mr. Jones." Ronald Smith spoke in a voice as devoid of features as his appearance. "I am the wrong person to help you with your dispute over grazing rights. You need to take that up with the government. Perhaps Mr. Forbes at the land office could be of more help."

"I already talked to him. He was as worthless as you." Stanley's voice held that same arrogance that had gotten under Kate's skin in the stagecoach. "Isn't there anyone that can help get our grazing land back from that sheep-farmer McCurdy?"

Kate gasped at the mention of Mr. McCurdy and startled backward. Her elbow hit the flimsy partition, bringing both men's attention to focus on her.

Stanley turned around and stood. "Well, well, if it's not the lovely Miss Donahue." He motioned for her to step around into the office space at the same time that Ronald Smith rose, pushing his chair back awkwardly as he came around his desk with his arm outstretched.

"Uh . . . uh . . . good morning, miss." Ronald Smith glanced at Stanley. "I believe there is nothing more I can do for you, Mr. Jones. Now if you'll excuse me, it appears I have another client to attend to." He gazed now at Kate as if she was something he rarely saw but wished he could see more of.

"Hold on there, Ron. Me and this little lady go way back, so don't get any ideas of honing in on my territory."

Kate bristled. "I don't recall ever giving you any indication that I was your territory." She turned to Mr. Smith, inching closer, placing her hand gently on his arm. She could feel it twitch under her fingers. "Mr. Smith, may I have a word with you in private?"

"Uh . . ." Mr. Smith appeared somewhat ruffled with her request. "Certainly," he managed to say. He nodded to Stanley and then to the door.

"I'm goin', I'm goin'." Stanley headed for the door, but not before winking at Kate and whispering out of the side of his mouth, "See you around."

"Unlikely," Kate said quietly through clenched teeth.

"Uh . . . what can I do for you?" Mr. Smith pulled the chair Stanley had been sitting in around to a better position for her to sit down.

"First, let me introduce myself. That might help me describe better what I need. My name is Katherine Donahue." She went on to describe how she'd seen the ad in the magazine and had chosen to come out west to set up her practice on the premise that they were in need of a doctor here in Craig.

His face expressed neither excitement nor distaste at her mention of being a doctor. That was a good sign. She hoped. She rambled on, feeling awkward with his stoic manner. Maybe this hadn't been such a good idea. "Well, Mr. Smith, you see—"

"Please, call me Ronald." It was the first thing he had said since she'd started her story.

"Well, you see . . ." She paused. It felt improper to use this man's given name—she'd barely met him. But maybe that's how they did things out west—

called even the opposite sex by their first names. "Ronald, I had heard that you came here based on the same hope, or misleading information, as I did—you too had learned that this new town was booming and was seeking professional people like doctors and lawyers to come and be part of the community. I was hoping that you could give me some tips on how I might set up my practice and/or get started, because obviously you're doing well."

"Well, Miss Donahue . . ." He paused, looked her in the eye for a moment, and then glanced away, staring at the bookshelf behind her. "I wish I could be of more help," he said slowly and without rise or drop in pitch. "But I really didn't set up this office. I didn't actually see an ad like you did. My uncle is one of the investors of this new town. He's the one who talked me into coming here." His words began to flow with less effort. "He told me he'd set me up in an office and pay me a little stipend until business trickled in. But I had to promise him I'd stick it out for at least three years. I've been here two. Not sure I can last another one. It's awfully lonely out here." He cleared his throat and stared now at his clasped hands on the desk. "Without my family, that is. You know, all my brothers and sisters and parents are back in Chicago. And business isn't the best. Out here, people take the law into their own hands. They settle things with guns, not lawyers." Now that she had him talking, it was as if he didn't want to quit. It was as if he'd thirsted for someone who could understand what he was going through, and now he'd found a kindred spirit. "It took me three months before I got my first case. And then I wasn't even able to help poor Lucas McCurdy."

Kate sat up straight in her chair. She brought her wandering mind back and focused on Ronald Smith's words. Lucas McCurdy? She bit her tongue from spilling his name out in surprise. "Uh . . . if you don't mind me asking, what happened?"

"Do you know the man?"

"No, I just arrived four days ago."

"Yes, yes, I knew that. Sorry. Well, I suppose I can tell you. The whole town knows, and you'll know about it sooner or later."

"Knows what?"

"His wife up and left him and took their little girl with her. After hurting for a year, I guess he figured he'd better get on with his life. At least that's what he told me when he came in to file for a divorce last year. When I had her served with the divorce papers, I assumed it would be no problem because it was no secret that she hated it out here. Homesteading didn't suit her well. But she surprised both me and Mr. McCurdy by refusing to sign them."

Kate couldn't rein in her curiosity. "Why?"

"I wish I could tell you." Ronald Smith stood. "And I wish I could have helped you with some advice on getting settled. I'm not really very good at much. No wonder no one needs my services." He escorted her to the door. "I wish I could visit longer, but I do have an appointment." He glanced around the partition. Kate looked too and noticed a large man with a clean cowboy hat. And a badge on his shirt. The sheriff. The doctor.

"But . . . uh, I would love to talk . . . some more." The sense of awkwardness had returned to his voice.

"Maybe sometime," Kate said, anxious to go now. But how would she get out the door without passing the big man with the badge, the one with the bedside manner of a badger? She stared at her feet and inched toward the door.

"Good morning, Sheriff Greene. You can come in now. Miss Donahue is just leaving."

The sheriff walked past. Kate could tell by the large boots scuffing across the wooden floor. She kept her face down but lifted it when Mr. Smith said, "Oh, Sheriff, this is Miss Kate Donahue. She's wanting to set up an office, she's a doc—" He cut his words short and sent Kate a nervous glance.

"Yes, a doctor. I already got wind of that," Sheriff Greene said in a rough voice. "Look me in the eye, gal."

Kate brought her eyes up—she refused to let this man intimidate her. The acne-scarred face of the sheriff was endowed with a large nose that looked like a plump, red plum.

A smile could barely be seen under his bushy, white mustache. "You're as pretty as they say. And you want to be a doctor, do you? In this here hole-in-the-wall?" He let out a laugh that rattled the front window. "Go right ahead, missy. But I gotta warn ya, you'll grow even skinnier than you already are. Why do you think I took on the job of sheriff? Folks around here got no money. You'll be lucky if they pay you in eggs. That's on a good day." He plopped down in the spare chair. "Hey, personally, I'm glad you're here. I can use the help. But unfortunately," he turned his back to her, "I doubt most men in these parts are as open-minded as me."

CHAPTER 6

KATE WIPED HER FEET ON the mat before entering the hotel. She wished she could wipe away the day's frustrations as easily as the mud had slipped from the bottom of her shoes. Yesterday, when she'd proposed the idea of subletting the back room of the land office, Mr. Forbes had sounded open to the idea. Today, however, he had exhibited the temperament of a boiler fire—it was probably best she didn't rent from him anyway. She'd just keep looking.

In stark contrast from her meeting with Mr. Forbes half an hour ago, Mr. Tucker greeted her with a warm smile. "Ah, Miss Donahue, you have a letter." He pulled an envelope out from room number three's cubby and handed it to her.

"Thank you." Kate accepted it graciously, but underneath she was wary. Had her parents discovered her whereabouts? A time or two, she had considered writing her mother just to say she was okay. For certain, she'd not include a return address. But the fear of her mother finding her and somehow forcing her to return to New York prevented her from writing that letter. She wasn't strong enough—in that way—to write a letter yet. Craig didn't feel like home.

She hurried and opened the envelope and unfolded the single sheet of paper it held. A quick glance at the letterhead brought a sigh of relief. Though she was a bit confused at seeing what appeared to be legal correspondence from Mr. Ronald Smith.

Dear Miss Katherine Donahue,

I am herewith requesting the pleasure of your company to join me for dinner at the Sunny Saloon, 590 West East Yampa Avenue. I will stop by the Craig Hotel at 6:00 P.M. to obtain your response. If you are amenable to this proposal, you can let me know at that said time, and we will promptly proceed to the aforementioned establishment.

Sincerely,

Ronald H. Smith

She held in an amused chuckle. Mr. Smith's apparent intent to court her almost endeared him to her. But at the same time his offer sounded as inviting as spending the evening with a dry tumbleweed on the barren hills east of town. A quick glance at the clock behind the front desk told her Mr. Smith would be here in about five minutes. Her brain scrambled for a polite way to refuse his offer.

As Kate deliberated whether to wait for Mr. Smith in her room or just stay in the lobby, Stanley Jones walked into the lobby with a bouquet of flowers in hand. From talking to the Tuckers that morning at breakfast, she knew the only other guest was a middle-aged government land officer with a gut that definitely had to be bad for his health. She knew those flowers weren't for him.

"Ah, Miss Kate." Stanley's face lit up, raising his continuous eyebrow high over both eyes. "You're just the person I wanted to see. I hope you're hungry."

"As a matter of fact, I am," Kate said truthfully, her brain switching gears.

"Good!" Stanley's lip curled up, wiggling his mustache.

"I hope Mr. Smith feels the same way, as he will be calling on me shortly to take me out to dinner—I mean, supper." Kate offered him a polite smile. "Perhaps we can chat at some other time." The door opened, and her eyes skirted toward it. "Ah, here is Mr. Smith now."

Ronald Smith walked in. His eyes lit up as they rested on Kate, though his body seemed glued to the wooden pillar next to the door. Then he noticed Stanley, and his eyes and body slumped.

"You're right on time, Ronald." Kate emphasized his first name, a bit uncomfortable but seeing possible value in dropping her long-embedded etiquette for the moment. "Punctuality is a good attribute. To Sunny's then?" She motioned to the door with her outstretched hand.

Stanley's eyebrow furrowed, and he glared at Ronald.

"Y-yes." Ronald's face expressed what looked like surprise. He held the front door of the hotel open for Kate and motioned for her to go first.

Kate could practically feel Stanley's glare boring into her back. She wiggled her shoulders to shake it off and walked outside.

There was a nip of fall in the air. She wished she had her fur stole to wrap around her arms, but she'd received a few too many stares when she'd worn it the other day. She felt like it had made her stick out like an expensive piece of china in a cupboard full of tin cups. That was the last thing Kate wanted. Her desire was to blend in with the people of Craig.

Kate rubbed her arms to keep warm, avoiding the elbow Ronald had sheepishly extended. He quickly pulled it back in when her hands remained fixed on her arms.

Kate felt bad for accepting his dinner invitation but not his arm. But then again, why couldn't they just be friends? She felt he was the person in this little town with whom she had the most in common. And being with him did bring a measure of comfort.

They strolled down the wooden sidewalk without talking, watching the sunset. As they approached a large building at the end of the block, Kate could barely read the sign that hung above the two swinging doors, but she knew what it said. She'd seen it the second day she was here, finding it almost an oxymoron— or at least that its two words didn't belong together. Sunny Saloon.

She and Ronald stepped inside the establishment. Kate coughed from the cigar smoke. So did Ronald.

He raised his hand and motioned to a large-bosomed woman. She had mounds of blonde hair piled atop her head and was dressed in red from the feather in her hair to the pointed shoes on her feet. He leaned toward Kate to be heard over the ruckus of poker games and men drinking and laughing at the bar. "Sunny has some tables at the back that aren't so bad."

"Ah, Sunny," Kate said with a lilt to her voice. "The owner's name. But wouldn't it be spelled . . . ?" She paused and looked to Ronald.

"She told me the man making her sign made a mistake and left off the apostrophe *s* and there wasn't any more wood for another. So she put it up temporarily. Then she realized she liked it better this way."

"Really now?" Kate gave a quiet laugh.

Dressed all in red, the woman Kate assumed must be Sunny moved across the saloon floor like a rose growing up through a pile of manure. Her pleasant face and smile didn't fit in this place, but Kate found it a welcomed sight. "A table for two, Mr. Smith?" Sunny asked.

Ronald nodded.

Sunny looked at Kate and radiated a pleasant smile. "You're that new gal, the one that arrived on the stage last Tuesday, aren't you? Did I hear right that you're a doctor?"

"Yes, ma'am." Kate wondered if there was anyone who hadn't heard about her. Gossip was something she would never understand. But maybe she should try to be a little more understanding of those who felt the need to do such and at least be grateful for it at the moment. Here was advertising she didn't have to pay for. She thought about her box under the bed and how she'd already gone through five dollars of her savings.

Sunny led them to the far corner of the saloon. "This here's my best table." She gave the round table a slap as Ronald pulled out a chair for Kate. "And I promise the beer's cold. I wish I had more to offer than cold sandwiches." She glanced at Ronald. "But that's coming. So is a new dining area. Being the boss now has its advantages. You're going to see a lot more changes around here."

Kate's interest was piqued. "I hear you run this place," she said as she lowered into the chair Ronald had pulled out for her.

"Sure do!" Sunny rested a hand on Kate's shoulder. "And, honey, I can't tell you how good it is to see another woman take the bull by the horns and do what she wants; prove to the world that we don't have to be a man to run a business." She picked up a postcard-sized menu from the table and handed it to Kate. "Pete, God rest his soul, never liked the idea of serving food in his saloon— said that's what men had their wives for. But I always felt there was a need for something like that here in town. Told him it was an opportunity just waiting for us to cash in on." She handed a menu to Ronald. "Now you two just holler when you're ready to order. Otherwise, I'll be back in a minute to do it for you. Ha!" With that, she was off to the bar, clearing off the empty glasses.

"I take it she recently lost her husband," Kate said, trying to make conversation because Ronald just sat there staring at her, not saying a word.

He nodded.

"So he left her the saloon?

Nodding again, he muttered, "In his will."

"She must have a head for business. It appears to be doing well."

"Yes, it does." Ronald went back to staring; only this time it was at the menu.

"Maybe she could help me," Kate said. "You know, give me ideas of how to solicit customers. I mean, patients." When Ronald didn't say anything, she added, "No, that's a silly idea. Just forget I said that. Maybe I should just turn around and go back to New York, like Mr. Forbes told me earlier today."

"No! You must stay." Finally, Ronald was talking. "We need you here. I nee—I mean, I . . . it's so nice to finally have someone who . . . I can talk intelligently with."

If you'd just talk.

The next morning, Kate washed her face and hands for breakfast, actually enjoying the refreshing cold splash of water she'd poured into the porcelain bowl. It woke her up better than the warm water back home. She thought again about what Ronald had said last night about how the town needed her. Though it was minimal, what little he did say had been the encouragement she needed to endure another day. She could "stick to her guns," as they said around here, and not think of returning to New York.

Or maybe Sunny had been the source of the encouragement.

It didn't matter. She was going to set up a medical practice here if it killed her. If for no other reason than to prove to her parents she could do it—all on her own. And to prove to Darwin that she didn't need him—or any other man. And to the men of this town that she could be just as good a doctor as any man!

She took her black leather bag from the dresser in her hotel room, pulled out her tools, and carefully laid them back in the drawer. This wouldn't fix her problem of not yet finding an office, but getting her doctor's bag fixed was something that needed to be done. She headed down the stairs, hoping that finding someone who repaired leather goods would be easier than setting up her practice. So far she'd found that every other business owner on Craig's main street, which she'd learned was named Yampa Avenue, had either built their place with their own two hands or had an investor do it for them.

She had neither of those luxuries. Determined not to let that stop her, she hurried to the kitchen, where she ate her meal with Mary's little girls to make it easier on the hotel's maid/cook and worn-out mother of four. In the past week she'd gotten to know the children somewhat, finding each of them delightful in their her way. But what she'd enjoyed most of all was chatting each morning with their mother.

"Are you sure you wouldn't like another flapjack?" Mary hovered a pancake on a fork over Kate's empty plate.

"Positive, but thank you, Mary. You are a sweetheart. I do enjoy your cooking so." Kate stood and gave Mary a quick hug. She stepped into the empty dining room, wishing Mary's social skills were as good as her cooking. The poor woman holed herself up in the kitchen of this hotel every day by choice, not caring to go out and mingle with the townsfolk. She'd wanted to ask Mary about a place to get her doctor's bag fixed but knew that would be as fruitful as asking Mary to enjoy living in Craig.

Kate had, however, noticed a saddle shop on the east end of Yampa Avenue yesterday as she'd strolled through the town. It had been a lovely day to check out all the businesses and then walk along the streets that had been staked out, awaiting the influx of new families. Most of those streets consisted of a swath of dirt cleared from sagebrush. Only a street or two to the north and a street or two to the south of the main street held any houses.

As she strolled down Yampa Avenue once again, enjoying the cool September air on her face, she tried to envision what the investors she'd read about had obviously seen: flourishing shops surrounded by blocks and blocks of two-story homes with white picket fences.

"Good mornin', Miss Kate."

The greeting startled Kate from her daydream. She turned to see a young boy sitting atop a horse, reining the animal in closer to the dirt path that served as the sidewalk at this far end of Yampa Avenue. It was the servant boy who had helped her with her luggage when she'd first arrived.

"Good morning—Logan, is it?" Kate said, not positive about his name.

"Yes'm." The boy lifted his hat and set it back down on his head while his eyes remained locked on Kate's face. "You sure are pretty, Miss Kate."

"Well, thank you, Logan. That's very kind of you to say." If the boy weren't so young, Kate might have been tempted to tip her head and blush. "You sure are good with that horse," she said, sensing the boy wanted to keep talking. "How old are you?"

"Almost thirteen." Logan looked away for a moment. He returned his eyes to hers. "I know—I'm small for my age." He squared his shoulders. "But I can ride better than any other boy in these parts. Go ahead; try to find one that rides better than me. You can't."

"I believe you." Kate thought about the boy's need to have her think highly of him, feeling sadness for his situation, especially for his crippled leg and the treatment he'd received from his apparent employer. That sadness warmed her heart for him. "Maybe you could help me, Logan."

"Anything, Miss Kate. You name it. You need me to ride you a message out to the farthest homestead in these parts, just say the word 'go' and I'll take off in a flash. Or if you want your stalls mucked out, I'll do it for free, Miss Kate."

"I had something a little simpler in mind." Kate smiled at the idea of her having a stall that needed to be "mucked out." She could only imagine what that meant. "I was hoping maybe you could help me find a suitable place I could rent. I need a place both to live and to set up a doctor's office." She figured it was a long shot asking a child, but he seemed to want to linger and talk to her. What could it hurt?

"I already heard you were lookin' for a place, Miss Kate." He grinned big. "And I been workin' on it right hard. Well, not real hard. It was easy. I know everybody in town. Talk to them all almost every week at least. Check in on them, make sure they're all right."

"That's very sweet," Kate said sincerely. She turned away from him and resumed walking down the street, determined to complete her task at hand.

Logan continued to follow her. "And—"

A cowboy barreled down Yampa Avenue at top speed, engulfing Kate and Logan in a cloud of dust. He whooped in a high voice, pulling his horse to a stop in front of the R. H. Hughes Mercantile. When he hopped out of the saddle, his waist barely came to the top of the hitching post as he wrapped the reins around the wooden bar.

"Whew." Kate fanned the dust away from her face. "He sure made lot of commotion for such a small cowboy," she muttered under her breath, trying not to be too unladylike, even though she was talking to a child.

"Oh, that ain't no boy, Miss Kate." Logan fanned at the dust too. "That's Rosie Decker." He motioned with his chin to the cowboy—cowgirl—removing her hat as she entered the store, letting her braided hair tumble down her back.

"Lavender's daughter?" Kate thought about the cheerful store manager's wife and the request she'd presented to Kate. *If you could maybe get to know her and have some of your fine manners rub off on her, we'd be beholden to you.* Kate's insides warmed at the thought of responding to Lavender's wishes. She didn't know if she had anything worth "rubbing off" onto Roselund Decker, but she was anxious to get to know this woman who worked as a ranch hand and rode a horse as good as any man.

Logan nodded. "Anyway, Miss Kate, I was about to say I found you a place maybe you could use."

"Really?" Kate offered the boy a sincere smile. "Where? Is it here on the main street?"

"Just keep walkin', and you'll be there." He pointed to the saddle shop where she was headed. "Talk to young Mr. Hoy there. He told me he might be interested in renting out his upstairs."

A gust of wind kicked up, and Kate grabbed hold of her hat as she resumed walking.

Logan glanced up at the dark clouds rolling in. "Sorry, I'd best stop talkin'. I've got a message from Sam at the store that I've got to deliver to Mr. McCurdy— his barbed wire's in—and I want to beat this storm."

"Lucas McCurdy?" Kate stopped. Why did just the mention of that man's name make her heart beat irregularly?

"Yes'm." Logan tipped his hat. "Gotta go." He took off, maneuvering his horse, an obvious relish of the task evident on his smiling face.

Kate figured helping others was the way the boy could feel whole and equal to everyone else. She wondered if she could help him. What had caused his deformity?

She lifted her skirt and hurried toward the saddle shop.

CHAPTER 7

KATE LOCKED THE DOOR TO her new apartment/office and danced down the stairs, elated at finally having a place to call home and a place to set up her practice. Mr. Hoy at the saddle shop had rented it to her the very day she'd come in to inquire about the vacancy. He'd just built a new home on Sixth Street, their two-room dwelling above his shop being too small to house the needs of his growing family. He'd been skeptical at first—a woman doctor obviously hadn't sat well with him. But Kate figured the dearth of renters in a place like Craig had made him change his tune and rent to her. By the end of their conversation, he actually sounded excited to have her as a tenant, telling her it would be nice to have another woman around for his Ethel to talk to. And a new doctor in town could come in handy. It seemed every time his wife needed to take their kids in for a broken arm or to stitch up a bad cut, old Doc Greene was hard to find. Plus, he didn't seem to deal well with children.

Last night she'd slept on a borrowed bed. She needed to head over to the mercantile and order herself a new bed and everything else she needed to set up her household. And then there was the matter of her office. She hoped the ad she'd torn from a magazine back home in New York was still valid, because she doubted Mr. Decker had a catalog of medical supplies sitting around in his store. She'd need to write the business that had placed the ad and order a medical supply catalog. She only hoped that the few patients who needed her services in the meantime would be content with being examined while sitting in a chair or standing up.

The bell above the door jingled as Kate walked into the store.

"Morning, Miss Donahue." Behind the counter, Sam Decker looked up from the screws he was counting out for a customer—a rancher, by the looks of him. "Be with you in a minute."

"Don't hurry on my account," Kate said, feeling rather comfortable in the store. Maybe having her own place had helped her to feel more settled, more of a sense of belonging. She was ready now to move ahead with her plans, determined to make this career choice work. "I'll just do some browsing," she said with a cheerful lift to her voice.

She strolled along the wall lined with shelves filled with towels, white goods, bolts of fabric, and nice things she loved. Though the choices were limited, they were sufficient. It actually felt good to make do, to be happy for just having that simple bar of soap she'd purchased last time, rather than to lavish herself with oils and fancy soaps of all colors and sizes and to have servants to administer them for her. But she had better purchase one or two, maybe three, extra sheets. It was doubtful she'd have time to wash and hang them to dry in between patients—first she needed to learn how to do laundry. Quietly she let out a nervous little laugh.

She did feel a sense of satisfaction in buying new bedding and setting up her own household. Glancing at the bolts of fabric stacked upright, starting with white on one end of the shelf and running through the rainbow until the colors darkened into black at the other end, a yellow print caught her eye. She pulled it out and examined it, envisioning it worked into a new dress. Did she dare tackle a complete dress? She wondered if she'd need to buy some more sewing supplies. It was most certain she'd need a good pair of scissors. She hadn't dared to take more than one spool of thread and a single needle from her maid, Lucy. It had been Lucy who had taught her to sew. Kate's mother wasn't even aware that Kate knew how to do something with a needle other than embroidery. Kate had preferred it that way, not wanting to upset her mother.

Kate looked up into the face of a dark-haired young woman about her own age. "Oh." Startled, Kate let go of the fabric she held in front of herself—she had thought it was just her, Mr. Decker, and the rancher in the store. And the woman's dark-brown eyes held a familiarity that Kate couldn't place.

The brown-eyed woman extended her hand toward a bolt of white fabric. "Would you mind if I reach past you?" she asked, barely above a whisper.

Kate stepped back and let her slide into the space next to the shelf holding the fabric. "Here, let me help you." Kate pulled the soft white fabric out for the woman to grab more easily. It felt like diaper flannel, not that Kate had much experience changing a baby, but in her medical training, they had used it to make bandages. It absorbed the blood well and could be bleached out if not allowed to dry before washing. "How many children do you have?" Kate asked, wanting to make conversation and get to know as many of the townspeople as she could.

"What?" The woman looked confused. Her expression then changed to one of embarrassment. "Oh, it's not for diapers. I'm not married." She turned her back to Kate, examining the fabric. "Probably never will be," she muttered softly under her breath.

The pain Kate detected in this young woman's voice cut Kate to her very core. She ached for her. What would make this young woman—whose dark hair and light skin, though not striking, held a subtle beauty; and her neat, clean clothing revealed a person who either worked very hard or had money—doubt she could find a husband? Especially out here? "I'm sorry." Kate placed a hand on the woman's arm, which seemed to calm her a bit. "I should never have pried. Please, forgive me."

"Oh, it's all right." The woman straightened her back as if shaking off a load. "You're Kate Donahue, that new doctor that's moved to town, aren't you?" she said with a glimmer of hopefulness in her eyes.

"How did you—"

"My brother hasn't stopped talking about you since he came back from Baggs two weeks ago. Apparently you made quite the impression on him. Though I doubt he'd choose you over Doc Greene if he happens to break his leg. Which I'd like to do almost on a daily basis. And once in a while, my pa's." She let out an exhausted-sounding breath. "Living in the same house as those two men is—" She rushed her fingers to her mouth. "Excuse me, I shouldn't have—"

"You're a Jones?" Kate cut in, knowing now why her eyes had looked so familiar.

"Yes, Susannah Jones." She held her hand out to Kate, accepting Kate's in return. As they exchanged a polite handshake, she continued, "But most people call me Clara."

Kate raised an eyebrow in response.

"It's my middle name. I prefer my given name, Susannah. But Pa insists on calling me Clara. He has ever since my ma died thirteen years ago." She looked off distantly with sorrow in her eyes. Chewing on her lip, she returned her attention to Kate. "I was thirteen, and it was up to me to take care of the family and the ranch house. Pa started calling me Clara, I guess as his way of dealing with the empty spot Ma left." She brought her fingers to her lips again. "Sorry, I shouldn't be boring you."

Kate grasped Susannah's arm to pull her fingers away from her mouth. "No, you're not boring me. I would really like to hear your story," Kate said, almost begging. She really did want to hear what had brought this woman of seeming wealth and position—at least for the high deserts of Colorado—such reason for sorrow. Maybe she could help. Even if in the smallest of ways.

"Oh, there's not much else to tell. I've tried to fill Ma's shoes since she died. And I'll probably keep doing so until the day I die. Or at least until Pa passes. Which could very well be after me. He's as healthy as a horse." She offered a weak smile. "He won't be needing your services unless he does break his leg. But he'd be more stubborn than Stanley about seeing a woman doctor. Sorry."

"That's okay," Kate said. "I'm getting a lot of that sentiment from men. But I think I've got a few convinced to visit my office if they find a need." Kate picked up the bolt of yellow fabric and shoved it back between two others on the shelf. "And I'd better quit dreaming about a new dress while I've got an office to set up." She inched away from the fabric shelf with the intent to speak with Mr. Decker. He now busied himself at the counter, his customer having slipped out the door. With a nod, she said, "Good day," but sensed Susannah wanted her to linger, as if she had more to say.

"Oh, well, goodbye then." Susannah stared at the floor. "It's been nice talking with you."

Kate realized that she had plenty more to say to this woman who had touched her heart so quickly. "How do you do it?" Kate needed her help, and now seemed to be a good time to bring it up, for already Susannah's eyes lit up with the prospect of continuing their conversation. Kate wondered how often Susannah talked with someone of her own gender. She feared it rarely happened.

"Do what?" Susannah asked with a hint of eagerness in her voice.

"Take care of a household? Especially out here in the West where there doesn't appear to be many of the conveniences available back east, like both cold and hot running water and boilers and radiators inside your houses? And washing machines and iceboxes and—well, I think you get what I mean. Frankly, I'm overwhelmed. I would appreciate any guidance you could give me."

"It's not hard." Susannah's eyes smiled, as if anticipating more conversation. "You can't miss something you've never had," she said in the most confident voice she'd used yet. She went on to instruct Kate what to do and not to do as she set up her little apartment and acclimated to life without servants.

Not caring that time passed quickly, Kate found the conversation both delightful and invaluable.

"Feel free to come out to the ranch anytime if you want me to show you firsthand anything I've explained." Susannah chewed on her lip as her eyes communicated once again that she had more to say. "I'll make you a steak dinner. I'm sure Stanley would come into town to fetch you. Just send word with Logan if you want to come. He's always easy to find, running errands like he does for everyone in town."

Kate thought Susannah's attitude toward their boy servant a bit odd but brushed it aside. She sensed Logan was not what Susannah really wanted to talk about now. Or steak dinners. Mr. Decker and her shopping list could wait a little longer. "Do you mind me asking—how did your mother die?" Kate said to keep the conversation going, hoping to dig a little more into what was bothering this woman. In this short half an hour or so of time, Susannah had already endeared herself to Kate. It wasn't just that she was close to Kate's own age or that she was without a husband or hope or desire to have one. Kate sensed this woman needed someone she could confide in.

"She died during childbirth. After Stanley and me, she had female problems. She lost two other babies at birth between Stanley and Logan. I think Pa still blames Logan." She rolled her eyes. "As if doing so would bring Ma back. It wasn't his fault she died. It was the doctor's. This was before Doc Greene. It was one Pa had to fetch from Hayden. But as Logan grew and his crippled leg became more noticeable, Pa associated it with Ma's difficult delivery and began to blame my brother more and more. How Logan maintains his cheery disposition despite his pa and older brother, I'll never know. I just wish I knew how he does it."

"Wait a minute," Kate broke in, glad to finally have a spot she could do so without sounding rude. "Logan's your brother?"

"Yeah. The best brother a person could ever have. But he's still no substitute for a woman." Susannah sighed.

"But the way Stanley was ordering him around that day by the stage-coach . . ." Kate could feel her blood warm and threaten to boil. "I thought he was a servant." A crippled servant who needed assistance, not to scramble for luggage the arrogant brute could get for himself.

Susannah ducked her head as if she were the sibling to be ashamed. "I despise how Stanley treats him—as if his crippled leg was an indicator of his worth."

Susannah fingered the white fabric she'd had her eye on earlier. Finally, she pulled it from the shelf and cradled it in her arms as she turned away from Kate and toward the counter. "Have you seen Mrs. Decker? I really do need some of this fabric, and Mr. Decker skimps on the yardage when he measures it out. Lavender always measures big." She leaned toward Kate's ear. "Not that I really care about the money right now, but I don't want Mr. Decker asking me the same question you did—you know, about the diapers. I don't want to explain the real reason I need this fabric."

A swell of warmth flushed Kate's cheeks as she realized why Susannah was buying the fabric. "I'm sorry about that. I should have thought past the obvious," Kate said, thinking about the muslin bag that she kept her feminine rags in during those days of the month. She'd never had to buy the fabric for them herself. Her mother had always taken care of that for her, or rather, their maid Lucy had purchased the absorbent fabric and cut it into convenient-sized rags. She thought about the tiny box filled with safety pins she used to pin them in place. Her mother had told her of the difficulties of that time of the month before the days of safety pins. Were such luxuries even available out here in the West? She hadn't noticed any on the shelves by the sewing supplies.

"That's okay." Susannah rested a limp hand on Kate's arm as if assuring her. "I just wish it was more acceptable to talk about such things." She looked off to one side and mumbled, "I really need to . . . talk . . . to somebody."

"Susannah." Kate said her name like she was speaking to a child who needed to listen. "Are you having problems with your menstrual cycle? I'm a doctor, remember. You can tell me."

"Men . . . stral . . . what?"

"The three to seven days a month when you flow," Kate said, trying to word it so Susannah would understand, realizing this poor woman grew up without a mother while going through this change in her body. It made Kate cringe and then ache inside for Susannah. She patted the bolt of white fabric. "It's the reason you're buying this fabric."

"Three to seven days a month?" Susannah repeated Kate's words as if she hadn't heard them right. Her eyes widened. "That's as long as it's supposed to last? That's about only how long it lets up each month," she said, staring at Kate, her eyes begging for help.

A quick glance around the store revealed another male customer had entered. Though he sorted through a bin full of nails on the other side of the store, Kate felt this matter should be handled in privacy. "Can you come over to my office? It's not really set up, but we can talk in private there. I could still give you an exam."

"Right now?"

"It sounds like you should take care of this as soon as possible."

"But I've got to hurry back to the ranch. Pa's expecting me by noon. He gets upset when I'm not back by when I've promised to be."

"Is there a time that would work better for you?" Kate offered her a smile, hoping to calm Susannah's fears, nerves, apprehension—whatever it was that caused her to be so hesitant.

"How about nine in the morning? Tomorrow?" Susannah sucked her bottom lip between her teeth before adding, "Pa and Stanley are usually out on their rounds about then."

I think I can squeeze you into my busy schedule, Kate was about to say to make the conversation light, but then she thought against it. "That would be fine," she said. This was no matter to be made light of. Though she finally had her first patient, one who could obviously pay, she wasn't as excited as she'd expected. She was worried. Her soon-to-be patient definitely needed her help.

But it was not just the medical issues that had Kate concerned.

How many other women in this town had reason to shrink from their true potential because of the men in their lives?

CHAPTER 8

MARY TUCKER HAD INSISTED KATE still take breakfast in the hotel's kitchen until she got fully settled in her new place. Kate nibbled on her freshly scrambled eggs while sitting between the two youngest Tucker girls. Her heart swelled with gratitude for Mary's thoughtfulness and the delightful company she enjoyed when she was able to share breakfast with her. Mary hadn't been able to join her and the girls—the hotel had three guests needing their breakfast. Kate missed her company but was glad to hear the hotel had some more paying customers.

After breakfast with the four Tucker girls, Kate rushed back to the saddle shop and shot up the stairs to her apartment. She hurried and changed the sheets on her bed in case she had to perform a pelvic exam on Susannah. A proper exam table would be preferred, but for now the bed would have to do. The one she'd ordered from back east wouldn't arrive for almost another month.

The stove needed another log to bring the fire up to what was required to boil water. She needed to fill her tiny sink with hot water. True, it was small, but she was glad to have the sink with a water pump—glad to have the second room that the Hoy family had used as their kitchen when they had lived here. Other places she'd looked into renting had no sort of indoor plumbing at all. As she stuffed the piece of wood inside, dirtying her hands, she cursed lightly then chided herself. Were the western ways of life rubbing off on her? She hoped not. She wanted to stay a proper lady no matter what life in the West threw at her. She lived in a two-room dwelling with a kitchen the size of a closet and a bedroom that also served as a drawing room and exam room, but she wouldn't complain. Especially after she'd tried so hard to find this place.

Her heart warmed as she thought of Logan, the almost-thirteen-year-old boy who looked like a ten-year-old, who had taken it upon himself to find her an office. The darling child seemed to have only one thought on his mind: the desire to help other people. She admired him. She could not think of a better attribute to have.

Kate put a pot of water on to boil and hurried back to finish making the bed. Logan's sister would soon be here—her first official patient. And unlike her littlest brother, Susannah didn't wear a constant smile on her face. An ache swelled inside Kate, spawning a deep desire to help this woman who was the same age as her but who had apparently lived through a lifetime's worth of trials.

With the final tuck of the sheet under the corner of the mattress, Kate heard a timid knock at the door. She rushed over and opened it, holding on tight against a gust of cold wind. Susannah stood on the landing at the top of the wooden steps, looking like she might turn around and head back down them at any second. Kate reached out and snagged her by the elbow. "Hurry, get in here out of the weather." Kate shivered and shut the door the moment Susannah stepped inside.

Kate stepped into the kitchen while she had Susannah strip down to her bloomers and bodice. Susannah's obvious hesitation made Kate all the more certain her decision to stay in Craig was the right one. She could only imagine how much more nervous this sweet woman would be if she were in Doc Greene's office right now. Or rather Sheriff Greene's spare bedroom. From what she'd been told, his office was no better than hers.

Kate had Susannah sit in a chair first and took Susannah's pulse. Then she listened to her heart and lungs and examined her throat—all the basics. To ease the anxiety of the pelvic exam, already suspecting what Susannah had, Kate tried some light conversation. "So, what do you do in your spare time? You know, for fun? I like to read, even sew a dress from time to time. How about you?"

"Nothing, really," Susannah said wrinkling her forehead. "If I ever get an extra minute, I usually lie down."

"Oh." That wasn't the response Kate was hoping for—another reminder that her patient was in need of medical help.

"I do like to read and write poetry sometimes," Susannah said timidly.

"Wonderful. I'd love to read some of the things you've written." Kate leaned in front of Susannah's face so she could see her eyes. "If you don't mind."

"Not at all." Susannah looked off to one side. "Men don't seem to like poetry. And that's who I usually keep company with, unfortunately."

"Yes, that is unfortunate. I need to come out and visit you. At least once a week. I too find myself in need of female companionship."

Susannah's eyes lit up, yet her voice sounded hesitant. "Really? You'd do that?"

"Absolutely." Kate knew it would be good to try to get a feel for what Susannah had gone through since her mother's death and try to figure out the other issues that were obviously bothering her. "For now, however, I need you to move over to the bed." She prompted Susannah with a gentle nudge at the elbow to rise from the chair.

Having worked with patients in a hospital her last year of medical school, Kate had seen all shapes, sizes, and genders of people in various stages of nudity. She found it a bit awkward this time, however, asking Susannah to undress from the waist down, but held a professional expression nonetheless. "When you're done, place this extra sheet across your bare legs and call for me. I'll just wait in the other room until you are ready." Perhaps it wasn't a good idea to get to know her patients on a personal basis.

She fought the negative thought away. *Yes, it is! This woman needs more than just a medical exam; more than a clinical diagnosis, she needs someone who cares about her.*

The exam went rather smoothly. After Susannah got dressed, Kate dug through the jars and vials of salves, herbs, and medicines she'd been able to procure before she'd left New York. She'd been collecting them for some time during her schooling in anticipation for this very day—though at the time, she'd envisioned it in a sterile clinic someplace on Long Island.

It surprised her when that memory of what she'd expected her life to be no longer visited her thoughts with gnawing pain.

Kate sat down on the edge of the bed and asked Susannah about her menstrual periods, the heaviness of their flow and duration, and some input about the accompanying cramping.

"So, can you help me? Can you make it go away? Or at least help me be normal?" Susannah asked in a hopeful tone.

"What you've got is a condition an Austrian doctor named von Rokitansky referred to in his writings as adenomyoma. Unfortunately, our understanding of the disease has not progressed very far since he discovered it thirty years ago. We just know it's a painful disorder in which tissue that normally lines the inside of your uterus—the endometrium—grows outside your uterus." Kate handed Susannah a jar of salve. "I worked with a patient in my last year of medical school who had the same malady. I found this salve through an herbal catalog. My advisors frowned on my using such practices, but nothing they had to offer seemed to help the woman. Both she and I figured she had nothing to lose in trying it, since it's just made out of wild yams in Mexico. Rub it onto your stomach where it hurts. It has naturally occurring plant hormones that mimic your own that are in short supply."

"And . . ." Susannah raised her eyebrows. "Did it work for her?"

"It took a few months of applying it every day, but she stuck with it, and it helped her immensely." Kate placed the jar in Susannah's hands. "Here, you take this home and try it for two or three months. I'll give you the address where you can mail-order some more. When you do, just order two jars—one for you and one to replace mine. Hopefully, you'll start to see some results before the first jar is through so you'll be apt to purchase more."

"Oh, don't worry, I will. I'll order it even if it hasn't started working yet. I have a little money saved away Pa's got no control over—a birthday gift from my grandmother, God rest her soul." Susannah looked at the floor. "She passed away five years ago, and I've been saving her gift ever since."

Susannah put on her coat and gathered her things. "Oh, thank you so much, Kate. How much do I owe you now?"

"Oh, nothing. This first visit is on me," Kate said. Realizing what she was saying, she wanted to kick herself, but she would have felt guilty asking her friend for money. She should be happy to help a friend in need without expectation of some kind of return. *But you're a doctor now. How else do you get paid if you don't charge for your services?*

Kate had confidence in her skills as a physician, but she realized she was definitely going to have to work on her business skills. Maybe a visit to Sunny's Saloon was in order.

"Are you sure?" Susannah asked.

"Positive," Kate said as she ushered her friend to the door. She couldn't renege on her offer now.

On the threshold of the door, with the morning air blowing the dark sky's cold inside, Susannah turned and gave Kate a hug. "Oh, and I was just thinking, maybe it's not such a good idea that you come out to the farm to visit me. I mean, uh . . . well, maybe I can just come into town more often, insist there's more shopping to be done. I'll come visit you then. Yes, that would be better because I know how busy you must be, being a doctor and all." She gave Kate another squeeze and took off down the stairs.

Busy? She knows I'm not busy.

Something had changed Susannah's mind. There was a reason she didn't want Kate to visit her on the ranch. All the more reason to find another excuse to go out there. She feared something worse than her female problems weighed on her new friend. What good would it do to help Susanna heal her body if her emotions were in peril of crippling her life?

But how can I get out there if I'm not invited?

There was an easy solution. Kate didn't like it. But she figured it would be the only way.

Stanley.

CHAPTER 9

"So you changed your mind and decided a trip to the Circle J was worthwhile?" The wind blew gently, ruffling the dark locks of Stanley's hair hanging below his hat at the nape of his neck.

Kate no longer found him as handsome as she'd first thought. Perhaps she could consider him attractive if it weren't for the brain that resided behind his face. "Yes, I suppose I did. But isn't that a woman's prerogative?" she said in an extra feminine voice she almost surprised herself by using.

He turned in the wagon's seat and smiled like she'd said exactly the kind of thing he wanted to hear. "I guess it is."

Should she really be leading Stanley on like this? But why on earth would a man like to hear such nonsense? Why wouldn't he want to discuss the price of tea in China with her? Or at least, when it came to Stanley, the price of beef on the open market? He talked about such things with men; she'd overheard him at Decker's store. Did he not think she was as smart as a man? Could she not comprehend what it all meant?

Of course she could.

Kate knew she must tone down her sarcasm as Stanley drove the wagon through the lowlands along the Yampa River, pointing out the way the leaves fell from the trees in shades of yellow and brown, and how all trees didn't turn red in the fall. She tried to come to a compromise in her voice, somewhere between overly feminine and on an equal standing with him.

There was one thing, however, she didn't understand and honestly wanted to know. So she asked, not caring if she sounded like a typical female this time, at least the kind Stanley was obviously looking for. "Stanley?"

"Yes, Kate?"

"Why do cattlemen hate sheepmen?" Kate hoped she had said that right. "Or whatever it is you call men who raise sheep for a living."

"I call them no-good varmints." Stanley smiled, but the dark shade of his eyes communicated he was more than serious.

"Seriously, Stanley, tell me why."

"You don't know nothin' 'bout sheep, do you?"

"A little."

"Well, obviously not enough to know that they graze the grass right down to the roots, nearly killin' it off. Sometimes it never grows back. And then there's the smell. You ever smelled the varmints?"

He gave her a glance and then returned his gaze to the road. "No, I don't suppose you have, bein' a city gal and all. But that's okay, you don't need to know nothin' 'bout sheep to live around here. In fact, the less you know the better. Besides, it's not fittin' for a woman to bother herself with such matters. Leave that to us men. You just stick with your house stuff." He gave Kate a strange glance. "Oh, yeah, you're wantin' to add doctorin' to your list of womanly duties." He snickered.

Kate couldn't contain herself any longer. She glared at him while imagining the satisfaction to be had if she were to kick him in the shins. Where did that come from? The West must be getting to her.

The roof of a house became visible in the distance. They turned off the main road—if one could call it that. To Kate it was not much more than a cattle trail times two. The carriage now bumped down two ruts cut into the sagebrush and rocky ground. As they neared the house, she could see a billow of smoke rising from the chimney. Large trees shaded the two-story frame house that had been painted white and trimmed in varying shades of blue. It looked quite delightful. She wondered if Susannah had some influence in the color. The thought made her smile.

The house looked larger than she'd originally thought when she'd first seen its roof. As Stanley pulled the carriage up to the front door, Kate became concerned. "Does your sister know I'm coming? Will it inconvenience her, having another guest for dinner?"

"Oh, don't worry yourself about Clara. She always makes plenty. Pa sees that she does—just in case one of the other cattlemen stops by. Which they do all the time. Pa's got himself a poker table in the rear parlor. We have a good time back there. Clara makes us drinks and sandwiches for our games all the time. She doesn't mind. 'Least she never says nothin'. An extra mouth won't put her out tonight." He looked at Kate, moving his gaze from her feet to her face. "Especially one that looks as if she eats like a bird." He jumped out of the carriage and ran around to Kate's side.

Reluctantly, Kate accepted his hand and let him help her. Once firmly on the ground, she let go of his hand and approached the door with apprehension. Why did Susannah not want Kate to come? And why did her brother insist on calling her by her middle name? Kate could understand her father's reasoning for calling her Clara, but why would her brother call her that too if she preferred Susannah? He would have never thought of his mother as Clara, so how would using that name for Susannah help him deal with the loss of his mother? Strange.

As Kate walked inside, she was greeted by all sorts of animals that had been stuffed and mounted on the walls. She felt like she was in a zoo for dead animals. Obviously, a woman's touch hadn't reached the inside of the house.

Logan appeared in a hall that spilled into the entryway. "Miss Kate, you did come! You did! It's so good to see you." He ran over and held out his hand for her to shake. "Welcome to the Circle J Ranch," he said with pride, as if he held a big part of the ranch and was important here. Kate knew differently. It made her admire the boy even more. He kept shaking Kate's hand, staring in her face with a big smile on his.

Stanley elbowed the boy in the ribs. "Stop ogling her, boy. She's well out of your league. Any girl's out of your league," he said with a laugh.

Kate felt like elbowing Stanley. Instead she said, "I appreciate your kind welcome, Logan. You have truly done the Circle J proud."

He beamed.

Stanley glared.

"Dinner's ready," Susannah's voice came in from a back room. Kate assumed it must be from the kitchen or the dining room. It sounded tired and like she'd said the phrase a million times over.

While no one was looking their way, Kate leaned toward Logan's ear. "Next time you're in town," she whispered, "and you have some extra time, stop by my office. I'd like to take a look at your legs—as a doctor, if that would be all right with you?"

"That would be dandy!"

"What are you two yakkin' 'bout?" Stanley motioned with a sweep of his hand for Kate to come.

"Nothing you'd find of interest," Kate responded as she followed Stanley through the arched doorway that opened into a spacious dining room with a large rectangular table set for four. Kate again hoped this wasn't a bad idea. How would Susannah react when she saw Kate there, unannounced? And then should Kate call her Susannah? Or should she call her Clara, and pretend for everyone's sake that she and Susannah had not yet met?

The smell of frying onions came in from the kitchen and added to the discomfort of her stomach. She hated onions. But Susannah didn't need a rejection of her cooking added to the surprise of Kate being there.

Susannah walked out of the kitchen through a swinging door, carrying what looked like soup, potholders covering her hands clamped to each side of the pot. She took sight of Kate, let out a slight gasp, and ran back into the kitchen, pot and all.

"I guess I should say I'm sorry, sis. But I'm not really." He glanced at Kate with a nauseating grin on his face. "But I brought myself a date to supper tonight. Grab another dish to slap on the table while you're in there."

"Ah, she's okay." A big, burly man in a crisp new cowboy hat strolled into the dining room. He pulled a chair out from the table with the toe of his boot and sat down. "Ben Jones here." He tipped his hat at Kate. "And you are?"

"Katherine Donahue, sir." Kate wondered if the men in this house had any manners at all. Did they wear hats at the dinner table? Did they ever notice the nice way their daughter or sister set the table with polished china? Were rude remarks like "slap another dish on the table" commonplace?

Susannah came back into the room. This time she held a new plate and bowl and some silverware, which she set neatly in front of Kate. She looked a little more composed, but she shot Kate a questioning glance.

"Sorry," Kate whispered when Susannah dipped low to set the table and her ear moved within range to where only she could hear Kate's apology.

As Susannah went around the table, ladling soup into each person's bowl, Stanley huffed out a breath. "Liver and onion soup? Agh! I was hoping for something decent. I told Kate here I would treat her to a good steak. We are a cattle ranch after all."

"I'm only the cook, not the butcher too, thank heavens." Susannah mumbled the last words under her breath. "I can only cook what you put in my larder. And right now, it's pretty bare." She turned to Logan. "Tell them I'm not lying." Then to her father, "I promise, the storeroom is running low. You need to kill me another steer."

Logan took a slurp of soup and looked over at his father. "Honest, Pa, the storeroom is near empty. I told you that you needed to butcher us somethin' a month ago."

"Why should I listen to you, boy?" Ben Jones glanced down at the bowl of soup set before him and picked up his spoon with apparent revulsion.

"Because she told you too," Logan said simply. There wasn't an ounce of spite in his words. He'd spoken them the same as if he'd said, "The sky is blue," with a smile on his face and sincere.

Kate would have rubbed an entire shaker of salt into her tone if those had been her words. Forget trying to behave like a well-bred lady. She was dealing with men here who had no breeding at all—unless she wanted to count cattle breeding. She was merely a guest at this table, but the tension was much thicker than the soup, and she had to do something.

"Well, I think it smells lovely," Kate said. "The soup," she added in case there would be room for confusion.

"Thank you, Miss Donahue," Susannah said, setting the pot of soup in the middle of the table and finally dishing up a bowl for herself. "Oh, sorry, I forgot the bread." She jumped out of her seat and dashed into the kitchen.

The sound of an oven door opening and the smell wafting into the room told Kate that the bread she was about to eat would be hot and fresh. If these men found some reason to complain about it too, Kate was unsure if she'd be able to maintain her bearing as a proper lady any longer. That was something she'd always struggled with as it was, especially in her youth. He mother had insisted that Kate always act like a lady, regardless of the circumstances. But Kate preferred her nanny's view. "Face the situation and adjust accordingly," Nanny Vincent had always said. And right now, she'd adjust to the situation.

"Excuse me, gentlemen," Kate said, some manners still insisting to be present. But they ended there. Her voice rose. "How can you expect a delicious meal placed before you by your sister or daughter—not a paid servant—when you don't even give her what she needs to prepare a decent meal? I've run into her at the store in town. She's scared to death to spend an extra dollar on anything, yet you live in this big house, have the biggest ranch in these parts, and expect her to feed you like kings. You deserve to be fed liver and onions— made with bad meat."

Her anger had added that last bit without thinking. But then, she hadn't thought much about the other statements either. They'd just flown from her mouth, spawned of emotion. "I mean," she hurried and tried to repair a little of what she'd said. Her words came out a bit softer now. "If you haven't butchered her any meat for some time, how could the liver be good?"

"Don't worry, Miss Kate," Logan spoke up. The other two men just stared at Kate with jaws slightly agape. "She used the dry stuff we store for emergencies."

Ben Jones burst out with a belly-rolling laugh. "Good gracious, Stanley, where'd you come up with this gal? You're gonna have to lasso her in like a buckin' bronco and always keep a tight rein on her if you're goin' to survive. But sometimes those feisty ones make for the best—"

"Sorry, here's the bread." Susannah's entrance interrupted her father's words.

Kate was more than grateful they had. She would probably explode if the man proceeded to explain something about matters that were best kept behind closed doors, between a husband and wife. She didn't doubt for a moment he was capable of debasing such matters in public too. "It smells heavenly, Susannah," Kate said as the platter of sliced bread was placed in the spot on the table in front of her. She didn't care to play it safe any longer, withholding the name by which she'd grown to know this unfortunate woman. "Susannah," she said the name again, putting a little extra emphasis on it for good measure. Or bad measure—unsure of how this would work out. "Sit down and enjoy your meal now. You've done enough."

Stanley leaned close to Kate. With a hand raise to his mouth to direct his words at Kate, he said, "She goes by Clara."

"But I call her Susannah too," Logan piped up.

Ben glared at the boy before focusing on Kate. "Pay the boy no mind. Around here, she goes as Clara. It's her name. It's who she is. She's gone by it for nigh onto thirteen years now. So whoever told you it was Susannah, well, they've led you astray. Sorry about that, Miss Kate." He picked up his spoon. "Now hand me a couple of slabs of that bread and some of that butter, and let's eat this slop." His words were spoken with finality, forcefully, and with eyes projecting his authority to every person at the table.

Especially to Kate. She dipped her spoon into her soup and sipped. It didn't matter if there were a million onions floating on that spoon, or a grainy bite of rehydrated liver. She'd eat it and shut up.

CHAPTER 10

THE REMAINDER OF DINNER PROCEEDED in silence, except for the clank of spoons against porcelain or the shuffle of cowboy boots on the wooden floor beneath the table. Ben and Stanley had second helpings. Kate was unsure if that was a result of her chiding or if they were actually that hungry. She could barely finish her small bowl. Logan ate three bowls.

"Thanks, sis," Logan said, wiping out his soup bowl with the last slice of bread.

"You're welcome, Logan." Susannah smiled at her little brother with eyes that communicated sincere appreciation.

"Yes, thank you, Miss Jones." Kate refused to call her Clara.

Before Susannah could respond to Kate, Stanley stood. "Come on, Kate. Let's get out of here." He pulled out Kate's chair and whisked her away from the dining room.

Kate didn't give him credit for pulling her chair out for her to stand. She was certain it hadn't been prompted by manners, but rather by his selfish desire to rid himself of the unpleasant dining experience—and his family—and have Kate all to himself.

As Stanley grabbed her hand and led her back into the hallway, her insides recoiled at his forceful touch, but she didn't dare resist. She'd caused enough trouble here already. But she'd much rather go back into the dining room and eat ten more bowls of that soup than be alone with Stanley.

Together they walked into a room paneled with dark wood. Numerous shelves lined one of the walls, each sparsely filled with books. A library? Kate envisioned it as a dream of Clara Jones, growing slowly because of the difficulty of obtaining books in this isolated high-desert town. Kate was willing to bet her entire savings that there hadn't been a book added since her death thirteen years ago. The room, however, seemed to be taken over by all things cattle.

A brown-and-white hide hung from one of the walls like a tapestry. The wall opposite the near-empty bookshelves had a map tacked to the paneling next to the room's lone window. A large desk sat squarely in the middle of the room as if saying, "I'm the most important of all."

"This is my pa's office," Stanley stated with obvious pride. "We've got the biggest ranch in these parts, and it takes a lot to keep it runnin'. He's trainin' me to take over. One day this will all be mine." He swept his hand around the room and pointed to the map on the wall.

Kate assumed it was a map of their ranch. She was impressed by its size, if the scale of miles on the lower corner was correct. Plenty of land to split three ways. "What about Su—your sister and Logan?"

"Nope, it all comes to me."

"Is that fair?" Kate clenched her fists, hiding them amongst the folds of her skirt.

"Clara's a girl." He let out a laugh and then said, "And Logan's hardly fit to run a ranch."

"So split up the land three ways and let them sell their portion and keep the money for them to undertake something more to their liking or abilities."

There was that laugh again. Kate's stomach muscles tightened at the noise coming from Stanley's mouth.

"Ha, like what? Clara doesn't like anything. The only thing she's fit to do is take care of the house."

"Well, then give her the house. You and Logan split up the land."

Stanley glared at her like she'd said the most absurd thing he'd ever heard. "She'll get her own house when she gets married. And as for my little brother, well, he can't do anything. But I'll do my duty and keep him on here at the ranch. He can work alongside my ranch hands."

Although Kate was boiling, at the moment, curiosity moved her on to a subject that was bothering her even more than Stanley's view of his brother. "Does your sister have many suitors?"

"Ha." Stanley's sickening laugh surfaced again. "No." Then he stopped to think about what he'd said, almost like he'd realized there was something wrong with that picture. "But I suppose I can keep her on here as well after I inherit this place. She can keep doin' the cookin'. That's something she does enjoy."

"A girl as pretty as Susannah, and no gentlemen callers?" Kate could feel her brain working, trying to make sense of it. "Something doesn't seem right with that."

Stanley scratched his chin and stared briefly at the cowhide on the wall without really looking at it. "I do recall a man or two from up north, Hoy's Ranch. They took turns calling on Clara a few years back. One of them was even Old Man Hoy's son. But Pa ran'm off after his third or fourth visit. Told Hoy he was just after his land, not his daughter; told him to never come back."

"What about the other gentleman?"

"Oh, he wasn't no gentleman. The man was just a ranch hand up there at Hoy's place. Clara did seem a lot more upset when Pa ran him off. Cried for a week. Never came out of her room to make us dinner or nothin'. The house was a mess."

"Why did your pa run him off? It sounds like she must have liked him a great deal."

"The same reason I would have," Stanley said, straightening his back like he was master of the ranch. "He wasn't good enough for a Jones!"

Stanley grabbed Kate's hand again and pulled her toward the map hanging on the wall. "See, just look at our ranch. It takes up a good portion of the Yampa Valley. Tell me a lowlife ranch hand deserves to have a part of our hard work just because he marries my sister."

Kate wasn't going to tell Stanley anything at the moment, or it might come out laced with profanity—something she rarely used. But then she'd never come across a case of such unfairness before. Kate concentrated on the map to help control her tongue. A blue line formed a large, crooked kidney bean shape in the center of the map. Through the middle of this area ran the winding Yampa River. Within the blue bean-shaped circle and below the river was a squarish area set off by a red line.

"What do the red and blue lines mean?" Kate asked, gladly pulling her hand from his grasp so she could point to the lines that encompassed the majority of the map.

"This is our actual property," Stanley said, tracing the red line that encircled a small section at the bottom left corner of the map. "It's the land we hold deed to." He smiled, revealing a piece of browned onion in his teeth. "It's bigger than most around here." He reached up and pointed to the blue line that lay just inside the border of the map. "This marks the land that we claim the right to graze our cattle on."

"So you don't own it?"

"No. Nobody does. It's public domain." His face grew solemn. Or was it anger she saw? "Dang government went and made a lot of the good grazin' land around here into national forest about ten years back. Now there's less and less of it to be had. Thankfully, they didn't make any of our grazin' land into their ridiculous forest. The Joneses have been raisin' their cattle on this land for nearly twenty-five years now—my grandfather started this place. Now if that mutton-lover McCurdy would just keep his sheep off the best parts," he said as he pointed to a section of the map that had a river running through it, "then things might not be so bad."

"But that's part of the blue section," Kate said, feeling an overwhelming urge to defend Lucas McCurdy. "I thought you said it was public domain. That means anyone can use it. Am I not correct?"

"Yeah, well, pretty lady, you'd be right on that account." Stanley reached out and touched Kate at the waist. "But we've been here longer, and everyone in these parts knows that it's ours to use. He with the most power deserves to take what he wants." His hand slipped farther around Kate's waist, forcing her away from the map and close to his chest.

Kate tried to resist.

His arm was too strong. He pulled her closer.

Her heart beat fast. Not from excitement—not in the least—but from fear. It froze her mind.

She hated this arrogant, cattle-loving, little-brother-hating monster for that. And for what his dark eyes told her he wanted from her.

She struggled some more.

His arm tightened, this time joined by his other hand. It ran along the waistline of her dress, letting his fingers caress each fiber of fabric as if he were envisioning it was something else. "I like how you don't wear one of those blasted corsets laced up so tight like so many other women do." His hand slithered around to her back, sending creepy shivers down her spine as it moved.

Kate felt a few of the buttons at the back of her dress pop open. Then a few more. She struggled harder. Her mouth opened to scream. "A—"

His hand flew to her mouth, covering it and part of her nose. She struggled for breath. He brought his mouth to her face, brushing his lips against her cheek as he moved it to her ear. Whispering, his warm breath crawling down her neck like a deadly spider, he murmured, "Don't scream. Pa'll be right in here if you do. But I want to be alone, don't you?"

Kate's mind spun, unfreezing her from fear and converting it into plans of self-preservation.

He let go of her mouth. His eyes bore into her with a warning, silencing her better than his hand. "That's better." Cold, calloused, and uncaring, his fingers slipped into the opening at the back of her dress, setting off every nerve ending in her skin with fear and disgust. His eyes fixed on hers, warning her not to, but almost daring her to scream.

Don't let him ruin your life.

Fight! Use what you know!

Every cell of her body filled with determination—and adrenaline. She jerked her leg up and brought it down with force onto his foot, digging her narrow heel into his boot. His grip loosened enough that she could lift her knee farther, and she thrust it upward into his groin.

"Aagh!" Stanley wailed, releasing his hold on Kate.

She dashed to the far side of the room. Panting, she spat out the words, "Don't you ever do that again, or I will call the sheriff and have you thrown in jail."

Holding his groin, he muttered, "Doc Greene does what we tell him."

"Then I will call on the federal marshal." Kate threw open the door. Hanging on to its knob, she said, "I am not one of your brow-beaten western women who cowers at your every word and looks the other way while she's abused." She stormed out of the room. Over her shoulder, she said to the sniveling man now groaning in the desk chair, more for her own sake than for his, "I'll get Logan to take me home. He's the only gentleman in this house."

CHAPTER 11

A<small>FTER</small> K<small>ATE HAD ANNOUNCED TO</small> the rest of the Joneses that Stanley didn't feel well and neither did she, Logan had happily offered to take her home.

For the next few days, her mind could not stop replaying the events of that horrible evening. After the first day, she'd been able to get past her ordeal, priding herself on her study of male physiology and the vulnerability of their reproductive organs. And by the priceless surprise—or maybe it was shock— on Stanley's face as her knee had made contact.

But her thoughts could not be pulled away or comforted when it came to Susannah. Kate longed to help her, but she had no idea how.

The only thing that Kate could find solace in was the idea of reaching out to all women of this area, to lift them if needed, from whatever kind of suppression they were subjected to. She could teach them to discover their own worth and then fight to have the men in their lives recognize it too.

She was certain a knee to the groin wasn't the solution for those other women. But they needed to believe in themselves, to see themselves as something of value. If Kate could do that, if she could help these women in just some little way to have a better life while living in this wasteland, then she'd feel she'd accomplished something even more valuable than setting up a medical practice in Craig.

Kate's stethoscope still lay on the table where she'd left it, along with her other tools, after examining little Nyda Tucker for an earache this morning. She pulled herself out of her daydreams to put her things away in preparation for her next patient, who wouldn't be here until tomorrow. Stewart Hoy, her landlord, had a cyst on his back that needed lancing.

Kate didn't have a sufficient number of patients to pay the bills yet, but it was a start. A few of them even paid in money, so she rarely had to dip into her box under the bed. But today she was paid with a free meal at the hotel.

Tomorrow it would be a reduction on this month's rent. It all helped. Kate couldn't complain.

Now if she could only figure out how to help Susannah. And Mary Tucker, who just needed to believe in herself. And then there was Roselund Decker, whom she'd only ever seen at a distance, but Kate knew Roselund's father vehemently opposed her choice to wear trousers and wrangle horses—or whatever they called it. Why couldn't the girl do what she wanted, as long as it didn't hurt her or anyone else?

Roselund fascinated Kate. Here was another female trying to do a man's work. How had she gotten her job on that ranch? How did other people view her choice? And how did she ride that horse with such skill?

An idea formed. It excited Kate—it would serve multiple purposes. She'd get Roselund to teach her how to ride a horse. That way she'd get to know Roselund better, and at the same time, she'd procure a method of transportation for herself. Living out here in the West, she doubted that many patients would be able to come into her office. She could be more productive if she could travel to them. And relying on someone else to take her, or even buying herself a buggy, didn't sit with her well. She knew a buggy was the acceptable way for a woman to get around. But she knew even riding in wagons, which were much sturdier than buggies, over the roads in Yampa Valley, would be precarious in poor weather. And the speed was that of a turtle. If there were to be an emergency, she'd need to get there as fast as she could. Especially if she were planning to be competitive with Doc Greene.

With an extra lilt in her step, she put away her tools and tidied her small office/living room/bedroom. She pulled on a sweater and took a glance in the mirror that hung above the dresser. She straightened her hair and then headed toward the stairs on a mission to learn how to ride a horse.

A knock on the door startled her a bit, though it sounded a bit timid. A new patient, maybe? Hopefully. She walked briskly to the door.

When she opened it, her heart slipped in an extra beat. "Mr. McCurdy."

"Uh, excuse me, lass, but I heard you were open for business now that you've got yourself an official doctor's office. Do I need to make an appointment for your services? Or can I just come in now?"

Kate realized she'd not moved, keeping the poor man out on the landing. "Oh, no, now is just fine. Come in, come in." She ushered him inside with a shaky sweep of her hand.

His boots were surprisingly clean, compared to most cowboy boots Kate was used to seeing. A worn leather jacket covered his broad shoulders, but was draped over one arm rather than being worn like normal. A limp was detectable in his walk as he stepped over to the chair she offered him.

"Have you hurt yourself, Mr. McCurdy?" Kate cringed as she said it. Of course he'd been hurt. Why else would he be here, walking with a limp, holding his arm close to his side with his jacket draped over his shoulder?

"Yes, Miss Don—" He paused, glancing up to her as he lowered into the chair. "I s'pose I should call you Doctor Donahue. I'm sorry."

Kate couldn't help but stare into his eyes, again finding their shade of blue as pure as a crystal-clear lake. But it was more than that. There seemed to be an indescribable light emanating from them, as if revealing something of his inner being.

"I hope you don't mind." He looked at her as if expecting a response.

"Oh, oh, no, don't be sorry," Kate said, realizing she had been staring and not paying attention. She cleared her throat in an effort to calm her nerves. "Now, tell me what happened before I start your exam." *Why am I so nervous? I've examined plenty of patients before now.* Maybe it was because he was her first adult male patient since she'd arrived here. That had to be it.

"My limp's nothing. 'Tis my arm that hurts."

She drew in a deep breath and helped Mr. McCurdy remove his jacket. Composure was a must. It had to be learned. She had another male patient tomorrow with her landlord, Mr. Hoy, and she'd better get over this fear right here and now.

As he described to her how his horse had tripped on a hole that he hadn't seen, throwing him and landing him on his arm on a rocky spot of land at the edge of his grazing rights, Kate's heart took on that familiar ache. She'd felt it for Susannah. She'd felt it for Mary. And even for Roselund, whom she'd not even met. It was an aching desire to help these unfortunate people. She didn't know that Mr. McCurdy's broken arm—as she'd quickly diagnosed it—had to do with his sad life, but the thought of him lying there in the middle of nowhere, all alone, with no one to help tend to his injury gave her a lump in her throat. He had to come all the way into town and seek out her help.

"From your description, I daresay you've broken your arm, Mr. McCurdy. Let me roll up your sleeve and examine it better to make sure." She took ahold of the sleeve of his shirt. It was made of blue plaid and had the smell of having been recently laundered with strong lye soap. She found the scent slightly medicinal but somewhat refreshing. Pleasant. Kate's hand brushed across his bare arm as she pushed up his sleeve. She felt him shiver. "I'm sorry. Am I hurting you, Mr. McCurdy?"

"Oh, no. Not at all." He smiled, peering off to a corner of the room.

"I'll try to be more careful." She pressed her fingers into the flesh of his arm, probing for the bones, feeling for any breaks. He winced. "Sorry." She felt some more, determining how she should pull his arm to set the bone properly—if need be. Unfortunately, his sleeve was in the way. "I'm going to need you to remove your shirt, Mr. McCurdy. I need to set your arm, and it is getting in the way of my work."

"I understand." He started unbuttoning the shirt with his good hand, opening a v-shaped view of his chest as he moved down on the row of buttons. The shirt fell away from his shoulders, and Kate gasped. A tingle ran through her.

"Is there something wrong, Doctor?"

"No. No, it's nothing," Kate said, admiring the way the muscles of his upper body stood out beneath his smooth cream-white skin—so much so, she could have identified each one of them with ease, if she'd wanted.

She held on to his lower arm, determined not to think about this married man's warm skin beneath her hands, chiding her body for the feelings surfacing because of him. And she was a doctor. She had an arm to set. A professional air must accompany her service. "This might hurt."

"I am accustomed to pain, lass."

Kate sensed he was referring to more than just the arm. Her thoughts couldn't help but jump momentarily to what that pain might entail. She'd seen it in his eyes before, hiding behind the sparkle in those alluring blue irises. His obvious suffering ripped at her heart. Could she possibly help him—with more than a simple setting of a bone could accomplish? "I'm sorry to hear that."

"Should ye want me to feel the pain?" He gave her a crooked smile. He looked down at his bare arm still cradled within her hands. "Right now it don't feel too bad."

"No. That's not what I meant." She felt herself blush. "I was just . . . it sounds like you've been through a lot. And I'm sorry for that."

Bracing herself so as to maximize her strength, she pulled on his arm, hearing a short cry of pain from him as she felt the bone move back into place.

"There. It can start healing properly now. Do you live alone, or do you have someone who can assist you with your chores?" Kate asked, fearing she already knew the answer but hoping maybe he did have help.

"I live alone." His eyes shone of determination, his fighting spirit endearing him to Kate. "But I can manage just fine."

"I imagine you can." She really could—and she did—picture a man pursuing the dream of owning his own land and raising sheep despite being a stranger in a strange land, having a neighbor like Stanley Jones, and a "witch" of a wife who hated this corner of the country. She wondered what his wife, Tempest, was doing now. Did her dislike of everything here in Craig include Lucas McCurdy? That was hard for Kate to comprehend, but if it was true, why hadn't Tempest signed the papers when Lucas filed for divorce?

After Kate wrapped his arm in gauze, she applied a layer of plaster. As she smoothed out the white plaster to form a cast, she felt grateful for having studied under a doctor in medical school who had learned while serving in the Crimean War this method of immobilizing a limb. He'd told her it wasn't a widely used practice here in America, which made her feel even more fortunate that she could help Lucas with the most effective treatment available. She braved a look at his eyes. "This will take a few hours to set up fully. Don't go riding your horse back out to your place until it's hard. Okay?"

He nodded.

"And don't get it wet if at all possible. You'll need to be careful with it. For the next few days, it will still hurt. If the pain gets to be too much, get yourself a strip of willow. Peel it off just under the bark and suck on it until it's dry. It has something in it known as salicylic acid. It helps with pain. Indians have used it for ages, but the western world is finally putting it into a pill form called aspirin. But that won't help you here. It's difficult to find, and definitely not on the shelves at Decker's store."

"Many thanks, Doctor Donahue. 'Tis something I'll do. There are plenty of them trees down by the river." He pulled his wet cast away after she'd finished wrapping it. He then picked up his hat with his other hand and placed it over his neatly combed hair, though the curly ends refused to be tamed.

"I'm glad to hear that." Kate didn't recall ever seeing his hair combed so neatly before. She was touched that he recognized her as a doctor and had come dressed with respect for her profession.

He struggled to put his good arm back into his shirt. Kate helped drape the other sleeve over his shoulder and assisted him with his coat. "Yer the kindest doctor this Irishman's ever met." He tipped his hat, adding a chipper, "Good day, lass," and slipped out the door.

After she shut the door with his departure, she clung momentarily to the doorknob. Then she hurried to the window overlooking the street and watched Lucas awkwardly untie his horse from the hitching post with his good hand before leading it on foot away from her office, making sure he didn't damage his unset cast. His horse, obviously a gentle creature, stood still throughout, patiently waiting for him to free the reins using just one hand. It was a beautiful horse, with an arrowhead of white above his nose and sandy-chestnut hair. She found herself longing for the exam to have lasted longer.

This is ridiculous. If she were to wish for all of her patients to sit with her and talk of the weather or about the grazing habits of sheep after their exams, she'd never make any money.

Money! She'd forgotten to ask for payment.

It was probably just as well. She'd probably have told him his first visit was free like she'd done with Susannah. Maybe even all of his future visits. Would there be future visits? She didn't want to wish a broken arm on anybody, but she wouldn't mind seeing him again.

And then it came crashing back down: a reminder more distasteful than liver and onions. She was longing for another visit from a married man.

She snatched up her coat and ran out the door, pushing her arms through the jacket as she scurried down the steps. Roselund! A nice, brisk horse ride was just what she needed right now—not that she'd ever done it before, but she needed some kind of diversion to scare the inappropriate thoughts right out of her.

CHAPTER 12

"I'm sorry to say Roselund's not here right now." Mrs. Decker's plump face looked rosier than usual, the heat from the oven flushing her cheeks.

"That's all right." Kate tried hard to keep her disappointment from her voice. She'd really looked forward to meeting the girl and discussing the possibility of horse-riding lessons. "I can come back later."

"I would really like you to meet her. I still think your gentle manner could rub off on her, help settle her down to be a proper young lady."

Kate cringed inside at Mrs. Decker's expectations for her. Proper young ladies do not knee men in the groin or daydream about married men.

"At least help her tone things down," Mrs. Decker continued, "so the menfolk will take notice of her. She's going on twenty-one now. Spinster is not a pretty word, or necessary in these parts, that's for sure."

"I'm honored that you think of me so highly. And I'd be glad to talk to her, if you think it would help. But, Lavender, I'm not sure I'm the right person to tell her to 'tone things down.'" Kate rushed her hand to her mouth. "Is it okay if I call you Lavender?"

"Certainly. It's my name. Wish more people'd call me Lavender. It's a lot prettier than Mrs. Decker, I daresay."

"That it is," Kate said, enjoying the aroma of baking bread as much as she would a field of the purple flowers after which Lavender was named. This woman always made her think of all things beautiful. "May I stay and chat for a while if your daughter is not expected to be gone too long?"

"I'd love the company."

"Wonderful." Kate took a seat at the table, looking forward to the company too. "What are you making?"

"Sweet rolls with cinnamon and walnuts. Sam loves them." She poured some sugar into a coffee grinder and turned the crank. "Making the frosting right now."

"In a coffee grinder?" Kate's voice reflected her confusion.

"Heavens no." Lavender wagged her finger at Kate. "I'm just grinding the sugar up real fine." She removed the powdery sugar and added it to a bowl with some butter. "You'll have to at least stay long enough to taste a roll after it's frosted. Old Sheriff Greene says they're to die for. I think they're pretty good myself. Keep telling Sam to let me put a pan of them in the store each time I make them. We'd sell out of them in no time. They'd bring in more money than his silly drawer of pocketknives. Most men already got themselves a good knife—wouldn't part with it for nothing. 'So why do they want to come in and buy a new one?' I tell him. 'In case they lose 'em,' Sam says. Well, I say they're not going to lose their knives as often as they're going to want to eat one of my rolls." She winked at Kate as she continued to give the frosting a good stir.

"I think you're absolutely right."

"It'd be nice to have knives that'd sell like cinnamon rolls—or something else that could fly off the shelves and bring in lots of money."

That gave Kate some concern. "Is your store not doing well?"

"No, it's doing as good as a hen gleaning a wheat field after harvest. Me and Sam could just use some extra cash."

Not wanting to be nosy and let all her manners slip by the wayside, Kate tilted her head slightly and looked at Lavender, hoping her eyes were enough to beg an explanation.

"Last week, Mr. R. H. Hughes offered to let us buy him out—at least for this particular store. We just need to scrape together some more for a down payment so we can get a loan from the bank. Did you hear? We're gettin' ourselves a bank here in Craig—should be finished sometime next year. They're setting themselves up a temporary spot behind the land office until it's built."

Kate didn't care about the news of a new bank—she cared about what this could mean for Lavender and Sam. "Is that something you and Mr. Decker want to do? Own your own place?"

"Oh, yeah, Sam's always dreamed of it, and I dream of keeping Sam happy." Lavender added a pinch of salt to her frosting.

Inspired by the smell of fresh bread and warm cinnamon, Kate spoke up. "Lavender, I've got a great idea!"

"What's that?"

"Start with asking Mr. Decker one more time if he'd be willing to let you sell your sweet rolls in your store. If he still says no, then go somewhere else to sell them." Kate almost clapped her hands at the idea. "And I've got just the place." She remembered the tiny menu devoid of sweets over at Sunny's—also the woman's apparent nose for business.

"Where?" Lavender definitely looked interested.

"Sunny's."

"The saloon?"

"It serves more than drinks now. You should walk on over there some day. Take a look. Buy a sandwich. Talk to Sunny. She's got some great ideas to make her place really successful."

"But Sam would die of embarrassment if I were even to go and talk with that woman, let alone sell rolls at her place."

"You wouldn't actually be selling them there at the saloon. You'd sell them to Sunny, who would pay you for them at a lower price and then sell them to her customers at a higher price. You'd both be making money. And helping each other out."

"I don't think Sam would like that either."

"Don't say anything until he says something to you about it." Kate stood and peeked in the saucepan to get a better look at the frosting. "Does he pay attention to you when you're baking, counting how many rolls you make each time?"

"No."

"There you go! You'll be fine." Kate wondered just how much attention Mr. Decker gave her outside the store—the R. H. Hughes Mercantile appeared to consume his life. Lavender deserved a little creative entrepreneurship to call her own. Not only would she help her husband obtain his dream, but it would boost her self-worth at the same time. "Just make extras every time you bake them for him, or even better, make them more often for him. And while he's out minding the store, you take them out the back door and across the street to Sunny's place. She'll pay you. With that money, you can replace the flour and sugar from your pantry, buy more to make more rolls, and put a little of it back in your pocket just for you. And because you already get your ingredients at wholesale prices, you'll most likely be able to put a fair amount back in that pocket."

Lavender's face lit up as the idea seemed to click in her head. "I think it just might work!" She leaned away from the hot stove and with a floured hand pulled Kate into a hug. "I knew I liked you since that first day I set eyes on you."

The conversation moved on to the weather, about how it was getting colder and Lavender warning Kate to buy an extra-warm coat to weather the winter. When Lavender's mitted hand pulled the pan of rolls out of the oven, the smell nearly made Kate lose all manners and snatch one out of the pan. After Lavender drizzled them with frosting, she dished one onto a plate and handed it to Kate.

The first bite was as good as Kate had anticipated, with a perfect blend of sweetness and buttery cinnamon. Kate opened her mouth, ready to fork in a second bite, when the back door next to the sink flew open.

"Howdy, Ma. Is that your sweet rolls I smell?"

"Sure thing, Roselund," Lavender said, licking her fingers.

"Ah, Ma, you know how I hate bein' called Roselund."

"It's your name, child."

"That's just it, when I was a child you called me Rosie. I liked that better."

"It's time to become a lady, Roselund. Besides, your pa don't think it's a fitting name, not with Rosy's house of ill-repute moved into town, bringing all those—those scantily clad—well, you know what I mean."

"Oh, Ma!" The young woman rolled her eyes, tipping her head back in the process and knocking the cowboy hat from her head. She caught it and slapped it back in place then appeared to notice Kate for the first time. Her eyes met Kate's momentarily as she approached her mother and motioned for a roll. "Servin' your rolls to customers back in the kitchen now, are you?" she asked. "I always thought that was a good idea." She snatched the plate Lavender offered her and plopped onto the chair at the table next to Kate, nearly dropping her roll onto the table. "Howdy. My name's Rosie. What's yours?" She held out her free hand toward Kate.

"I'm Katherine Donahue." Kate accepted her hand with delight and gave it a shake. "I'm the new doctor in town. I moved here from New York about a month ago"

"You don't say! That's great!" Her eyes seemed to twinkle with delight. She turned to her mother. "See, Ma, this lady's doin' the job of a man. Why can't I?"

"You know it's not me that's against it. It's your pa. What other people think is not what bothers me. I worry myself sick all the time that you're going to get hurt. That's why I don't like it."

Rosie punched her mother in the arm. "Ah, Ma, I love you."

"Love you too, girl." Lavender wagged a spoon at her. "Now if you can just stay safe . . . slow that dang horse of yours down, for heaven's sake!"

"Lavender!" Mr. Decker's voice carried in through the door that led out to the store. "I need your help out here."

"You two girls talk. Eat another roll," Lavender said. "I've got to go put out a fire out front, it sounds like." She tucked the spoon into a sink full of dirty dishes and darted through the door.

"Speaking of horses," Kate said, feeling she'd better bring up the subject before Lavender came back. "I'm trying to find someone to teach me how to ride a horse. I was hoping maybe you'd be willing to take on the job?"

Rosie looked at Kate, glancing from head to toe. "I'm sure you could find a hundred cowboys in this town who would climb over each other to get the job. Not to mention a few punches thrown to win that chance," she added with a smile.

"I don't want them to teach me," Kate said, recoiling at the thought of Stanley helping her up into a saddle. "First off, they would try to talk me out of it, telling me to use a buggy. Secondly, I know I'd be more comfortable learning from a woman."

"My turn for a question." Rosie leaned close to Kate. "Why do you want to ride?" She glanced over her shoulder at the door that led outside. "I haven't met a woman yet in this town that wanted to do it. I even offered to learn them. And you're some fancy lady from the East. I don't get it."

"I'm a doctor. I need a fast, efficient way to get to my patients—without having to rely on someone else."

"Gotcha!" Rosie slapped Kate on the back, hurling her into the table.

Kate caught herself, bracing her hands on the table at each side of her. "How soon can you start?"

"Right now. Or at least as soon as I finish this." Rosie held up her half-eaten sweet roll. She took a bite. With her mouth full of bread and frosting, she said, "You got any trousers?"

"No."

"You're going to need trousers. Can't ride in a dress. And sidesaddle don't work. It's as worthless as teats on a boar hog."

"I guess I could buy a pair from your parents' store," Kate said, trying to guess how much they'd cost and how much that would leave in her savings. She hated buying a pair of pants when she had so many extras skirts in her closet. And then there was the factor that she wanted to look professional as she traveled out to treat patients. She took a good look at Rosie. She wore a man's plaid shirt tied into a knot at her waist. It accentuated her narrow waistline and struggled to cover her ample bosom. The pants she wore had been cinched up with a length of rope; no doubt, a man's belt was probably not small enough to work with her girlish figure. Rosie looked like a girl having fun, but she was not even close to looking professional.

"Do your parents have dressier pants in their store?" Kate pointed to Rosie's mud-caked denim trousers.

"No." Rosie tilted her head to one side and stared at Kate. "You're wantin' somethin' more fittin' for a doctor, ain't you?"

"Yes. I was hoping for something along those lines."

"You could take a skirt and split it up the middle, fit it to your legs, and then sew it back up. Ma hated it when I used to cut up my dresses to do that. Finally, she bought me a pair of men's trousers from the store without Pa knowin', tellin' me she'd give them to me if I'd promise to quit cuttin' up my dresses. And at least wear a dress to church on Sunday."

Kate wasn't bad with a needle and thread, but "cuttin' up" her skirts was beyond her abilities. Still, she wanted to do it. She couldn't even imagine her own mother's reaction to such an action. *It doesn't matter—that's behind me now. Like so many things.* "Can you teach me how to do that too?"

CHAPTER 13

LATER IN THE DAY, AFTER Kate had eaten two of Lavender's cinnamon rolls, Rosie came over to Kate's apartment.

"I brought Ma's scissors," Rosie said the moment she closed the door behind her. She held them up and walked toward Kate's wardrobe. "Show me the skirt you wanna cut up. Let's hurry and get to it, 'cause it's a dang gorgeous day outside. You'll not find a better one in September—perfect for your first ridin' lesson."

Kate approached the pine wardrobe she'd purchased secondhand from a family on Fourth Street the day she'd moved into her place. It was crudely made, but served its purpose, holding all the clothing she'd managed to pack and bring with her. Though the small wardrobe brimmed with dresses, skirts, and blouses, she'd had to leave twice as many back home in New York. Each article of clothing was precious and needed to last her indefinitely—she had no idea how long it would be until she could afford to purchase more. To cut into one of her skirts, and possibly ruin it, made her uncomfortable.

She opened the pine cabinet and sorted through each garment she'd draped upon wooden hangers purchased along with the wardrobe, looking for her oldest, most worn-out skirt. "How about this one?" She pulled out a black cotton skirt she knew had a frayed spot on part of the hem.

"No." Rosie waved a hand at it. "That one's too narrow. We need something with lots of gathers and plenty of fullness. Trust me, those kind work best for butcherin' up a dress. Especially if you want it to still look like you're wearin' a skirt when you're done—not a pair of trousers." She sorted through Kate's clothing. "That is what you're goin' for, ain't it?"

"Yes, it is." Kate only hoped this would work.

Kate watched Rosie pull out her favorite skirt—her dark-blue one made of the finest wool and the most expensive article of clothing she'd brought with her. "Are you sure that's the one I should use?"

Rosie nodded. "If you want to do this right."

Kate gulped to ease her unsettled stomach. "Okay, let's do this."

Rosie took the dark-blue skirt and spread it out on Kate's bed. She pulled a box of straight pins from her pocket and proceeded to pin them in a straight line, from the hem up the middle and past the center of the skirt. "I'm markin' where you're gonna cut. I want you to do it 'cause I want you to learn. You might find you want to do this to a heap of dresses." She shot Kate a taunting grin.

Kate bent over the bed and cut carefully into the fine fabric, cringing less and less with each snip of the scissors.

"I ran into an old friend on my way back to town today." Rosie stood at Kate's side as Kate continued to cut. "He had a newly plastered left arm. Said it was you who doctored him up right nice."

"That would have been Mr. McCurdy," Kate responded, maintaining her concentration on making small, precise cuts with the scissors.

"Yeah, Lucas was wearin' a smile as wide as the Yampa Valley. He couldn't say enough good things about you. If I was a bettin' woman, I'd wager he's sweet on you."

"What?" Kate clamped the scissor handles together, cutting a full inch past the last pin. "Gracious! What have I done?" She fingered the disastrous cut.

Rosie took the scissors away from Kate. "Calm your horses, girl." She leaned over and scrutinized Kate's cutting job. "I purposely put the pins short of my mark 'cause I knew you was a beginner at this." She punched Kate in the arm. "It'll be fine. But what in tarnation made you do that? You was cuttin' so careful-like at first." She leaned back up and looked at Kate while a mischievous smile curled the ends of her mouth. "Time for another wager here. I'm bettin' your sweet on him."

"Him?" Kate felt a flush of warmth creep across her cheeks. "What are you talking about?"

"Lucas McCurdy. Who else?" Rosie raised her eyebrows. "The man with those soft, golden locks of hair that curl 'round his hat. And that soft heart of gold of his that would curl any girl's toes."

"It sounds to me as if you're the one who's sweet on him."

"Naw, Lucas and me are just friends. He moved here at the same time as me and my ma and pa—about five years ago. I was sixteen; he was pushing twenty-three. I'd always help Pa fill his orders at the store so I could drool over the man like a dog over a lazy butcher's soup bone." Rosie hitched up her chest. "Hey, I was just a dumb kid."

"So he doesn't make you drool, as you say, anymore?" Why did Kate hope he didn't?

"Heck, no." Rosie stared at the ceiling as if picturing a dream. "I want a man who's as tough as a maverick stallion, one who answers only to the land but is secretly waitin' to be tamed like a buckin' bronco by a girl just as stubborn as him." She returned her gaze to Kate. "Lucas is a worn-out horse that's long since been broken—broken by a tempest named Tempest. You can have him."

"I don't want him—I mean, I'm not looking for a man, I—" Kate could feel her face flush ever warmer than before. "This is ridiculous. Why are we even discussing Mr. McCurdy?"

"Darlin', you were the one who went haywire with the scissors when I mentioned his name and then drooled with your eyes when I described him. Okay, only as much as a dog over a dry bone, but still, I can see it in your eyes. He's pokin' at your heart with a big pitchfork."

"Even if he was—which he is not—it doesn't matter. Nothing is going to happen between Mr. McCurdy and me. You forget he's a married man."

"True." Rosie sat on the edge of the bed and unraveled a length of black thread. She bit it off with her teeth. "But if a woman had a fine horse and browbeat him every day, told him how much she hated him, and then abandoned him out in a cold, lonely field, with nothing, I'd say she no longer deserved that horse. Wouldn't you?"

"Horses and people are two different animals." Kate offered a weak laugh. "Things are not that simple with us."

"Well, that's the problem with people—we let too many things get in the way of our lives. Sometimes I wish we were all horses." Rosie wet the end of the thread with her tongue and threaded it through a needle.

"Speaking of life," Kate said, remembering Lavender's request to help settle her down to be a proper young lady. She doubted her abilities to do that, especially since Kate's polished manners grew more tarnished by the day, but she could give her some advice. "When you do meet up with a man who is your 'maverick stallion' as you say, it wouldn't hurt for you to let your feminine side show through. No matter how tough a man might seem on the outside, on the inside he's still a regular, run-of-the-mill man. And men like women—their softness, their curves, their gentle nature, and most of all, they like for the female to need to be protected by their male counterpart. That doesn't mean you can't be strong or work at the things you love. Just remember that women and men are meant to be different—equal, mind you, but different."

"I s'pose." Rosie squirmed and pulled a portion of the cut fabric onto her lap. "Let's get this skirt of yours stitched up so we can get you on top of a horse the way God intended a person to sit there."

An hour later, Kate stepped out into a fall breeze wearing her new "riding" skirt, pleased with how it had turned out. "I'm so excited," she said to Rosie as they hurried down the steps. Yet, she was nervous at the same time.

"Well, you should be. There's nothin' that beats ridin' your own horse. The control, the freedom, the speed—you're gonna love it. Of course, you won't be ridin' your own horse today." They rounded the corner of the saddle shop, and Rosie pointed to one of two horses tied to the hitching post. "I borrowed you a mare from Hoy's ranch to learn on. Sometime soon though, you'll wanna get you one that's yours."

The two oldest Hoy boys stood behind the hitching post, petting the lowered nose of the horse Rosie had just pointed to. "What are you doin' with Grandpa's horse, Miss Rosie?" asked Douglas, the biggest boy.

"I'm gonna teach Miss Kate how to ride today."

"You're going to teach me right here? On Yampa Avenue? In front of all these people?" Kate swept her hand toward the center of town while taking several quick breaths.

"Where else?" Rosie raised her eyebrow.

"I thought maybe out on some secluded corner of your ranch." Kate liked that idea much better.

"First off, it's not my ranch. I just work out at the Hoy place. Second, how in tarnation was I supposed to get you out there? Put you on the back of my horse and ride ya all the way out there then ride you all the way back to town when we was done? Blasted waste of time that'd be. Plus, if you're gonna get up into a saddle, it may as well be your own, and we may as well start now."

"Don't worry, Miss Kate." Douglas stopped petting the horse and looked at her. "Daisy, here, she won't buck you off. Grandpa says she's a kid's horse, that she don't care who her rider is or how stupid they are. She's who I always ride when I go out to the ranch."

"Thank you, Douglas, I appreciate your information." Kate hoped it was accurate and ignored that he'd just insinuated she was stupid.

"Come on, let's do this." Rosie motioned for Kate to come to the left side of Daisy while she unhitched the reins from the post. "Now, watch what I do. I take the reins in my left hand, grab onto her mane with the same hand, and with my other hand, I hold onto the saddle while I stick my left foot in the stirrup. Then I pull myself up and swing my right leg around and then sit in the saddle." Rosie moved in one fluid motion into the saddle.

Kate hesitated.

"You can do that, Miss Kate. It's easy." Douglas looked up her, his six-year-old eyes brimming with confidence in her behalf.

"You're right. I can." Kate stepped over to the horse as Rosie dismounted, determined to mount the animal quickly and easily—just as Rosie had done. She took the reins from Rosie. Keeping them in her left hand, she latched onto a tuft of Daisy's mane. She stretched her leg up as far as she could and managed to slip the ball of her foot into the stirrup. *I'm getting this; I'm doing it!* She grabbed onto the back of the saddle and lifted herself up. When she went to swing her right leg over, she realized her hand was in the way. When she let go of the back of the saddle so she could throw her leg over, the horse moved. She lost her balance and fell to the ground onto her back, barely managing to pull her leg from the stirrup in time.

The two little boys laughed.

That hurt worse than the pain throbbing in her backside. "I thought you said this horse wouldn't buck me off."

"She didn't buck you off." Douglas laughed even harder. "She took a step. You just didn't hang on right!"

Kate looked to Rosie, whose smile looked to be holding back laughter. *She don't care who her rider is or how stupid they are.* Little Douglas's words cut into her thoughts, adding humiliation to her pain. Kate had graduated from medical school at the top of her class. Surely she could learn how to mount a horse. And ride it. She had to! "What did I do wrong?"

Rosie stepped over to Daisy and patted the back of the saddle. "First off, you grabbed hold of the cantle." She moved her hand over to a metal handle of sorts that stuck out from the front of the saddle. "You should have grabbed onto the horn, like I did. That way your right arm's not in the way for sittin' down. Now watch again."

Kate made detailed notes in her mind, scrutinizing every motion Rosie made as she mounted Daisy a second time.

Kate tried it again. As her right leg swung over the horse and she sat down on the saddle, a euphoric feeling rushed through her chest and she couldn't hold back a smile. "I did it!"

"Don't go struttin' your stuff like an old rooster yet." Rosie mounted her horse, sitting level with Kate now. "The hardest part's yet to come, darlin'."

After quick instructions on how to use the reins, Kate rode side by side with Rosie down Yampa Avenue.

Kate could practically feel the townspeople's stares penetrate her skin, trying to irritate her nerves as she rode past each individual—not just one or two, but at least two dozen. Everyone else in town seemed to be out enjoying the last of the good weather before winter set in.

Then she decided to welcome the stares, hoping more women would follow her lead. Why wouldn't they want the convenience men had to go where they wanted, when they wanted, without having to hitch up a wagon? Plus, sitting high off the ground, feeling the breeze brush past her face as she moved effortlessly forward exhilarated Kate. No wonder Rosie liked it so much.

Then, without warning, in front of the mercantile and half a dozen onlookers, while Kate tried to maneuver past a stray dog in the road like Rosie showed her, she accidentally leaned to one side too heavily and Daisy bucked her off. With her pride bruised as badly as her backside, Kate wanted to become invisible, lie there in the dirt, and wait for a year until she got back onto that horse. Rosie dismounted in a flash and rushed to Kate's side. *How sweet; she's here to console me.* Surely, Rosie would tell her it was okay to quit for the day.

Rosie grabbed her by the elbow and pulled. "Get up, darlin', and get back on that horse."

"But—"

"If you don't do it now, you'll never want to try again. Believe me."

Kate trusted Rosie. Sore in more ways than one, Kate climbed back up on Daisy and followed Rosie to the outskirts of town.

They rode fast, and they rode far.

The next day they did the same.

And the next day. And the next.

On the fifth day of riding lessons, Rosie showed up at Kate's place with a different horse. Tied to the hitching post in Daisy's usual spot stood a fine-looking mare with a light-chestnut-colored coat. It reminded her of Mr. McCurdy's horse, only a little darker and without the white arrowhead marking between the eyes. Then that reminded Kate of Lucas. She hoped his arm was mending well and that no more mishaps had befallen him. Poor man, having lost his wife and child through no fault of his own. "Where's Daisy?" Kate asked, trying to bring her thoughts back to the matter at hand.

"This here mare's almost as gentle as Daisy, but she's for sale. Old man Hoy said he'd give her to you for a good price if you're interested."

"Me, buy a horse?" Kate hadn't thought that far out.

"Yeah! What else you gonna do? Someone comes to fetch you to come out into the toolies to do some doctorin', and you to tell them, 'Hold on an hour while I go rent me a horse and saddle'? I don't think so. You need your own horse, darlin'."

Kate knew Rosie was right. She petted the horse's snout, and it nudged Kate's hand for more attention. Its big brown eyes looked at Kate as if to say, *I promise to love you if you love me.* "How much is Mr. Hoy asking?"

"Fifty dollars. That's good for a horse of her bloodline." Rosie gave the horse's flanks an affectionate pat. "I'm sure Stewart Hoy'll give you a good deal on a secondhand saddle. And I arranged with Gus over at the livery stable to give you a good deal on boarding her. Only four bits a week."

Kate knew she had the money sitting in that box beneath her bed. But would that leave her enough for everything else she needed—and to survive on—until she could gain enough paying customers? But Rosie was right. She needed the convenience of her own horse and saddle. It could be as crucial to her practice as a proper exam table. "I'll take her," Kate said, knowing she'd still have a little nest egg left in her jewelry box. "And tell your boss thank you."

"Well, let's get to practicing with your new mare." Rosie mounted her horse and nodded for Kate to do the same. As the two of them steered their horses away from the saddle shop, Rosie asked, "So, what name you gonna give her?"

"Doesn't she already have one?"

"Yeah, but I'm not gonna tell you. She's yours now. You need to come up with your own name for her—one that means something to you, something that she reminds you of. My horse," Rosie patted the neck of her brown-gray spotted stallion. "He makes me feel happy, same as the sunshine does. So I call him Sunshine."

Kate thought for a moment, glad that she could actually ride her horse down the street now without having to concentrate on the mechanics any longer. "I think I'll name her Lucy, after my lady's maid. She encouraged me to become a doctor when everyone else in my life said my dream was ridiculous. Now this Lucy will help me to be the doctor I need to be. She'll transport me to my patients in a fashion everyone else may consider ridiculous." She found it interesting how her heart ached more to see her former maid than her parents at the moment. In the short time she'd been gone from home, the gaping hole in her life—created by the sudden absence of her parents—had healed to the point she rarely hurt from it anymore.

"That's a perfect name!" Rosie motioned forward with a wide sweep of her arm. "Come on, Lucy, let's take Kate out and teach her some more about ridin'."

The next day Kate pulled the money from her box without the least bit of regret or hesitancy and paid for Lucy.

A week later, after only a few more tumbles to the ground and a few lessons on how to saddle a horse, Kate felt like she could take Lucy out and ride her all by herself. And she did. She spent an entire first day of October roaming the streets of Craig and the trails on the fringe of town, getting to know her new home better and better.

The following day, Logan stopped by her office.

"Miss Kate, Miss Kate!" The words penetrated the door between knocks.

From the sound of Logan's voice, he wasn't here for a casual visit.

Was she going to need her horse? She had a niggling fear that she would. Was she ready?

It didn't matter. She was a doctor, and if people needed her, she would go.

CHAPTER 14

KATE HURRIED OVER AND OPENED the door to see the boy shivering on her doorstep, huffing for air. "You shouldn't have pulled yourself up these stairs. There are plenty of people you could have sent up to get me. I would have come down in a flash." She pulled him inside and rubbed his shoulders. "And where is your jacket? You'll catch cold!"

"I couldn't wait to find anyone, Miss Kate. I's in a hurry." Logan gave no resistance when Kate lowered him into a chair by the stove. "It's Mrs. Castillo; she's about to have a baby. It's her first one, and she's scared. Mr. Castillo came to our ranch and asked me to go fetch the doctor 'cause he had to run back to help her." He smiled big. "All the way to town I knew was going to fetch you. I figured Mrs. Castillo would rather have you delivering her baby than the sheriff. I know I would."

Kate gave Logan a hug. He deserved a thousand more, but she needed to gather her things. "Where do the Castillos live? I don't know that family."

"They're homesteading a piece about fifteen miles southeast of our ranch. Twenty miles from here." Logan looked up at Kate, his body still shivering but his eyes sincere. "You want me to come with you? Show you the way?" His grin grew even bigger. "I heard you'd gone and learned to ride a horse." The smile faded. "You could've asked me. I would've taught you."

"I'm sure you could have, Logan. And done just as good of a job as Miss Decker."

"Rosie?" Logan's smile returned. "I like Miss Rosie. She always talks nice to me."

Kate rushed over to her dresser. "Let me get you a coat; at least something to ward off the cold if you're coming with me."

She bundled him up in three of her sweaters and helped him down the steps. Thank heavens he at least had a hat with flaps that folded down to warm his ears.

The sun had warmed the fall morning by the time Kate followed Logan south out of town. "I'll take things slow," Logan said over his shoulder. "So you won't have trouble keeping up."

"That's okay, Logan. We can go much faster. I'll be just fine," Kate said, knowing that babies don't wait for slow doctors. When Logan didn't increase his speed enough for Kate, she dug her heels into Lucy. The horse darted forward. Kate scrambled to hang on.

Logan was at her side in a second, a scared look on his face. "Pull the reins up harder. You gotta slow her down. There's a ravine up ahead."

"Oh, thanks." Kate struggled to slow Lucy down; the horse seemed to love the freedom Kate had just given her.

"Over this way," Logan yelled, sweeping his hand in another direction.

Kate reined Lucy to follow him, the horse still determined to race. Logan was at her side a moment later, somehow working with his horse in a way that slowed Lucy down.

Finally, Lucy returned to a safe gait.

"We'll just have to get there when we get there," Kate said to Logan, who now trotted his horse at Kate's side. "I won't try to lead the way anymore." She reached over and touched Logan's arm. His face lit up. "You're an excellent horseman, Logan. Please know that. Take pride in that. It will take you places someday if you continue to believe that."

"Thank you, Miss Kate. I'll do that." Logan's mouth pinched into a straight line momentarily, as if he were thinking out his next words. "I've been stewing a lot on what you said, Miss Kate—about you takin' a look at my legs . . ." He gazed ahead, taking his time before continuing. "I'd really like that, but . . . I don't think . . . Pa would ever pay out money for that."

Logan's last declaration was spoken in innocence and without even a hint of guile. It tore at Kate's heart. "You don't worry about the money. You've done plenty for me already to more than pay for an exam. Besides, I'm not at all certain if I can do anything for your legs."

"I still wanna come," Logan said, his eyes filled with hope.

"And I still want you to." Kate gave him a reassuring smile. "The next chance you get—when I don't have to rush off to deliver a baby."

After a little less than an hour of riding, they made a quick stop at the Circle J Ranch for Logan to grab a decent coat. Kate waited on her horse while Logan ran inside. She moved to the cover of the drooping branches of a willow tree, hoping and praying every second of her wait that she'd not have to see Stanley or his father. She heard the front door open. With anticipation, she bent low beneath the branches, hoping to see Logan heading toward her. Her stomach tightened when she saw Stanley step onto the porch. At that same moment, two cowboys approached from the direction of the barn, pulling with them an extra horse. Kate recognized it as the one Stanley always rode. It was loaded down with strange-looking wire and had several red cylindrical objects sticking out of one of the saddlebags. Dynamite?

"You ready?" one of the cowboys said as he pulled both horses to a stop a few feet in front of Stanley.

"Darn right I'm ready." Stanley mounted his horse, seemingly concentrating on the task the three of them were about to undertake. "Ready to rid this land of those varmints once and for all." He dug his heels into his horse and took off, the two cowboys following close behind.

Kate pulled Lucy out from beneath the cover of the willow tree, grateful Stanley hadn't seen her. Though relieved by that bit of luck, the nature of Stanley and his ranch hand's impending task left her ill at ease. What kind of animal required dynamite to remove it from one's land?

The front door opened again, and Logan hobbled down the steps waving a coat over his head. "Got it, Miss Kate."

"Good, the wind is kicking up," Kate responded, buttoning her own coat up to her neck. "Now hurry and put it on and let's get going."

The remaining fifteen miles seemed to take forever, but the clouded sky, the trail of green cottonwoods lining the river, and the stark landscape with a unique beauty of its own intrigued Kate with its breathtaking views. Every so often, Logan would point out landmarks in case Kate had to ride back without him so she'd be able to find her way. "I can't wait for you to see things in the spring, Miss Kate. It's like a new world then."

"I can't either, Logan," she responded, determined she'd make it until then.

The afternoon had nearly slipped away by the time a small gray wooden house became visible in the distance. It took a good half an hour after spotting it before Kate and Logan hitched their horses on the post in front of the humble dwelling.

Kate dismounted, hearing her stomach rumble as her feet touched the ground. She'd not thought about bringing food, a foolish action she'd definitely have to rectify the next time she set out on her horse. She could never know what she'd run into or how long things would take. There were no subways out here, cabs to hire, shops to slip into for a bite to eat. She needed to be better prepared.

The door to the small home flew open. A dark-haired man with several day's growth on his jaw dashed outside. Upon seeing Logan, the man's face relaxed into an expression of relief. Then he took one look at Kate and his demeanor drooped.

"I asked you to fetch the doctor, boy!" The man Kate assumed was Mr. Castillo sounded like he wanted to punch Logan.

"I am a doctor, Mr. Castillo," Kate said in the kindest, most reserved voice she could muster. She was tired and hungry and knew her sources of exhaustion had just begun. "How is your wife?" she asked. She walked toward the door without an invitation. "Do you know how far apart her pains are? Have you been timing them?" Of course he hasn't. How would he know? Kate kept walking, holding her head high as she passed by the open-mouthed Mr. Castillo on her way through the door.

Once inside, her eyes had to adjust to the darkness. "We're going to need more light in here," she yelled over her shoulder to Mr. Castillo. She breathed a sigh of relief when she heard the panting sound of a woman in a far corner of the one-room house. Kate had arrived in time. "Mrs. Castillo," she said in a calm voice. Delivering babies had been her favorite part of her medical training, one in which even the toughest instructors had praised her. "I'm here to help you with your delivery." The farther Kate walked into the house, the clearer she could see the bed in the corner and the beautiful, fair-skinned young woman it held. Strands of long black hair clung to the sweat on the woman's face; a face that was obviously in pain. When her dark eyes looked up and met Kate's, she gave a momentary look of confusion. "I'm a doctor," Kate said. The woman's troubled expression melted into one of relief.

In a light Italian accent, the woman said, "I'm so glad you're here, Doctor . . . ?"

"Donahue."

"Dr. Donahue," the woman forced out the name between breaths.

Kate realized she didn't like the sound of that. Too many D's. The name didn't roll of the tongue but rather clunked off in clumsy fashion. "Please, call me Kate," she said.

The woman nodded. "I'm Maria." She took a few more quick breaths. "Miss Kate, I'm scared," she said. "I've never had a baby before. I didn't think it would hurt so badly. Am I going to be all right?"

"You're going to be just fine." Kate sat down on the chair at the side of the bed. "Pain is a normal part of the birthing process. But I will check you to make sure all is in order."

Mr. Castillo hung two lanterns from the rafters near the bed and lit them. Kate appreciated the extra light as she examined Maria, determining the woman had only begun to dilate.

"This might take some time," Kate said to Mr. Castillo. He sat with Logan on a battered sofa on the other side of the room. She turned her attention to Logan. "I fear it's too late for you to set off now. You're going to have to stay the night. I feel bad. Your father is probably going to be worried sick when you don't show up back home soon."

"Oh, he never notices when I'm gone. Or when I'm there. I stay overnight at people's houses all the time. It happens a lot with all the messages I deliver for folks. This valley's awful big."

Kate turned her attention back to Maria, angry at Logan's pathetic father who'd just ruined a beautiful moment for her. She was here to bring a new life into this world, not to taint her thoughts with the knowledge that there were people out there who didn't value some lives simply because they didn't match their expectations.

By morning, Maria had still not delivered. Through much persuasion, Kate convinced Logan to go on home without her, telling him she had no idea how much longer this would take. "Babies can take days sometimes to make their way here," she told Logan. "And it's best if you're not here to have to listen to Mrs. Castillo become more and more exhausted."

"I understand, Miss Kate," Logan finally said, with a look of comprehension clicking into place upon his face. He left immediately after that.

As Logan pulled his horse onto the trail, leaving a cloud of dust in the morning air, Kate wondered if she'd been wise in telling him about Maria's slow progress in order to get him on the road in good time. Was he barreling down the dirt trail now, wondering, worrying that the little baby about to be born might take so long it would exhaust its mother to the point where she'd give up and die, like his mother possibly had?

Maria Katherine Castillo was born that evening at 5:05 p.m.

Exhausted, Kate cleaned and swaddled the baby in a clean blanket cut earlier that day from a larger one, and placed the perfect little girl into her mother's arms. Mrs. Castillo accepted the wiggling bundle with trembling arms and a weak, but joy-filled, smile. Kate knew her own exhaustion was nothing compared to what the mother's must be.

Kate stayed the night, helping with the baby all she could so Maria could rest, also training her how to nurse her child and tend to the baby's healing naval. By late morning the next day, Kate set out, figuring she had sufficient time to make it back home based on when she and Logan had left Craig to go to the Castillos.

Taking notice of the landmarks Logan had pointed out earlier, Kate made good time at first. About two-and-a-half hours into her journey, she felt her head nod. The desire to lie down and sleep took over her entire body, including her brain. She fought it, urging Lucy forward.

Large trees with sweeping limbs of lush, green foliage surrounded Kate. Their leaves turned shades of red and orange. And then they turned pure white. They fell from the trees, sprinkling gracefully down upon her and Lucy. As each leaf touched Kate's face, they turned to ice, chilling her skin.

Kate blinked her eyes. She was back in the high desert. Snow was falling, not heavy, but wispy flakes here and there. Panic seized her as she realized she'd fallen asleep. She surveyed the landscape, searching for familiar landmarks. Not much could be seen but sagebrush growing gray in the setting sun hidden behind the clouds.

She tried to determine north by the sun, but it was too shrouded by the clouds. The fading light appeared a little stronger in the direction of a patch of short trees up ahead. She took hope that the setting sun was actually there, trying to send her a few rays of extra light to help her find her way. She adjusted Lucy accordingly and headed in the direction she thought was northeast based on that weak glow of light. But even if she were headed northward, how far east or west of the trail was she? There was no way to know how far off the trail Lucy had wandered while Kate had dozed off.

She whispered a quick prayer for help and continued on.

Daylight slipped further away. With its disappearance came the cold. She rubbed one arm at a time with her hand, her other hand holding fast to Lucy's reins, longing for the warmth of movement as well. Why had she not thought to bring a pair of gloves?

Frantically, she scanned the barren landscape, hoping to see a spark of light, anything to indicate life other than the coyotes that roamed the high desert.

Nothing.

She began searching for a makeshift shelter, an outcropping of rock, a grove of trees—anything to offer protection from the fast-approaching frigid air and animals possibly worse than coyotes. Travel would be impossible before the next hour expired. With the clouds blanketing the moon and stars, complete darkness would surely engulf her.

Her heart jumped when she spotted a light almost straight ahead. She urged Lucy forward, hoping the horse could feel her way through the sagebrush, unable to guide her with any measure of skill in the darkness. The light grew stronger, giving Kate hope that it was perhaps a hearth glowing through a window of some homesteader's cabin. Even the bonfire of a rancher would be welcome at the moment.

The outline of a white-framed home came into view. It appeared somewhat larger than the Castillos' home, but that was no matter. There was a light shining from a front window. It meant shelter, possibly food, and definitely the warmth and light of a fire. She urged Lucy to move faster.

Then she pulled the reins back. She knew nothing about who dwelt within those walls. Not all homesteaders were married. Many were single, lonely men in want of a wife, in want of a female to satisfy their desires. Memories of Darwin attempting to take some husbandlike privileges during their courtship, and then of Stanley, of his hand moving where it didn't belong, raced through her mind, paralyzing her in the saddle. She couldn't go in. She wouldn't go in.

Her eyes scrambled, searching the dark-gray landscape again for a patch of trees or rock where she could bed down. Maybe behind the pile of firewood next to this homesteader's corral. Hopefully, he had enough wood on his front porch that he wouldn't have to come out that far for more. She'd leave first thing in the morning, before he could notice her there. If she survived the frigid night. Already her arms shivered within her long coat.

She dismounted Lucy several hundred yards from the house, leading her by the reins in a sweeping arc out and around the house toward the small corral. Taking careful steps, watching the ground as best she could, she and Lucy approached the homesteader's horse. The last thing she wanted to do was to spook the animal.

As Kate moved closer, the horse turned in her direction. She felt as if the animal was looking at her, scrutinizing her. *It's a horse—just stare back at him!*

She did. As her eyes focused on the animal's head, she noticed it had a patch of white that ran from his eyes down to his nose in the shape of an arrowhead. She'd seen this horse before. Where?

Lucas McCurdy!

She wrapped Lucy's reins around a post of the corral's fence and ran toward the house, her heart pounding. Once on the doorstep, she stopped, gasping at her thoughtless actions. Lucas McCurdy was still a married man. This was horribly inappropriate. How could she do this? Ask to spend the night with him, only the two of them, all alone in this house that couldn't be larger than two, maybe three rooms?

A wolf howled in the distance.

Kate raised her hand to the door and knocked.

CHAPTER 15

THE DOOR CREAKED OPEN.

Lucas McCurdy stood there with lamplight behind him, illuminating the tips of his chestnut curls, turning them to gold. His face was in the dark, but lit enough for Kate to see the absolute surprise in his eyes.

"Katherine?"

Not Miss Donahue? Or Miss Kate? Kate was pleasantly taken back at his response.

"What are ye doing clear out here? And at this time o' night?"

"I'm—I'm horribly . . . sorry, Mr. McCurdy." Kate struggled for words. "I was delivering Maria Castillo's baby, and I thought I headed out with plenty of daylight left, but I got lost. And then it got dark. I was elated when I saw the light in your window. I apologize immensely, but please, could you possibly allow me to bed down in a corner of your house? I've got nowhere else to go. I promise I'll be no bother to you."

"Uh—uh . . . well . . . ah . . . certainly." He opened the door farther, motioning for her to enter.

She stepped in, and he closed the door behind her. A fire flickered in a large stone hearth. Above it, stretching across the stonework, lay a wooden mantle carved with designs she couldn't distinguish in the poor lighting. She imagined he'd built it himself. From what she knew, most homesteaders built the entirety of their own homes, learning the necessary skills as they went. But this fireplace looked like the work of a craftsman. It gave her a sense of awe as she gazed at it, considering what it must have taken to build it. She presumed he'd also made the large rocking chair in front of the fireplace. A small table rested to one side of the main room with a sink tucked into the adjacent corner—more like two tubs hooked to a low table. She imagined there was a pump somewhere outside from which he drew his water. On the other side of the room she could see a door leading into a second room—a bedroom, she surmised. She noticed a rag rug in front of the fireplace. "I'll be glad to just lie down there," she said softly, pointing to the rug, feeling awkward at his obvious lack of words. "Or, if you'll lend me a blanket, I'll bed down by my horse."

"Uh . . . no, no, ye cannot sleep on the floor." He finally found his voice. "I shan't hear of it. Or having ye spend the night outside. Winter is almost here; 'tis much too cold for someone like ye to be outside at night."

"I'm stronger than I look." Kate bristled slightly at his words. Was he going to be another typical male that immediately thought she was a helpless, fragile thing?

"I am so sorry. I meant nothing by that. I was just saying—I meant . . . 'tis not fit for anyone to be outside right now. Ye can sleep in me bed tonight." Despite the darkened room, his face appeared to blush. "I mean, ye sleep in there." He pointed to the door to the other room. "I shall sleep out here by the fire. There is a stove in there. I shall get ye a good fire going before ye bed down." He raked a hand through his hair and pulled at it. "I was getting ready to have a bit of supper. Would ye care to join me, Miss Donahue?"

So now he was calling her Miss Donahue. What was that all about?

It didn't matter—she was out of the cold, and curiously enough, she felt safe. "Thank you, I would love to join you," she responded, not realizing how hungry she'd been until she saw the plate of meat and potatoes on the table. "But, do you have enough? I'm sure you weren't planning for company."

He grinned, stretching a lopsided smile across his face that sent tingles down to her toes. "No, that I was not." He pulled a chair out for her to sit at the table.

Near the end of their quiet meal, Kate looked up from her mutton and noticed he was staring at her. "I'm sorry, have I done something wrong? Is there a more proper way I should be eating my mutton? This is the first time I've had it. It is delicious, by the way."

He laughed. "No. I was just . . . well, I guess I am so lonely for company out here, 'tis me who has a bit o' bad manners. Sorry for staring, lass. I was just thinking how grateful me heart is for finally having someone else in the house for a change."

"Your manners are fine—and I daresay I would be in need of company as well if I were living out here all alone." Unable to meet his gaze, Kate looked down at her hands resting in her lap, feeling herself blush and weighed down by his pain at the same time. She focused on the scrape on her knuckles from

Lucy's reins. She rushed her palm to her forehead. "Oh! I completely forgot about Lucy."

"Lucy?"

"My horse. She's still tied up to a post in your corral." She jumped to her feet.

"I shall take care of her." He stood, stepped over, and nudged her back into the chair. "I need to see to me own horse anyway."

Kate got up as soon as he left and started doing the dishes, grateful once again she'd hung around the kitchen often as a child, begging the servants to let her experience the dishwater on her hands and the food slipping through her fingers as she scrubbed the porcelain. She was wiping the last plate dry when Lucas returned.

"It appears your mare has taken a liking to me Dublin," he said with a sly grin as he walked over to the table and sat down.

Even Kate knew his horse was a fine animal. "Lucy's got good taste," she said, hanging the dishtowel to dry on the edge of the tin tub. She also knew she wanted to bring up the subject of his wife sooner or later—to offer some words of comfort. But how could she approach such a delicate subject?

She turned around, intent on joining Lucas at the table. Their eyes met. It seemed as if sparks flashed from his gaze, electrifying the space between them. It knocked her off balance. She sank into her chair. "I'm . . . I'm sorry about your wife." The words tumbled from her mouth before she could prevent them.

"Then you've heard?" A strange expression formed on his face. "But how? I just barely found out a few weeks ago, and I've told no one."

"But I thought your wife left you two years ago."

"Oh, is that what ye are referring to?"

"But of course," Kate said. "What did you think I meant?"

"That she's passed away."

"What?" Kate felt something stab her heart. Was it from the sorrow of a person passing? Or that this man was free from the bondage to which his wife had subjected him? What about his daughter? "How can that be?" she said, at a loss for something more fitting of the situation.

"I just received a letter at the end of August from me mother-in-law in Boston." Lucas moved the salt shaker out of the way. Resting his cast on the table, he ran his finger through a pile of salt left behind on the table. "I had tried to keep in touch with her and me wife—for me daughter's sake." He paused and then said, "I do not know if ye knew I had a daughter."

"Yes, I had heard," Kate said, careful not to reveal the fact that she had latched on to everything anyone in the town had said to her concerning the McCurdy family. "How old is she? What does she look like?" she asked, sensing the admiration the man had for his child.

"The wee child is four; she'll be five at Christmastime." His eyes lifted up to the ceiling as he spoke. "A beautiful lass, she is. Got light hair—strawberry blonde. And dark skin like her mother—not the kind that burns with a mere touch of the sun, like mine." He shook his head slightly and returned his gaze to Kate. "Anyway, at the first of the summer I got a letter from me mother-in-law telling me that Tempest—that's me wife—she was ill. Some disease I had never heard of."

"Do you remember the name of the disease?" Kate asked, her medical curiosity aroused.

"No, I do not remember. Sorry, Miss Donahue."

Kate wished he'd go back to calling her by her first name. Not Kate, but Katherine. Nobody ever called her that. But the way it fell from his lips made it sound like the most beautiful of names. She pinched her arm beneath the table where he couldn't see her hands as they rested on her lap. *Why am I thinking like this?*

"The name of the disease isn't important," she said quickly. "I'm sorry for interrupting you. Continue with your story, Mr. McCurdy."

"No need to apologize," he said with his lopsided grin. "We have time to burn. The nights are long out here. Ye can interrupt all ye want, quote pages out of yer medical books if ye'd like. I would take that o'er the silence any day."

Kate preferred this over the silence too. She liked how he rambled on with seeming ease now.

Lucas continued to trace his finger through the salt. "Two weeks ago, I got another letter from her. 'Twas very short. No small talk at all." He handed Kate a folded piece of paper.

She opened it and read,

Lucas,

Tempest is dead. She died of her nasty illness. I'm keeping Celeste, so don't come after her.

Regretfully yours,

Mrs. C. H. Wentworth

Kate was at a loss for words. She felt sorry that Lucas's wife had passed away. But from what little she'd heard of Tempest, she was glad for Lucas that the woman was out of his life. The saddest part of it all was that it sounded like the grandmother wanted to keep Lucas's child away from him. "She can't do that," Kate said. "Your mother-in-law. She can't take your child from you."

"What do you mean?" Lucas took the letter from Kate and stuffed it back into the envelope. "She has already got her. Celeste and Tempest have been living with her in Boston ever since Tempest left me."

"What I mean is, legally." Kate wiped the salt away so Lucas would concentrate on the story. "With your wife now deceased, your daughter should automatically come back into your care. Actually, she should have remained with you from the very beginning. The father automatically gains custody of a child in a divorce, or even if the couple is just separated, unless the mother petitions a judge and the judge awards her custody. Did that happen?"

"No." Lucas ran a hand through his hair. "Me wife just took Celeste and I didn't go after the child. I didn't know I could."

Lucas stared at Kate with a curious look in his eyes. "How do ye know so much about these things? Ye are so different from any lass I have ever met. First a doctor, now an expert in child custody laws."

"I'm hardly an expert." Kate knew she should have toned down the new, fired passion she felt burning within. Every time she had adopted a cause, her mouth had spouted out information or advice that had seemed to intimidate the people around her. Yet . . . her unladylike opinions didn't appear to be offending her gracious host for the night. A pleasant, warm feeling pressed out from her chest. "I just happened to be engaged once," she continued. "To a man who was a lawyer—before he went into politics. I guess I learned it from him." Kate's stomach twisted at the thought of Darwin. The pain of his pretended love was still fresh. There was something else she'd learned from Darwin—to dislike men.

So what was she doing talking with this man she hardly knew about things so very personal to him, possibly leading him on as if she were interested in him—especially now that he'd declared his availability with the news of his wife's death?

I'm talking to him because he's a human being, one who's hurting. She had no intention at the moment of exploring these curious, warm feelings she was experiencing. She didn't need to get involved with another man, and that was that! But she could, perhaps, help him get his daughter back. "You need to fight for your daughter. That is, if you want her back."

"Aye, of course I do!"

"Very well, you should get the law involved. She deserves to be here with her father."

"I would not know where to start." He hung his head.

"I'll help you write up a letter. Then we'll have Mr. Smith look over it."

For the next half hour, they worked on the letter. Once finished, Kate tucked it in her bag so she could take it into town. She fought a yawn. "It's getting late. I should retire before it'll be difficult to get up in the morning. I'd like to make an early start."

"Absolutely." Lucas rose from his chair. "I shall go change the bedding for ye."

"Please, allow me to do it. I'm the one putting you out."

"But I do not mind."

"I insist. Making up a bed with one's arm in a cast is not recommended by this doctor." Kate rose too. "Besides, I'll feel better about barging in on you like this if you allow me to do it."

"Well, then be me guest." He pointed to a high shelf attached to the back wall. It held blankets and a pillow and a few boxes of who knew what. "You grab what ye need while I stoke the fires."

"My pleasure." Kate took the footstool from the rocking chair and scooted it over to the shelf. She stepped up on it and stretched her arm as far as it would go. The bedding was still out of her reach. Rising up on tiptoes, she reached out and grabbed hold of the pillow. Exhausted, her ankle gave way as the three-legged stool wobbled beneath her feet, and she could feel herself falling.

"Ahhh!" The pillow flew across the room.

"Whoa!" Lucas hollered.

Kate had thought Lucas was at the fireplace, ten feet away. But she felt his sure arms scoop her up midair.

With their faces just inches apart, his eyes gazed into hers. Her heart pounded. He stood motionless, cradling her next to his chest. She could feel his muscles flexing to hold her, yet not straining even though his arm without the cast carried most of her weight. His arms felt confident, strong, and protective; Kate wanted to linger there and bask in the moment.

Then she felt his muscles tense, and he carried her toward the bedroom.

A million things raced through Kate's head; some good, some bad.

Her body stiffened.

Lucas stopped. "What was I thinking? I should have fetched ye a sturdy chair to climb upon. Ye could have broke a leg." He turned with a jerking motion and carried her toward the big rocker by the fire. "Sit tight, lass. I'll fix yer bed up. Me cast is not in the way much." As he set her in the chair, he looked toward the bedroom as if trying to avoid her eyes now.

Awkwardness rose like a wall between them. Kate had to say something to stop it from growing. *This is ridiculous.* It made no sense. They'd been talking so freely just minutes ago during dinner and—at least she—had been enjoying it thoroughly.

"Do sheep kill the grass when they eat it?" she asked, thinking a topic other than herself or Lucas would be good to get a conversation going.

"Did Stanley Jones tell ye that?" Lucas's voice carried in from the other room with a slight edge to it.

"Uh, well, yes."

Lucas stepped out of the bedroom. "'Tis as expected," he said with a somber look on his face. He plopped into one of the chairs at the table. "He tells everyone that. And 'tis possible—if ye do not move yer flock constantly. But I nay let me flock graze the same spot for long. If Mr. Jones would only take a wee bit o' time to talk to me or inspect the land better, he'd find that to be the case. The fact is . . . he does not want to."

"Why?"

"He needs an excuse to get me off the public land. Can I help it that I saw to obtaining a proper permit to graze there, and he did not?"

"You have a permit?" Kate crawled out of the rocking chair and walked over to the table, the cogs in her brain spinning. "And he doesn't?"

With his hands clasped together, looking as if they were preparing to pray while resting upon the table, he looked up at her and nodded.

She sat down on the chair across from him. "Then you need to fight him."

Lucas raised an eyebrow, tilted his head, and gave Kate a curious—yet adorable—gaze.

"I don't mean fight, like in punching Stanley," Kate said, remembering this was the West and the word fight out here literally meant using your fists. "I meant fight for your rights." She pinched her lips together, thinking she had been coming across a bit bossily this evening, telling this man how to run his life—as if she had all the answers. That was certainly not the case. *I'm just trying to help.*

"Ye do not know Mr. Jones like I do, lass."

Kate placed her hands over his, hoping to offer him support—she could at least do that. She let them linger as he continued.

"Fighting Stanley would be like itching a mosquito bite. The more ye disturb it, the worse it gets. Speaking o' mosquitos, there are none of the pesky critters in the Yampa Valley come springtime. Oh, 'tis a bonny place to set your eyes on that time o' year. You shall love it." He paused. His hands never moved; at least, he never tried to shake hers off. What little movement he made seemed to be in response to her touch, as if seeking to find the perfect position so as to be cradled entirely within her hands. "Ye really think there'd be a chance to get me wee lass back?" His voice had become serious.

"Of course I do." She discovered the feel of each snag of rough skin, each bend of his knuckles as they pressed against her palms, generating an over-whelming desire to embrace his hands further and send him what little comfort she could.

"What if me mother-in-law will not let Celeste go? I could nary afford to hire a lawyer. Not now. Things have been a bit rough."

"I believe Mr. Smith would be willing to do a trade." She gave his hand a squeeze. Unfortunately, she was unsure what Ronald could do with mutton or wool. "Or maybe he would extend you credit. He's a very considerate man."

"Perhaps 'tis best I not bother Mr. Smith." Lucas chewed on his lip. "'Tis me fear I shall not be able to care properly for the wee lass anyway. She needs a woman's touch."

His eyes peered into Kate's as he spoke. Was he merely making a statement—or was he seeking her help? And as a friend? Or was he looking for something more now that he was free to marry again? Was he interested in her that way?

Was she interested in him that way?

No! She was not interested in marrying any man at the moment.

But she had to admit she loved the feel of his hands in hers, the comfortable conversations they fell into so easily, and the way his mere presence spun her emotions into a tapestry of delightful feelings. She'd noticed the way he'd appeared nervous at times but other times seemed relaxed. Like her. Most likely, he was just as confused about his feelings as she was about hers.

The fire had died down to embers, having been neglected by the time they said their good nights. Kate's heart, however, glowed with warmth. She felt no worry for her safety as she walked into the bedroom with only the moon for light and shut the door—a door without a lock. Her inner sense told her Lucas was not like Stanley at all. Or Darwin. She had thought she'd loved Darwin, but the feelings dancing inside her now were nothing like those she'd experienced even on her best day with her ex-fiancé.

Kate woke to the smell of sausage. She hurried and slipped on her stockings, blouse, and riding skirt and opened the door a crack to peer out. The small kitchen table was set for two with a mason jar in the middle holding a few sprigs of wildflowers. Lucas stood at the potbelly stove in the middle of the larger room, tending to a pan of eggs.

He looked up from the stove. "Good morning. Sleep well?"

"Yes, thank you." Kate inched out of the doorway and over to the table a few feet away.

"This shall be ready in a minute. Have a seat."

"I feel like I should be making breakfast for you, not the other way around. You've already done so much, feeding me and taking me in for the night."

He gave Kate a mock warning glance, like he'd stand for no more of that. "I do not mind cooking—I kind of even enjoy it."

Kate felt her eyebrows rise. What a refreshing surprise this man was. Was it possible? Could he be just as open-minded about her doing the work of a man . . . if . . .things were to work out . . . between them? *Stop it!* she chided herself. The man's wife had barely passed on. She needed to be careful with her feelings toward Lucas. It wouldn't be proper to indulge them.

Lucas brought over the frying pan and set it on the table. "It certainly comes in handy when ye live alone—or when ye've got to make an old piece of mutton taste like a meal when there's nothing else in yer larder. Which happens way too often," he mumbled under his breath as he sat down.

Kate and Lucas ate slowly, chatting about his hens and how some were better layers than others.

Lucas finished his breakfast first. He stood from the table and headed for the door. "Aye, let me saddle yer horse while ye finish yer breakfast."

"You've already done so much," Kate protested. "Please, don't bother yourself."

"'Tis no bother, but a privilege." He flashed her that endearing, crooked smile of his. "Please, allow me the pleasure, lass."

How could she refuse? "Thank you, Mr. McCurdy. I would appreciate that."

Kate finished off her tasty plate of scrambled eggs and sausage, gathered her things, and went outside. Seeing Lucas secure her saddle into place on top of Lucy prompted a smile and warmed her insides. Like her, Lucas too appeared to gain fulfillment by helping others.

No words passed between them as Kate mounted and turned her horse to leave.

"Goodbye," Lucas finally said. He waved as she maneuvered Lucy onto the trail.

"Goodbye." Kate waved back and headed toward town, thinking.

He'd definitely stirred something inside her. She couldn't deny she was attracted to him. But how could things work with him way out here on his homestead while she had her practice in town?

They couldn't.

So why let her thoughts go down that avenue? She wouldn't, because more than anything, she wasn't ready to love again. And she'd just begun to enjoy the freedom of being her own person, able to choose for herself what she wanted to do and be. Would Lucas make her give up medicine if she were to become his wife? Just because he liked to cook didn't mean he'd support her in her profession.

And what was she thinking? His seeming interest in her may have just been her imagination. She didn't really know how he felt. After all, even after their intimate discussion last night, he still insisted on calling her Miss Donahue.

Kate dug her heels into Lucy's side. She had Mr. Hoy's cyst that needed lancing and flyers to hand out around town—compliments of Sunny's business mind. Kate was gaining acceptance in Craig more and more each day. She could feel it. If she just worked at it a little harder, she'd be able to pay all her bills without dipping into the box under her bed at all. Which was good, because Lucy had taken a good portion of it. Still, she felt she had enough for several rainy days.

CHAPTER 16

THE McCURDY PLACE SLIPPED OUT of sight. Kate could keep her eyes focused forward a little more easily now. She kicked her heels ever so lightly into Lucy's flanks, wanting to get back to town.

Up ahead, a stand of willows grew at the base of a hill. Kate hoped it was as Logan had told her, that anything taller than sagebrush out here meant there was likely a source of water. Horses needed to drink often. She reined Lucy away from the two ruts in the sagebrush that comprised the road and headed for the trees.

As she approached the base of the hill, sure enough, she could see a small stream of water. Lucy must have seen or smelled it too, for she trotted faster without Kate's command. As soon as they were upon it, Lucy plunged her head into the flow of water, causing Kate to grab hold of the saddle and hang on. As she tried to regain her balance, she looked downstream. Several yards away, nestled in the cottonwoods, was another horse taking a drink. A cowboy emerged from behind a tree and stepped over to the horse. The way he stood, with his back erect and hand on his gun, looked familiar. He lifted his hat and scratched his head.

Stanley.

Kate grabbed Lucy's reins and pulled her from the stream. Lucy whinnied.

The man turned around.

"Well, well, if it ain't our dear Kate Donahue," Stanley said with his lip curling up in a sneer. "Been out at the McCurdy place doin' some doctorin'?" he said the last word with an unsettling emphasis. He stared her in the eye. "I saw you leavin' there this mornin'. Don't tell me you traveled in the dark so you could arrive there bright and early first thing in the day to check up on his broken arm. He's a married man, you know. That won't go over well with your new patients back there in town. Craig's got a lot of God-fearin' people—folks with morals. They trust that Doc Greene would never stay the night with one of his female patients. Now, mind you, I'm open-minded. I just wanted to warn you most folks around here aren't." He lifted his hat and offered the most sinister-looking smile Kate had yet seen upon his face.

She shivered on the outside while boiling inside. "I'll have you know, Mr. Jones, that I had been delivering a baby out at the Castillo place. I thought I'd left early enough to make it back to town by nightfall, but I'm unfamiliar with this territory and I'd judged wrong. I had no choice but to beg Mr. McCurdy for a spot on the floor of his house—I hadn't come prepared to sleep amongst the sagebrush. I'm sorry, Mr. Jones, but I'm not accustomed to bedding down with coyotes and the cold," she said in the most defiant voice she could muster. It came out rather weak.

A sickening laugh escaped his mouth. "Oh, but who are you accustomed to beddin' down with, pretty lady?" His eyebrow lifted at the insinuation. "I'm sure the townsfolk will find out soon enough." He laughed again as he mounted his horse. With the disgusting smile still on his face, he rode off.

Kate sat there on Lucy, unable to move, stunned, scared. Though Stanley had taken off in the opposite direction she needed to go—thank heavens—she knew with every fiber of her being that it would only be a matter of time until he saw fit to tell the whole town what he'd witnessed this morning—and add his editorial to it.

It took great effort for her to urge Lucy forward and ride into town. Would Stanley head back around and warn the city before she arrived? If he did, every eye would be on her when she arrived, judging her, whispering to their neighbors, "You don't want to go to her as your doctor. She's a wicked woman."

The gray sky didn't help lift her spirits as Lucy clomped along down the road. *I didn't do anything wrong. What other choice did I have?* She wasn't that sort of woman! Surely the townspeople would recognize that—and the fact that there were no hotels along the road for a traveling doctor to stay in at night. They'd have to see Kate's side over Stanley's.

Her defiant thoughts offered little solace—even though they were true. Stanley was a Jones. His family had been here since the beginning.

❦

By the time Kate made it back into town, there wasn't enough time before her appointment with Mr. Hoy to heat water on the stove and fill the round tub for a bath. She took a towel and dipped it into the small bit of cold water she'd pumped into the sink, and sponged down her sweatiest spots.

After she got cleaned up, she sat down on her only piece of living room furniture, a secondhand armchair she'd purchased from Sunny. Business had been doing so well for the woman that she was able to refurnish part of her living space above the saloon. Bringing in Lavender's sweet rolls hadn't hurt.

Kate glanced again at the clock sitting on the shelf above her bed. "Where is he?" she muttered when she saw that Mr. Hoy was ten minutes late.

Ten minutes later she jumped from her chair in frustration. Stanley couldn't possibly have made it back to town before her and warned her patient not to show up. *Then where is Mr. Hoy? It's not like he's got that far to travel.*

Maybe the man had just forgotten. That had to be the reason.

Kate kept telling herself that as she slipped on her coat, intent on heading down the stairs and talking to her landlord.

Once inside the saddle shop, Kate looked around for Mr. Hoy. She saw Mrs. Hoy, with her youngest son clinging to her skirt, standing behind the counter. They were the only ones in the shop. "Excuse me, may I ask where your husband might be?" Kate asked, trying to look calm and collected as she walked toward Mrs. Hoy. "I had a three o'clock appointment scheduled with him. We were going to take care of that cyst on his back."

Mrs. Hoy was a ragged-looking woman in her thirties with light-brown hair that always managed to sneak out of its pins in wisps and fall onto her face. The woman looked up from the leather belt she was polishing with a puzzled look on her face. "Didn't he tell you, Miss Kate?"

"Tell me what?"

"This morning he got called away to his family's ranch. His ma is at death's door. His brother came and fetched him to come and say his goodbyes to her before she passed on. He told me he was going to run up and let you know he'd have to reschedule. I guess he forgot or something. Sorry, Miss Kate."

Kate felt like reprimanding herself for thinking harshly of Mr. Hoy—and thinking Stanley had kept him away. "Oh, please, don't be sorry. I'm the one who should apologize for barging in here all upset. And I'm more than sorry to hear about his mother. So she's not going to make it, they think?"

Mrs. Hoy shook her head. "Naw, I don't think so."

"So my heading out there probably wouldn't help much, then, would it?"

"No, not at all. Especially since Doc Greene is already out there." Mrs. Hoy twisted her face. "Sorry, but Stewart's pa is really old-fashioned. Plus, he and Doc Greene go way back."

"No need to apologize," Kate said, reaching across the counter and patting the woman's hand. "I understand. Not everyone is open to a woman doctor. I just appreciate you and your husband's open-mindedness."

Kate brushed a wisp of hair out of her eyes. "Well, it sounds like Mr. Hoy's mother will be in good hands as she passes on," she said. "One person passes out of this life, and another one comes in. Life is marvelous the way it works, isn't it? I just delivered a new life into this world yesterday—a healthy baby girl, to the Castillos. They're homesteading out past the McCurdy place, about twenty miles south of here. Do you know them?" Kate asked, hoping to at least establish her side of the story to ward off the gossip soon to follow.

"Yes, he's stopped in here a time or two, but I've never met his wife." Mrs. Hoy's eyes lit up with her faint smile, a look of something wanting within them. "A little girl, you say? All's I could manage to bear were boys."

"Well, they are fine boys, all four of them." Kate ruffled the hair of their youngest as he continued to cling to his mother's side. "And I understand why you have never met Mrs. Castillo. It's a long ride out there to their place. More than half a day's journey at a good pace. As a doctor who can't always plan on when she has to head out on the road, I am glad there's a house or two dotting the trail to offer shelter if need be. I probably wasn't back yet when your husband stopped by this morning. I had to spend the night at one of the Castillos' neighbors on my way home. It got too dark to keep riding safely."

"I think it's marvelous that you've got yourself a horse, Miss Kate." Mrs. Hoy's grin spread wide. "How's the saddle Stewart sold you? It was an old one someone traded in, but he fixed it up right nice, I thought."

"Oh, he did a good job on it. I like it just fine." Kate took a deep breath, her fears having settled down for the moment. "Please tell your husband he can reschedule his appointment when he gets back." She turned and walked to the door. Upon opening it, she turned back and looked at Mrs. Hoy, desirous to share the feelings swelling inside her. "And thank you so much for giving me a chance. I know a female doctor takes some folks a little getting used to."

Mrs. Hoy looked up from the belt she continued to work on and offered Kate a quiet smile. "Not for me," she said.

❧❦

For the rest of the week, Kate kept hoping Mr. Hoy would pound his big cowboy boots up the stairs and set up another appointment. It never happened. Several times, she considered going down while he was in the shop and asking him to reschedule, but she felt awkward. On Friday morning, she finally heard a knock at her door. She hurried over to open it, wondering if it was Mr. Hoy or one of the two other appointments she had scheduled for that day.

Logan stood on the landing wearing a reluctant-looking grin and his fisted hand ready to knock again. "I got some messages for you, Miss Kate."

"Come on in." She motioned for him to step inside. "Messages from whom?" she asked once she shut the door behind Logan.

"Mrs. Swanson says her cough is better, so she won't be coming in today. And Mr. Hiatt, the blacksmith, says to tell you his wife needs to cancel her appointment."

"Did she want to reschedule?" Kate asked, her fears becoming reality.

"Nope." Logan shook his head. He looked around her place, his eyes lighting up like it was the first time he'd taken notice of all her medical paraphernalia. "Sorry about those people not coming." His eyes came to rest on her diagram of the muscles of the human body that hung on the wall next to her medical cabinet. "But if you're not too busy, maybe now would be an okay time to look at my legs?"

"No, I'm not busy at all." Kate let out a sigh. "Right now would be a good time to do that." She glanced at the beat-up boots and worn pants he had on. "But I'm going to have to ask you to shed your shoes and your trousers." She stepped over to her bed/exam table that had been made ready for her other patients and patted the thin blanket she'd folded and placed on the corner earlier on. "I'll step in the other room while you remove your pants," she said, wanting to treat Logan with the same respect she would have any of her adult patients. "Use the blanket to cover yourself up—except for your legs. Holler when you are ready."

A minute later Logan called out, "I'm ready."

Kate stepped back into the room, seeing at a distance enough of Logan's shrunken leg to immediately pierce her heart with sadness. She hurried over to his side and examined the two malformed legs in more detail, confirming her fear. Picking up the smallest leg she poked his quadriceps. "Can you feel that?"

"Yes, Miss Kate."

"Try your hardest to squeeze this part of your leg."

He winced. "It's hard—and it hurts."

She felt it tighten slightly under her touch. "But you're doing it." She moved her hand down to the major muscle in his calf. "Now do the same with this one."

Again he winced, but she felt the muscle respond.

She then ran her hands along each of his legs, feeling each muscle and prompting them to move. "It's as I feared." She ran her fingers across her forehead to brush away a wisp of hair. "But it's not all bad."

"What? What's not all bad?" Logan's voice begged for explanation.

"True, you were born with one leg shorter than the other, but the shorter leg has no reason to be shriveled and useless—except from neglect. I can show you how to exercise your weak leg, and if you commit yourself to work your muscles every day like I show you, no matter how hard it is, I think you can eventually obtain a level of function so that you'll be able to walk somewhat normally." She paused. That was a lot to promise. "Maybe," she emphasized.

"Maybe is good." Logan's eyes widened to where she swore he was looking at the whole world, and differently, at that moment.

"Well, we'll need to get you a special boot made with a thicker sole for your shorter leg. And the foot of your stronger leg is misshapen and will most likely always cause you to limp, but . . . given time and lots of hard work, I think you can certainly move around with much more ease than you are currently."

Kate proceeded to work on Logan's small, nearly atrophied leg, showing him exercises to do and pushing him to his limits. By the time he left, he was exhausted but excited, promising to work his leg every day just as she'd shown him and stop back at her office now and again to learn some more exercises.

As she watched him hobble down the stairs, after two hours' worth of physical therapy, she sensed he was exhausted but, at the same time, more optimistic than she'd ever seen him—if that was even possible. She faltered inside and dropped into her soft chair, overwhelmed by myriad things. It was amazing how worthless his leg had become, simply because it was believed to be worthless. Since his birth, Logan himself had been considered worthless by two-thirds of his family, but he didn't believe it and was the most cheerful boy she'd ever met. The power of just one person's love was amazing.

CHAPTER 17

THOUGH SHE WAS HAPPY FOR Logan, Kate kept to her apartment the rest of the weekend, not wanting to go out in public and face the townspeople, afraid of what they might say. It was easier to stay out of sight and hope over time they would all forget about the nasty things with which Stanley had obviously filled their heads.

By Monday, Kate's supply of food had run dangerously low. She put on her coat and wrapped a scarf around her head and part of her face, partly to ward off the wind but mostly to hide, and ventured down the stairs. Staring at the ground as she walked, she moved briskly toward Decker's store. At the end of the block, she heard a horse come up and trot alongside her. She glanced up and saw Logan riding on his usual white and gray horse.

"Hi, Miss Kate. I've been doing my exercises," he said with an excitement that warmed the air around her.

"I'm glad to hear that," Kate said sincerely, glad his weekend had gone well.

"I'll stop by tomorrow to learn some new ones, like you said. But for today I've got a message to give you, and then I need to be going."

"Oh," Kate responded, wondering for a moment if there was someone else who was using Logan to cancel their appointment. Not possible—she had nothing more scheduled.

"Susannah sent me to find you. She's in town today 'cause Pa and Stanley are in Baggs on business, and she wants to talk to you. She's over at the new eating place Sunny's opened up at the side of her saloon. Will you go over there for me? I promised her I'd make you come."

"Of course I'll go, Logan. Thank you for telling me." Kate abandoned her plans to go to the general store for the moment and headed for Sunny's.

Still atop his mount, Logan remained by her side, walking his horse slowly to match her speed. "Miss Kate, I still like you."

"Well, thank you, Logan. I like you too."

"What I'm trying to say, Miss Kate, is that I don't care what other people say about you, especially Stanley. I don't know why he'd want to say such mean things about you and Mr. McCurdy. You two are some of my most favorite people."

"That's very kind of you to say." Kate would have liked to give the boy a hug if he hadn't been out of reach atop that horse. Curiosity prompted her next words. "May I ask, what kinds of things is he saying about me? And Mr. McCurdy?"

"I don't really understand most of them, and the thing that seems to upset people the most and makes Stanley smile the biggest is . . . well, to be honest with you, Miss Kate, I don't understand why it's any big deal at all. He's telling folks that you spent the night at Mr. McCurdy's house and slept in his bed."

Kate cringed.

"Like I was sayin', Miss Kate, I don't know what all the fuss is. Of course you stayed at Mr. McCurdy's. If you left too late from the Castillos', you would have had to, or else slept outside with the coyotes," he said with a smile. "And of course you'd have slept in his bed, because Mr. McCurdy is a nice man and would never let you sleep on his floor. He would have given you his bed and slept on the floor himself."

Kate couldn't help but smile at the boy's innocence. She only wished everyone else in town had a mind and heart as pure as his. "Thank you, Logan. I appreciate your confidence in me." She picked up her pace, feeling a little energized just by Logan's vote of confidence. "Do you know what Susannah wanted to see me about?"

"She didn't tell me much—just that she's worried about you."

When Kate and Logan reached the saloon, Logan tipped his hat to her. "I've got another errand to run now. See you around, Miss Kate." He kicked his horse and raced away.

Kate walked around to the side of the saloon. The building sat on the corner of the block, its side facing Sixth Street. A new door, with a window on each side, had been built into the wall of the saloon. Kate had watched the remodeling take place but had never used the new door or had a chance to visit the improved cafe portion of Sunny's business. Kate was proud of Sunny's spunk and vision as she stepped onto the new wooden sidewalk that ran the length of the saloon on that street. When she stepped inside, she treaded with a certain amount of elation across the newly polished wood floor, checking out all the improvements.

She spotted Susannah sitting in a booth that butted up to the end of the bar. She wasn't alone. Kate couldn't see who Susannah was sitting with, only the top of his cowboy hat over the back of the booth.

Susannah's eyes lit up when she saw Kate. She motioned for her to come over and join them.

Kate couldn't imagine who Susannah shared her booth with. The unfortunate woman had no friends, nor did her father appear to allow her to entertain suitors. Had Susannah finally decided to stand up to her father? That would add a bright spot to Kate's bleak week, that's for sure. It also made her feel better about Susannah wanting to meet her at Sunny's rather than come up to her place above the saddle shop. She'd worried that maybe Susannah didn't want to be seen going there, just like Kate's canceled appointments.

"Kate!" Susannah held out her hand. "I'm so glad you came. We've been worried about you."

"We?" Kate squeezed Susannah's hand and turned to see who else could possibly be worried about her.

"Yes, we." Rosie Decker slid over on the wooden bench of the new booth to make room for Kate.

Kate sat down. "Why would you ladies be worried about me? I'm fine. Never been better." She drew her handkerchief from her pocket and waved the clean white cloth in front of their faces. "Clean as clean. Not even a sniffle here."

"You know what we mean." Rosie took off her hat and set it on the table. "You been holed up in that cracker box of a place for the last several days."

"That's not good for a person," Susannah added.

"And there's the pot calling the kettle black," Kate said, looking straight at Susannah.

Susannah ducked her head. "I know, I know." She pulled it back up, staring at Kate with a speck of defiance in her eyes. "But I've been a recluse forever. It's who I am. You"—she took a breath as if it were spawned by admiration—"you aren't like that. You stand up for yourself, for what's right."

Rosie leaned forward to join the conversation. "So why aren't you doin' that now?"

"What are you talking about?" Kate didn't want to talk about it, actually.

"Do you really not know?" Susannah blinked rapidly.

"Of course she does," Rosie said, looking at Susannah. "Kate's as smart as they come. She's just toyin' with us." She glanced at Kate. "Now you just stop that."

Susannah reached across the table and gathered Kate's hands into hers. "I know it's my brother who is behind the vicious rumor. It is so much like him to do something like that. He's a horribly jealous man. Whatever it was you did to him that night he brought you out to the ranch really made him mad. And if I had a hat," she lifted Rosie's from the table and placed it on her head, "I'd take it off for you. Nobody's gotten the best of Stanley Jones like you did that night. So when I heard the nasty statements flying around the dinner table a few days later, about you and Lucas McCurdy, I knew they were just Stanley's way of dealing with it. And so I knew they weren't true. But I also knew that Stanley wouldn't stop at our dinner table. He'd make sure he told the whole Yampa Valley."

"And he has," Rosie said. "He came into my folks' store the next day. I happened to be helpin' Ma sort out a box of buttons when Stanley came strutting in there, like he was the most important man in town, chest out, nose high, and proceeded to tell everyone in the store about how he saw the town's new doctor comin' out of Lucas McCurdy's house bright and early in the mornin' that day. He knew she'd spent the night there because he'd seen her go in the night before. And how he didn't doubt she'd spent the night in the man's bed because he'd seen the way she looked at the 'mutton lover' and the lust in her eyes—and the way McCurdy made eyes at Kate—and he still bein' a married man, no less."

Kate felt a spark warm her insides for a moment at the thought of Lucas noticing her. She quickly smothered it. Both of their reputations were on the line. "How did they react?" Kate asked, not anxious one bit to actually hear. "Your folks and the people in the store?"

"Like you'd expect in this little close-minded town," Rosie said. "Women rushed their hands to their mouths with an, 'oh, dear me,'" she mimicked their voices with hers raising in pitch several steps. "The men just frowned, but I knew they were soppin' up the gossip like a dry piece of bread on a plateful of gravy."

"Did he go anywhere after that? Or tell anyone else that you know of?" Kate removed her hands from Susannah's grasp and slipped them beneath the table to her lap where she could clench and wring them without being seen.

"I'm sure he did, though I can't say." Rosie blew out a long breath. "But he didn't need to. Matilda Forbes was there."

Susannah sighed and raised her eyebrows as if things made sense. "Now I know how Stanley spread his nasty rumor so fast."

"Who's Matilda Forbes?" Kate had neither heard of nor met this woman.

"The wife of the man who runs the land office."

"He and his wife are about as friendly as a pack of coyotes on the prowl." Rosie rolled her eyes. "She won't ever wish you a 'good morning,' a 'good afternoon,' or a 'good evening,' but she sure as shootin' will tell you about everyone who's not havin' a good day."

Kate was overwhelmed by the goodness of these women sitting next to her. It was obvious they hadn't thought Kate should quit her medical practice and go apply for a job at Rosy's brothel at the edge of town, like other Craig citizens might. "I appreciate the two of you inviting me to lunch and believing in me." Kate glanced from Rosie to Susannah. "I didn't even know you two ladies knew each other."

Rosie punched Kate in the arm. "This is a small town, city girl. Everybody knows everybody. And I've been calling Susannah Susannah for long as I remember. I didn't care that her pa told everyone she wanted to go by Clara. I knew it was a lie." She glared at Kate. "And I knew it was a lie when I heard Stanley spout off about you and Lucas."

"How did you know?" Kate asked, wanting desperately to sop up whatever morsels of encouragement she could from these sweet ladies who had kept their minds open to the truth.

"Because, I've gotten to know you." Rosie folded her arms tight across her waist. "Seven days straight I watched you struggle to get on a horse and then get bucked back off. That didn't squash your determination to ride an animal that you'd never had contact with except to pat its nose. And why? So you could get to those people in need out on the farthest homestead in the valley. That says a lot about a person in my book—not a two-minute tattletale from a man who's got the ego of Pike's Peak." She glanced at Susannah. "Sorry, I know he's your brother."

"No need to apologize to me. I know him better than you do." Susannah turned to Kate. "We invited you here"—she held out her hands, indicating the small eating area of the saloon—"rather than came to your place above the saddle shop, for a reason."

"When Susannah came into the store this mornin', we got to talkin'," Rosie said. "We'd heard how you don't come out of your place anymore. Kate, that's not good. It's only got people talkin' more. They say it shows you must be guilty. Don't you see? I think they're open, maybe even wantin' to believe the truth—"

"Except for Mrs. Forbes," Susannah cut in.

Rosie waved her hand at Susannah's comment. "I think they're open-minded because everyone knows how spiteful Stanley can be. And they know that you went out to the Castillos' to deliver a baby—"

"Logan let people know that," Susannah cut in again.

Rosie gave her a frustrated look, and Susannah ducked her head. "Anyway, as I was sayin', everyone knows it's a long way out to the Castillos', and if they were travelin' that road and it got late, and it's a cold October night, they'd be knockin' at McCurdy's door for a place to bed down too." She grabbed Kate by the wrist. "But don't you see, darlin'? By stayin' away and duckin' your head, you're makin' yourself look guilty."

Susannah tipped her head up and locked her gaze onto Kate's. "You're the one that told me to stand up for myself and be myself. And I'm starting to do it. Sort of. Slowly. And it's liberating. I don't know how I'll ever thank you."

"Yes, you do," Rosie shot Susannah a look. "That's why we're here: to tell you to take your own advice—leastwise the advice I learned from your example. You taught me to be proud of who I am, not worry about what others think of me and what I'm doing with my life as long as I'm doing good and not hurtin' anyone. I only have to answer to myself and God."

"As I started to say," Susannah jumped back in. "That's why we wanted to meet with you here, so people could see that we're honored to be in your company. That we believe in you—not my brother's sick twist on your trip home from the Castillos'."

"You two are absolutely right." Kate pulled Susannah's and Rosie's hands into hers. Releasing them she said, "I can't believe how foolish I've been. It's so unlike me to cower so."

"Don't beat yourself up," Rosie said with a mischievous grin forming on her lips. "It's easy to be rattled when dealin' with somethin' so close to your heart."

Kate disregarded Rosie's last statement and concentrated on the first. "Thank you. I will try to hold my head up and go back to living my life."

"That's the spirit!" Rosie picked up a menu. "Now let's get ourselves somethin' to eat, okay?"

"Absolutely," Kate said, feeling better than she had in days. "And I insist on paying. No arguments. You're two of the best friends I could ever ask for." Kate thought of the shallow friendships she'd had back in New York. Even with this little episode of gossip, she never wanted to return there. She doubted even her mother could talk her into it now—although she still wasn't ready to write her mother just yet.

"But is that wise?" Susannah tipped Kate's menu down, forcing it onto the table. "Can you afford it, Kate? Even if we can convince people to ignore the gossip, it may take time before you see a return of patients."

"Don't worry; I still have a fair amount of savings." Kate straightened her menu back up.

"Where?" Rosie glanced at Kate with a look of confusion. "The bank ain't finished yet." She gave a nod in the direction of the new bank across the street that had yet to receive its roof.

"Locked up in an old—" Kate caught herself before she divulged more than was needed. "Let's just say it's tucked safely away. I've dipped into it numerous times, trying to set up my practice, but I have a sufficient amount left. I'll be fine. The same with all the gossip—I'll be fine." She thought about Logan's "useless leg" and how it had pretty much become so because he'd believed it was fact. She wasn't going to let that happen to her. She was strong and could recover from this gossip; she believed that. "Things are going to pick up, so stop your worrying."

A man sitting at the edge of the bar jerked, tipping his drink over and into their booth.

"Ah!" Susannah jumped off her bench and stood up, wiping beer from her shoulder with obvious revulsion. "You clumsy fool!" she shouted—at least, for Susannah it was a shout.

Kate watched her friend's spunk with awe as Susannah spun around to glare at the cowboy who had spilled his drink on her.

Susannah let out a gasp as the cowboy in the light hat turned his face toward them.

Kate gasped too. He was the spitting image of Stanley.

"Sorry, Miss Clara," the man said in a low voice that held little remorse. He turned his head back toward the bar. "Sunny," he yelled. "There's a mess over here that needs cleaning." He returned his attention to what little beer remained in his glass.

Sunny was at their booth in a flash with a rag in hand. "So sorry, gals." She mopped off Susannah's shoulder.

"Don't worry about it, Sunny. It's not the first time someone from the Circle J has spilled beer on me." Susannah motioned for Sunny to wipe the spill from the bench.

As Susannah slid back into her seat, Kate couldn't hold back the question. "You know that man?"

Susannah nodded.

Kate leaned forward and whispered this time so he couldn't hear from his perch above them at the bar. "It's kind of creepy how much he looks like your brother. Is he your cousin or something?"

"Yeah, creepy." Rosie leaned in too.

"He's a ranch hand out on our place. His name's Will Pewtress. And thankfully, he's no relation, and I don't have to see him very often." Susannah let out a cleansing breath. "He's as personable as my brother. I'd forgotten how much he looks like Stanley if you see him at the right angle." She shuddered.

"Two peas in a pod, eh?" Rosie added.

"Unfortunately." Susannah picked up her menu again.

As soon as the three of them got back to the task of deciding on their meal, the man who'd spilled his drink slammed his emptied beer mug on the bar and slid off his stool. He dashed out of the saloon as if he were in a hurry.

"Good riddance," Rosie muttered, glancing up at the vacant spot at the bar.

After a lunch of a cold roast beef sandwich and one of Lavender's sweet rolls, Kate bid Susannah and Rosie goodbye and headed back to finish her errands. She walked with head held high across the road to the R. H. Hughes Mercantile.

With her back straight, she stepped into the store.

Lavender stood by the stove in the middle of the room, stoking it with a log. She looked up. "Good afternoon, Kate," she said as if the past week had never happened.

Kate had the urge to rush over and give that sweet woman a hug. "Good afternoon, Lavender." She felt a smile form on her lips. It felt so good.

As Kate set to her task of replenishing her supplies, Mr. Decker emerged from the back room. He ignored her at first, which wasn't normal for him. Kate kept her head held high and wished him a good afternoon. Several minutes later, he grunted a response to one of Kate's questions. By the time Kate had gathered her dried beans, flour, and lard, and set them on the counter to ring up, Mr. Decker at least wore a cordial expression on his face as he worked the cash register. Kate took her purchases, wished him a good day, with a smile, and headed for the door.

"You have a good day too, Miss Kate." Mr. Decker's voice rang in her ears like music as she stepped outside.

On her way home, she stopped by Ronald Smith's office. She'd just wish him a good day and see if he was okay. Once inside, she poked her head above the partition. "I heard you had a nasty cough. I thought I'd drop in and see how you're doing."

He looked up from his desk. "Oh, Miss Donahue! I assure you I am fine. Thank you for inquiring."

By the brightness of his face as he smiled, Kate could tell he was no longer affected by the gossip—if he ever had been at all. "That's so good to hear. I'll leave you to your work. Good day, Mr. Smith."

"Good day, Miss Donahue. And thank you again."

She stopped at the saddle shop before heading up the stairs. With more confidence than she'd felt in a week, she approached the workbench where Mr. Hoy was busying himself polishing a saddle. "Good afternoon, Mr. Hoy," she said in the most pleasant voice she could muster. Though her confidence had been increasing all morning, she still had jitters inside. Especially here. Her landlord had been particularly cold to her once the gossip had begun. And he never had rescheduled his appointment. Kate worried that he might not allow her to stay in the apartment above his shop.

"S'pose," Mr. Hoy muttered as he continued to rub down the leather.

"I can't tell you how much I appreciate my little apartment above your shop. I couldn't ask for a better landlord than you. And your dear wife, when she comes over here, is such a delight to talk to. I do hope business is going well for you."

"It ain't too bad." Mr. Hoy looked up, his face softening a bit. "Saddles are kind of a necessity around here."

"You sure do fine work." Kate ran her fingers over the new piece of leather he'd added to the saddle he'd repaired. "What made you decide to choose such a profession, Mr. Hoy? From what I hear, your father has a big ranch north of town. Almost as big as the Circle J. I would have thought you'd be a rancher and take over when your father passes on, like Stanley Jones."

"First of all, I'd never care to be like Stanley Jones—even if it's just as you're talking about here, with inheriting a ranch and all." His face softened further and a smile emerged, like it had wanted to show up long ago but had held back because of uncertainty. "Secondly, I never did care much for the ranching business. I'm the youngest of four brothers. I always got sent to do the dirty jobs—mucking out the stables, heating up the branding irons, saddling my brothers' horses in the wee hours of the morning while they sat in the warm kitchen eating a big breakfast that I hadn't had a chance at yet. But one job I really liked was taking care of the saddles. Learned to do it real good. Taught myself how to make them too. So when Pa started talking about how he was going to split up the ranch when he died and most of it was going to Paul, my oldest brother, I decided to take less than my little portion of inheritance by receiving it early. Then I set this shop up in town. I wanted to be in control of my life and my family's future, not beholden to my brother for my livelihood the rest of my life, being just a glorified ranch hand."

"That is most admirable." Kate loved his story. "I'm impressed. I truly am." She clutched her purse, ready to leave. She knew it held two ten-dollar gold pieces and a bit of change, reminding her how helpful it would be if she could still take care of his cyst in exchange for next month's rent. "I wish you the best of luck with your business, Mr. Hoy."

"Thank you, Miss Kate."

"Oh, and if you get a chance, perhaps we could reschedule your appointment. It would be best if you got that cyst taken care of before it becomes infected."

"Right. How about tomorrow afternoon?" Mr. Hoy scratched his chin. "And speaking of business, I think you had a patient stop by this morning while you were out. I heard his boots on the steps." He patted the wall that held the stairs to her apartment on the other side. "I swear he was trying to tiptoe up the creaky things, but no one can go up those stairs without me hearing every step of his foot."

"I wonder who it was." Kate felt her spirits lift further. Maybe business would start to pick up again. "Well, good day, Mr. Hoy. I need to get going." She hurried out the door after Mr. Hoy had given her a smile and nod of his head in farewell.

She clapped her shoes on the wooden steps in a hurried fashion, all the time wondering what they sounded like inside Mr. Hoy's shop. A tickle of excitement pulsed though her as she realized that her exam table should be arriving by stagecoach any day now. She couldn't imagine how they'd ever get that thing on top of the coach and get it back down. It would probably have an inch of dust on it when they delivered it to her. She would need to find someone to help her get it up the narrow stairs. Yesterday she would've thought that a difficult task, but the townspeople were already starting to thaw toward her.

Once on the landing, she fumbled in her purse for her key. When she inserted it into the lock, she realized the door was already unlocked. She opened it and stepped inside, a little rattled. It was so unlike her not to lock the door when she left. The key fell from her hand. Her jaw dropped as she caught a glimpse of her apartment.

Clothing lay strewn from one end of the room to the other, the drawers to her wardrobe having been pulled out, emptied, and discarded on the floor. She rushed over to her bed. Shaking as she knelt, she looked underneath for her old jewelry box. Gone! Frantic, she looked around the room. A glimpse of the box's delicately carved wood poked out beneath the tangle of bedding atop her bed. Still on her knees, she grabbed the box, and with a sinking feeling, she pulled the necklace that held the key from around her neck, doubtful it was still locked—the keyhole had been damaged.

Fear clenched her stomach and twisted. Without even opening it, she knew what she'd find. She opened it anyway. Gone! It was all gone!

CHAPTER 18

K<small>ATE RAN DOWN THE STAIRS</small>, huffing more from panic than lack of oxygen. She burst into the saddle shop. "Mr. Hoy, did you get a look at the man climbing my stairs earlier?"

"Never set my eyes on him, just heard him." Mr. Hoy's face took on a look of concern. He tilted his head and considered her more carefully than when she'd first stepped in. "Why? What's wrong? You see a ghost or something? You look like you've been scared out of your wits."

"Worse. I've been robbed." Kate struggled to hold back the tears.

"Robbed! I'm so sorry, Miss Donahue."

"It had to have been that man you heard going up the stairs. I haven't been gone that long. Unless you've seen or heard anyone else go up there? I've been gone since eleven."

"Nope, just that one set of footsteps." He sat down his tools and held out his empty hands. "I wish I could be of more help, but that's all I know."

Kate clenched her fists. "I can't believe someone would just break into my home and take all my money!"

"Sorry to tell you this, Miss Kate, but this here isn't known as the Wild West for nothing. There's men out here that can pick a lock easier than using a key. And would just as soon rob you as put in an honest day's work. You gotta keep your valuables better hid. At leastwise until we get that new bank built." He offered a weak grin. "But those get robbed too."

Kate gathered her skirt, ready to go. "I won't allow this. I just won't."

As she scurried to the door, she could hear Mr. Hoy say, "Not that Sheriff Greene could do much now that the man and your money's long gone, but you want me to fetch him anyway?"

"I'm headed there right now, but thanks for the offer," she muttered as she stepped outside. She leaped into the street and shot in the direction of the makeshift town hall/jail one block down. Sheriff Greene had always intimidated her, with his six-foot-plus husky frame and bushy white mustache that concealed the smile or frown on his face. She forced her feet to move faster, telling herself with every hurried step that she was going to see Sheriff Greene, not Doctor Greene, and so this had nothing to do with any physician rivalry.

She hesitated outside the building, staring at the single-story wooden town hall that bore two signs above its two doors. On one side the sign read Craig City Hall; the other read Yampa Valley Land Office. She could see the man she knew as Harlow Forbes through the window of the land office sitting behind his desk. He'd been so rude last time he'd spoken to her—and he'd probably be worse now after an earful of his wife's gossip. Kate squared her shoulders. It wasn't Mr. Forbes she was seeing; it was the sheriff. She couldn't see anyone through the other window, just an empty desk at the front and two jail cells through a doorway into a back room. A wave of disappointment hit her. As much as she hated the idea, she needed to see Sheriff Greene. There was some movement in the back room. Sheriff Greene's white hair stuck out amongst the brown and gray of the two rooms.

Feeling a small measure of relief that the sheriff was in after all, Kate took in a deep breath and plunged through the door under the Craig City Hall sign.

"Ah, if it isn't Dr. Donahue, our little lady from out east. What can I do for you? Wondering if maybe this old man needs a checkup?" Pathetically, he let out a laugh as if he found himself funny.

Kate held back the urge to offer a quick retort. "I need to report a robbery," she said, trying to sound calm, wanting to appear as strong as possible.

"Really now?" The sheriff lifted a white eyebrow. "You witness someone taking something that didn't belong to them?"

"No! I've been robbed," she said with more energy than she'd planned. "And I want you to find the perpetrator and do something with him!"

"Perpa-what?"

"The criminal."

"And what did this person take?"

"All of my savings. Every last dime I had locked away in a jewelry box under my bed."

"And how am I supposed to find this person? Did you see him take your money, and did he take the box too?"

"No. But the money's gone, and my place is a mess as a result of him looking for it. And Mr. Hoy heard someone going up the stairs to my apartment while I was over at Sunny's."

"Having a sandwich? Or one those finger-lickin' sweet rolls?" The sheriff lifted his eyebrows while he smacked his lips.

"Does it matter?" Kate was losing patience.

"Did Stewart see the fellow? The one you think took your stuff?"

"No. Like I said, he just heard him on the stairs."

"So I'm supposed to find your bandit based on the sound of his footsteps, is that what you're asking?" he said simply.

"No!" Kate realized how puerile she sounded.

"I'm afraid you're going to have to give me more to go on than this." The sheriff's voice finally sounded serious. "Did anyone else know about this jewelry case that you kept under your bed?"

"I've never told anybody about it or let anyone see it," Kate said a little too defensively. She needed to tone down her voice. Then it hit her. "Except for hinting about it to Susann—I mean, Clara Jones and Roselund Decker. I was telling them about my tiny savings while we were having lunch at Sunny's today. And just after I mentioned it to them, this cowboy seated at the bar next to us spilled his beer. He must have been listening to our conversation!"

"Do you happen to know the name of this man, the one who might have been listening in?"

"That I do," Kate said, relieved that this investigation was finally going somewhere. "Will Pewtress. That's what, uh, Clara said his name was."

"Will Pewtress, eh?" Sheriff Greene pulled out the chair to the desk marked "mayor" by a name plaque resting on its surface. "He's handy with a lock pick, that's for certain." He sank into the chair, pushed it back farther, lifted his legs, and crossed them upon the desktop. "It wouldn't be the first time I've locked him up for robbery."

"Then you'll arrest him?" Kate felt a weight lift off her shoulders and tossed aside.

"Hold on there, girl." Sheriff Greene let his feet drop back to the ground. He looked Kate in the eye. "Just because you think the man overheard you tell the whereabouts of your money doesn't make him guilty. Not even in my book."

"But the man's a known thief. You said so yourself."

"I caught him red-handed those times." He put his feet back on the desk and leaned back in his chair. "I'll go talk to him 'cause that's my job. But don't go gettin' your hopes up that he'll confess and give your money back. Just to let you know, until you get me some solid evidence, Will Pewtress will remain the free, lowlife of a man that he is."

"So you're saying you can't help me?" Kate's shoulders straightened.

"No, I'm sayin' all's I can do is talk to him."

Kate turned on her heel and stormed out the door.

Not knowing what else to do, without giving it much thought, she ran toward the livery stable where she paid four bits a week to keep Lucy housed and fed. Where was she going to come up with the money now to keep Lucy? Those two ten-dollar gold pieces wouldn't last forever. She couldn't give up her horse. How else could she get around? Who else would nuzzle her cheek when she was down and love her unconditionally? She had to get that money back. And if the sheriff wouldn't help, she'd go get evidence on Will Pewtress herself!

◈

The wind whipped Kate's hair into her eyes as she prompted Lucy into a gallop and let her anger push caution aside. She pulled Lucy from the main road off onto the less-traveled trail that led to the Circle J Ranch. Susannah would surely help her get the evidence she needed to have the sheriff throw Will Pewtress in jail. She'd already tried to recruit Rosie's help, but she'd been told her friend was out on the range, and it would have taken too long to find her.

The faster she rode, the colder her arms became, but the more her determination heated. If she had to, she'd go into that bunkhouse where all the ranch hands stayed, walk right up to Mr. Pewtress, stomp on his filthy cowboy boot, and demand he give her money back. She knew he'd taken it, all right. And she was going to get it back.

The Circle J Ranch house, with its surrounding outbuildings, came into view. Kate slowed Lucy down, first to a trot and then to a walk.

Reality set in.

If Will Pewtress was truly the kind of man who would steal a poor woman's money, he wasn't about to just hand it over to her. He'd demand evidence too. The sheriff was right; she had none.

Kate started to pull Lucy around, recognizing how foolish approaching Mr. Pewtress directly would be. She hesitated for a moment then reset Lucy back on the trail to the Circle J, hoping Susannah could still help her or at least give her some moral support. Heaven knew she needed it at the moment to deal with this catastrophe.

Lucy whinnied as Kate wrapped her reins around a corral post near the ranch house. "I know. I don't like this place either. Let's just hope Susannah didn't decide to spend all day in town, and Mr. Stanley isn't back."

Kate crept toward the front porch, apprehension dragging her footsteps to where they each took a concerted effort to move. Once on the huge porch, she pushed herself toward the door and knocked.

The door swung open.

Kate had half-expected a maid, some sort of servant, to open the door. In that same second of false expectation, she remembered that Susannah was the maid, cook, and butler all rolled up in one. Her anger didn't have time to boil at that injustice; fear rushed in. In her anger, she had not thought this through.

"Well, well, if it isn't my little lovely lady, Kate Donahue." Stanley leaned his outstretched arm against the doorframe and batted his eyes. "What brings you out my way? A change of mind? You've realized yer mistake and you've come crawlin' back to ask my forgiveness? I am a forgivin' man, you know." He reached out and brushed her cheek with the back of his hand. "If you agree to the right things."

Repulsed by his touch, Kate jerked her face away. She was just glad that she could see a number of ranch hands out in the nearby corrals so she wasn't alone with this man. But they work for him. Her body tensed. "I've come here to see Susannah." Kate refused to keep calling her friend Clara in front of Stanley.

"You mean Clara?" Stanley's momentary confusion only made his face more disgusting.

"No, I mean Susannah, your sister. I need to ask her help on something."

"Well, she's not here," Stanley said with an edge to his voice, his honey-sweet façade having faded with her recoil from his touch. "But if there's anything you need, I'm sure I can help you better than her anyway."

Kate quickly weighed her options: turn tail and run, or proceed with her original goal.

She'd always prided herself on her strength—she had to resolve her dilemma. Besides, if Stanley Jones had even a shred of decency in him, and she hoped he did because she hated to think any man could be so evil inside, then he'd at least question his ranch hand. "Yes, I do believe you can help me on this."

Stanley's eyes lit up ever so slightly. "Finally, you see the light." He widened his grin to stick out on each side of his black mustache. "What can I do for you, my pretty lady?"

"You have a man working for you by the name of Will Pewtress," Kate said, trying to sound confident and businesslike.

"Yeah, what of him? You want me to set you up with Wild Will?" Stanley's grin twisted. "Sorry. I draw the line there. If any man on this ranch gets you, it's gonna be me."

Kate tightened her hands into fists. "Nobody's getting me! I came here to call your man, Mr. Pewtress, out. Ask him if he stole my money. Because if he did, I want it back."

As Kate proceeded to tell Stanley about the box with her savings, how the lock had been picked and now lay empty, and her suspicions on who took it, his eyes wandered from her face down to her waist and back up again several times. "Are you even listening, Mr. Jones?" She raised her hand and shook it in front of his face. In that same moment, her mind cleared of its anger and a bigger picture took form. Did she seriously think a man who would assault and defame her without batting an eye would help her out now? Of course not! She'd been so intent on getting her money back—and being strong and doing it herself since no one would help her—that she had not thought things out sufficiently. She'd always equated strength with fixing problems. Now she could see that being strong could just as well mean being able to weather one's problems with gracefulness. And that's what she should have done here.

If only she could go back an hour or so and put into place her newfound bit of wisdom.

Stanley grabbed her hand. "I'm listenin' to you. Loud and clear. Every single word out of those beautiful lips of yours." He pulled her close. "I'm sure I could convince Wild Will to cough up his spoils. But if I do that for you, what are you going to give me in return? How about this for starters?" He held on to the back of her head and forced his mouth on hers.

Kate ducked, pulling herself free from his hand and lips. She stepped away, cocked her arm way back, and flung it at his face. Slap!

Stanley stumbled back into the ranch house, holding his cheek. His eyes glared with more than their usual darkness; this time they were filled with what Kate could only describe as a storm of venom. "You think a little friendly gossip was painful," he said, practically spitting out his words. "You just wait, pretty lady. You ain't seen nothin' yet. That mutton-lovin' man you got your eyes set on is goin' to wish he'd never set foot in cattle country. I've just been waitin' for a better excuse than just his ugly face to get rid of that foreigner once and for all." He rubbed his cheek. "Now you've given it to me." He slammed the door in her face.

Too stunned to move, Kate stared at the door, the wheels in her mind churning at top speed. What had she unleashed? She'd come here intent on reclaiming her money—a task her gut instinct had told her was unrealistic. Now, she was not only leaving without her money but with the fear that her bullheadedness had cost her a lot more. If she were the only person about to become the target of Stanley's venom, she'd find a way to deal with it. But Stanley intended to get back at her by ruining Lucas McCurdy. The unfairness of it weakened her knees and she nearly collapsed.

Forcing herself from the doorstep, she stumbled to her horse, contemplating a hundred and one horrible things a cattleman could do to a sheep rancher to drive him off his land. Again, the injustice of it all overwhelmed her. This poor sheep rancher had been nothing but kind to her. And now, Lucas McCurdy would meet with a storm of hatred because of her. Because Stanley Jones's Pike's-Peak-sized ego had to blame someone for Kate's rejection.

Kate crawled up into the saddle in a daze. How could she fix this? Her mind churned in rhythm with the clip-clop of Lucy's hooves, grappling for ideas. Not a single viable way came to mind. She couldn't fix this problem—a problem she'd created, no less.

CHAPTER 19

IT HAD BEEN A FULL week since Kate's money had been stolen. After her episode with Stanley at the Circle J Ranch, she'd come home and wanted to lie on her bed and cry for a good two hours. But she didn't. She'd straightened the wrinkles in her dress as if she had taken that cry, and told herself to get on with her life. Now she stood by her sink, washing her few breakfast dishes, worried about what the next week would bring. The more she talked to people, the more she was certain she'd never regain her stolen money.

You can do this; you can weather this. Kate's thoughts churned, calculating every way she could save a penny and any way she could bring in extra ones until her medical practice became profitable. She lowered a plate into the warm dishwater. It washed up easily, she having licked it clean of its single fried egg at the breakfast table. Limiting her meals and not wasting a morsel of food were small ways she could save. But they wouldn't be enough for her to survive the winter. She had only her two ten-dollar gold pieces and a few bits' worth of change left to get her through. A shiver ran down her back as she considered the cold weather that soon would befall Craig. Mr. Decker and Mr. Hoy both had described the need for a well-stocked woodpile and pantry because there'd be days on end that "any sane person wouldn't want to venture out of their homes."

Kate's heart sank as she glanced over at the pile of wood next to her stove, sitting there like a family reunion back home in New York—lean, with little chance of more showing up.

It had been some time since she'd thought about New York. That was one good thing that had come from the chaos that had befallen her. But right now thoughts of her Long Island home rushed to the forefront of her mind. She knew she need only write a simple letter to her mother describing the misfortunate theft of her savings—and beg for forgiveness—and her mother would wire her money.

No, I'm not going to do that!

That would surely come with the stipulation that Kate pack up and return to New York. At the moment, she wasn't sure if she was strong enough to resist her mother's pull.

She pushed the temptation of writing home to the back of her thoughts. Doing so caused that niggling worry for Mr. McCurdy's safety to surface again. She tried to push it down just like the saucer she plunged into the dishwater. This time, her concern for Lucas refused to be buried. The fact that Kate had felt no repercussions from her slapping Stanley's face a few days ago gave her huge cause to worry. She knew Stanley Jones well enough to be certain that his threats of retribution were not empty words. If she wasn't receiving his wrath, then someone else was.

Oh, poor Lucas.

Her heart refused to quit aching for his sake. She wished she could help him, even if in the smallest of ways. But how?

A knock at the door pulled Kate out of her painful musings. She dried her hands on her apron and dashed out of her small kitchen into the living room/bedroom. When she opened the door, her heart took an extra beat. "Mr. McCurdy!"

"Are ye open?" he asked in an apologetic voice.

"Open?" Kate was still trying to process seeing this man who filled her thoughts standing on her doorstep as if her mind had willed him here.

"For doctoring." Lucas held up his arm crocked at an angle. A portion of his cast stuck out past the sleeve of his coat. She barely recognized it as such, the white plaster having turned gray-brown from obvious use of his hand. "I think 'tis time to take the thing off. 'Tis itching something terrible." His lips curled up into his crooked smile. "Plus, I need to settle with you."

Kate felt her eyes widen as she stared at him, uncertain what he meant.

He pushed back his sleeve and waved the cast back and forth. "Take care of me payment."

A gust of wind slapped Kate to her senses. "Oh, yes. Yes, of course. Come in, come in." She motioned for him to step inside. "It's awfully cold out there, isn't it?" she said after she'd shut the door, bouncing on her toes.

"'Tis a mild day for mid-October," he said as he removed his coat. Before he hung the threadbare coat on the hook, he reached into one of its pockets. He pulled out his hand, clenching something in his thick fingers. "I know 'tis not cash. 'Tis not even something ye need to get ye through the winter. I apologize. But I hope ye understand. Those things are in short supply at me place too. Next spring, after the wool's been shorn, I promise I shall make good on my bill. For now, though, I'd like for ye to have this . . . to show my appreciation." He held out his hand, letting its contents tumble down, maintaining hold of a very thin strip of leather. At the end of the strip hung a wooden bird, about the size of a ten-dollar gold piece.

Kate stared at it, unable to form words on her tongue or in her head. Disappointment fueled the silence—she needed money. Then a sense of awe swept away all feelings of discontent. The beauty of the intricately carved animal became more apparent as she let it rest in her palm and pulled it up to her eyes. With strips of brown, as dark as coffee, next to ones that looked like caramel, the wood grain filled out the bird's outstretched wings with an illusion of feathers.

"'Tis a necklace. It reminds me of you." His voice was timid.

"A bird?" Kate said.

"Not just any bird. An eagle." He took the necklace from her palm and looped it over her head. "Independent, strong, and beautiful creatures they are." His hands reached under her hair, brushing against her skin, evoking a heavenly tingle as he lifted her hair away and let the strip of leather rest on the back of her neck. He stepped back and viewed his work.

Kate looked down at it resting against her skin barely above the lace-trimmed neckline of her dress. "It's beautiful," she said softly.

Staring at her wearing his necklace, Lucas murmured, "Aye, lass, that it is."

A flush of warmth spread through Kate. She turned away, focusing on the gray sky through the room's lone window. "Nasty weather, isn't it?"

"You nay have spent a winter here yet, have you, Miss Donahue?"

"No, I haven't." Kate stepped over and sorted through the cabinet of her medical tools. "And please, just call me Kate, or Miss Kate," she said over her shoulder. "That's what everyone else calls me." And Miss Donahue sounds so forced coming from your mouth. She continued looking for the pair of large shears she'd purchased at Decker's store when she first got here. Mr. Decker had told her they were for cutting chicken wire, but she'd seen them as a means to cut off plaster casts.

"I'd rather call ye Katherine, if ye don't mind. It fits ye better." He walked over and stood at her back as she rummaged. "Regal name, it is. Katherine," he spoke her name like it was a privilege, letting each syllable roll from his tongue with reverence. Accompanied by his light Irish accent, her name sounded like music coming from his lips. "But only if ye call me Lucas."

Kate could feel his presence, sensing the heat from his body on the skin of her back. She kept fumbling, picking up the same scalpel over and over again, forgetting what she was looking for. The fog cleared from her mind enough to spot the shears. She grabbed them and turned around. "Okay, Lucas it is," she said, convincing herself that she was merely falling into the informal ways of the West—not that she desired to call him by that name.

He didn't move. She faced him now, her face just inches from his.

Kate's heart beat rapidly. She willed it to slow. There was work to be done. Finally, she had a patient to tend to, and she couldn't have her silly emotions get in her way. She pushed her free hand against his chest, intending to move him out of the way. The action instead sent tingles up her arm and made her step back. The medical cabinet rattled as she backed into it. "Oh, my," she blurted out, feeling heat rise to her face. "Let's step over there," Kate said in a shaky voice, pointing to the center of the room. "It'll be easier to get the job done."

He stepped back.

Kate swore she detected reluctance in his eyes. Did he want to be next to her as much as she desired to be near him? She shook her head to dislodge the unprofessional thought and pointed to the kitchen. "Could you get that kitchen chair and bring it here?" she said in a firm voice for her own sake. "It will be easier if you're sitting down."

Lucas pulled away from her and rushed into the kitchen, returning quickly with Kate's single kitchen chair in tow. He set it in the middle of the living room and slipped onto it in one continuous movement. "Okay. Ready, doctor," he said, smiling his crooked smile and gazing into her eyes. He caught sight of the shears in Kate's hand. With an eyebrow lifted and his face twisting in an expression of humor, he said, "If I'd have known ye was to use those, I could've asked me neighbor—if I had one—to cut this darn thing off long before now." He held up his casted arm despite his comment.

"But mine are clean." Kate wiggled them in front of his face. "They haven't been left out in the chicken coop for the past year, collecting chicken manure and feathers." She chewed on her lip for a second and gazed at Lucas more seriously. "Actually, you're the first patient I've tried these on. I do hope they work okay, because we certainly don't have the time for me to send for a set of actual medical shears." She raised her fingers to her mouth and muttered under breath, "Or the money to do so."

Lucas reached up. Resting his hand momentarily on her arm, he said, "I heard about your savings. I am so sorry. Truly I am. And I promise I shall pay ye properly as soon as I can."

His hand could have stayed there permanently as far as Kate's fluttering insides were concerned, but her head was relieved when he removed it. And her head had to step in and control the conversation. "Thank you, I appreciate your concern, but I'll be okay. And the necklace is fine payment. I should be the one concerned about you." Kate couldn't keep back the worry any longer. "How have things been going for you out at your place?"

"'Tis the same as usual." He ducked his head slightly. "Maybe a wee worse." He flipped it back up, his eyes focusing on Kate's. "But I am fine. I have friends like you, do I not?" he said in a tone portraying a sincerity that touched Kate.

She was glad to be considered a friend. That's why she had to tell him. She had to warn him in case it could help him prepare somehow for the wrath of Stanley Jones. She had to tell him it was all her fault. "Mr. Mc—Lucas, I've got to tell you something." She set the shears down on the end table next to her lamp. "I've upset Stanley Jones something terrible. And for some reason, he seems set on taking it out on you. I'm so sorry. I can't understand why he'd want to do that, and I feel just horrible about it. I wanted to warn you so maybe . . . it would help you prepare for . . ."

"His mischief?" Lucas said with a wary smile.

"That's too gracious a way to put it, but I gather you know what I mean." Kate sighed in frustration.

"Oh, yes, I am quite familiar with Stanley's mischief." Lucas no longer smiled. "'Tis growing passed mischief though, I must say. A week or so ago, he used dynamite to scare me poor sheep off the public land."

"Seriously?" Kate said with a slight raise to her voice. Then she remembered seeing Stanley's horse loaded with blasting material. "I still don't understand why he's set to punish you because of me. We barely know each other. Surely he's intelligent enough to see that the night I spent at your place was no different than times he's inevitably bedded down at a gracious homesteader's along the trail."

"Oh, he's smart enough. 'Tis why I did not let myself worry for a minute about the gossip he spread right after it happened. Folks around here know 'tis a common thing. Ye did right in holding your head high. Proved to people ye had nothing to hide. 'Tis all they needed."

"How did you know about that?" Kate swore she hadn't seen him in town since she'd stayed overnight at his place.

"Logan. The lad tells me everything. He's like me eyes and me ears to this town." He looked away, staring at the blank wall above the medical cabinet. "And to you."

"Me?" Kate whispered in surprise.

He paused. "Unfortunately, Stanley has a way of getting to Logan, forcing the lad to tell the things I have told him in confidence. Not just about me land, but about you. I should really learn to button me lip, but the lad's my only visitor and it gets awfully lonely out there. I long too much for conversation. So, unfortunately, Stanley knows how I feel about you, and it appears that has just given him one more reason to despise me."

His declarations startled her. Had she heard him correctly? "Oh" was all she could think to say.

"Since the day I met you, I knew ye were cut of different wool than any other lass. 'Twas a struggle to push ye from my thoughts. But being a married man, I knew I must. When I received news of my wife's passing, I beat myself up near a week at being relieved rather than heartbroken, as I should have." He turned his attention away from the wall and faced Kate. "But I have the right to move on now, do I not? To love the kind of lass that sets my heart on fire with her beauty and strength—and a gentle heart that don't usually go with the aforementioned traits."

"Uh . . ." Kate picked up the shears. She didn't know what to say. What to feel. This couldn't be happening. Lucas wasn't the first man who'd shown interest in her since she'd sworn off men forever. But he was the first man who had interested her. *There, I've admitted I'm attracted to him; I could fall in love with him. But I can't, not now!*

Kate wasn't ready to risk having her heart ripped from her chest and trampled once more. If she were to let down her guard and openly love Lucas and court him properly, Stanley would only make things worse for Lucas and his sheep. And she couldn't bear knowing she'd been responsible for his homestead's demise. "Let's get this cast off your arm."

"Very well." Lucas looked at the floor and held out his arm.

She pushed up his sleeve past his elbow to have access to the full length of the cast. The shirt sleeve had been ripped to accommodate the cast. Knowing that he had no money for a new shirt, Kate's heart ached for him. She wanted to help. "If you want to leave this shirt with me, I'd be glad to mend it for you. I'm fair with a needle and thread."

"Thank you, 'twould be helpful."

The chicken wire sheers struggled through the plastered gauze. Lucas helped with his good hand after Kate's hands grew sore. When the cast finally fell away from his arm, his hand and arm flexed, celebrating their release from prison.

Kate had expected to see a spindly wisp of an arm, like she'd seen with other patients when she'd removed their casts, but the muscles in his forearm flexed firm and strong as he moved it. It did, however, look pale and smaller than she'd remembered. Instinctively, she massaged his arm, trying to stimulate its circulation, sincerely wanting to help her patient. Her fingers moved over his wrist. She could feel his pulse. It beat rapidly. Too rapidly for a man sitting in a chair.

She let go of his arm abruptly. "Uh . . . hopefully that feels better—I mean, that your arm will get back to normal soon." She turned away quickly and headed for the dresser. "Let me get my needle and thread, and I'll get that shirt of yours sewn back up," she said over her shoulder.

With her back to him, she sifted through her sewing supplies, taking longer than she'd expected to find her package of needles. Once found, she grabbed them and a spool of white thread and turned around, expecting to see Lucas still in the chair wearing his torn shirt, awaiting with outstretched arm for her to stitch it up.

Lucas stood by the chair, holding his shirt, bare from the waist up.

Kate let escape a quick gasp. She'd forgotten what an absolute stunning example of the human body Lucas McCurdy's torso was, with all its muscles perfectly in place. But now was not the time and place to be admiring it. She grabbed the spare blanket she kept folded at the foot of her bed and wrapped it around his shoulders. "Here, wear this while I fix your shirt. I don't keep my place warm enough for such lack of attire."

Kate settled into the armchair with needle and thread and torn shirt. Lucas pulled the kitchen chair close, and they chatted as she mended his shirt. She took care to make neat, small stitches, wanting to make her work the very best she could. The desire to give all she could for this bullied, lonely, unfortunate man, burned strong within her, as did a need to know more about him. "What made you want to leave your homeland for this stark Colorado desert?"

"Aye, the yearning to own me own land." Lucas's eyes sparkled. "When I learned I could purchase 180 acres for eighteen U.S. dollars, the next day I booked passage on a ship bound for America. I bade a fond farewell to me brothers and sisters and, with my life savings in me pocket, I left me homeland behind and set out in search of the opportunities to be had in the wild frontier of the big open West." His volume had increased, and the last several words came out with a bit of dramatic flair.

"What about your parents?" She wondered if his parents were against him chasing his dreams the same as her parents were. Why else had he not mentioned them?

"Both of them are gone. I was the youngest of eight children. Me brothers and sisters had enough to worry about with their own broods, they nay had much time to fret over my future."

Though their reasons for leaving were as different as night and day, she still felt a certain kinship to the man in that they had both come here following their dreams. "So what did you do when you got here?" she asked, wondering if there were times he too had been tempted to return to his homeland.

"When I landed in the east, I was told Colorado was the place to go. So I came out here, staked out me homestead outside of Craig early on, before many other homesteaders had come. Then I purchased a wee flock of sheep and struggled for the next five years, surviving off the wool and what I could raise in the way of food on me land, not wanting to sell off any of me flock— so they would multiply."

"Did you ever want to give up, go back to Ireland?"

Lucas hesitated with his answer, staring off into the distance. "Only once. The day me wife left me and took wee Celeste with her. 'Twas two years ago." He shook out his shoulders and looked again at Kate. "But this coming year should be the year I can afford to sell off some of me flock without affecting me wool production. That is, if I lose no more sheep to mischief," he said with a slight hint of his crooked grin.

"We need to make sure of that," Kate said, unsure how to do that. The only thing she could think of was to make Stanley believe that she was totally out of Lucas's life. She concentrated on her stitching, wanting to finish up this shirt as quickly as she could.

"I had hoped to become friends with the Joneses," Lucas continued, "drawing from their knowledge of this new landscape, so desolate and much colder than the countryside where I learned the shepherd trade from me grandpa back in Ireland. But I soon came to learn cattlemen and sheep farmers mix worse than oil and water, always fighting over the public grazing lands."

Sadness weighed down Lucas's eyes. "Then I went through the trouble and money to get a permit to graze me sheep on a certain section of land, but 'twas all for naught. The Circle J claimed that land was theirs because they had been here first and had been grazing their cattle on it for years."

"No, that's not fair; it's not right!" Kate's body stiffened.

"Aye, and 'tis not the worst of it." His mouth twisted into a feeble version of that crooked grin that always seemed to weaken her knees.

Now, however, it gave her the desire to cup his face in her hands and offer a caress of comfort. How could he muster a smile in the middle of such a story?

"Last winter the mischief resumed. After they'd burned down me house that first year, I had hoped 'twas the last of it." The weak smile hung on as he continued. "But no. I came home from me rounds one chilly evening to find me eye-high woodpile down to one log high. Just a wee time later, I came home to a broken window and a rock sitting inside me house amongst the shards of glass. This summer a brush fire was set on me deeded portion of land."

"Did you tell the sheriff about these things?" Kate set down her mending. It only needed a few more stitches to finish her repairs, but this—this maddened her. The rift between the cattlemen and sheep farmers needed to be repaired. "Could he not arrest these cattlemen for their vandalism? Because it's as plain as the nose on anyone's face they were behind it."

Lucas smiled his crooked smile wide this time. "I love how you stand up for the little guy. How you fight injustice." His smile faded. "But I have to tell you, lass, your feisty spirit will not get ye far when pitted against the Joneses or any other of the big cattle ranchers. I know; I tried at first. But the sheriff's their longtime friend, and Mr. Forbes at the land office just laughs at me for lack of proof and says, 'This is the West, Irishman. If you want to settle a dispute, it's best you go buy yourself a gun to wear on your hip.'"

"But if you have a permit, this shouldn't be happening; you can prove the land in question is yours to use, not theirs, and they should leave you alone."

"Oh, Katherine." Lucas chuckled. "If only everyone were as pure and sweet as you." He reached out and touched her hand. "I do not have a copy of that permit, because it burned when my house burned down the first year I got here. That was before my wife came out to join me. I think the culprits were at least decent enough to not try it again with a wife and wee babe in the house thereafter. But even if I did have a copy, the lawmen around here would not see fit to help me uphold it. 'Tis cattle country. Even the folks in town who don't touch a cow—'cept with their forks—have longhorn blood flowing through their veins." He hung his head. "'Tis a battle I shall have to fight on me own."

"What about your little girl?" Kate's ache for Lucas's situation grew another notch, yet this ache was laced with a bit of hope. "Have you heard back from your mother-in-law? Is she going to send the child to you?"

"Aye, I heard back." Lucas ran his hand through his hair, causing the blanket to fall from one shoulder. "Tempest's mother won't allow it; 'tis too dangerous a place for wee Celeste,' she says. The lass is only four." He chewed on his lip and sighed. "For once, my mother-in-law is right." His sad eyes stared out the window as he mumbled softly, "Especially with all that's happening."

"I'm so sorry." Kate's words couldn't even begin to express the sorrow she felt for Lucas. Her heavy feelings only added to the fear that she had made his trials worse. She bit the end of the thread from the shirt, having finished its mending. She handed the shirt to Lucas, letting her outstretched arm sag in the process. It was as if it too felt the heavy weight of hopelessness permeating the room. "I wish I could help. This whole situation seems so unfair."

He took the shirt and stood, letting the blanket fall from his shoulders and giving Kate cause to look away to prevent her heart from fluttering. "Your friendship helps." His deep voice, rich with warmth and sincerity, pulled Kate's eyes back to him.

"I'm glad," Kate responded, grateful his shirt covered his body—except for a long, narrow V of skin below his neck where skiffs of golden-red hair grew on his chest.

His newly un-casted hand fumbled with the buttons. Kate's instinct was to rush in and offer to help, confident that her small, nimble fingers would be able to finish the task much more easily. She held herself back. It would only fuel the attraction. And attraction would lead to romantic involvement. She wasn't ready for that. And she couldn't have Lucas. She couldn't add more fuel to the Joneses' hatred of this poor sheep rancher. It would be best if she returned to her original plan of locking up her heart and tucking it far away from men.

Lucas finished buttoning his shirt and walked over to where his coat hung by the door. Kate followed at a distance. After putting on his coat, with hand on the knob, Lucas lingered at the door. He turned to face Kate, who was an arm's length away. "Thank you so much."

"My pleasure."

"Really?" he said with a hint of that mischievous smile that had surfaced earlier.

"Really." Kate offered him a simple but sincere smile.

Lucas lifted his hat from the hook, hovered it over his head, and then put it back on the rack. He took a step closer to Kate, their bodies now inches apart. "Aye, this might be burning a bridge here, but life's uncertain, and 'tis a bit of a chance I have got to take." His arm slipped around her back and pulled her body close to his. Standing just inches taller than her, his neck bent slightly as he pushed his lips against hers.

Kate succumbed to their softness. Her body went limp. His arms lent support, pulling her against his chest. His lips pressed against hers with a strong, yet gentle force that opened her mouth and made it welcome the passion that followed.

Lucas ended the kiss abruptly. He steadied Kate on her feet before grabbing his hat. "I'd better be going." He put on his hat, opened the door, letting the wind rush in, and stepped outside.

Kate closed the door behind him. Hanging on to the doorknob, she lowered herself to the floor. A million emotions coursed through her. She didn't want to have beautiful feelings like these for Lucas. It only complicated an already complex situation.

CHAPTER 20

KATE STOMPED OUT OF THE land office. Mr. Forbes had been about as much help as a hemorrhoid. She may as well have gone and talked to Stanley directly and asked him, "Pretty please, will you stop harassing Lucas McCurdy, stop trying to push him off the grazing land that is rightfully his to use?"

Yesterday, she'd sat on the drafty floor next to the door after Lucas had left, crying to the point when she had soaked the front of her dress, angry with herself for leading Lucas on. Why had she not resisted his kiss? How dare she enjoy that kiss beyond any others that had ever touched her lips? Why didn't she stop to think her unprofessional actions could very well put Lucas in further danger? She'd known she was not ready to give her heart to anyone. Marriage was years down the road—if ever at all. Yet she'd let him kiss her like a man she was about to marry.

That was yesterday. Today was a new day, and she had to move on. It was best that she and Lucas McCurdy avoid any and all romantic involvement, but that didn't mean she couldn't still be his friend and advocate. The best way to do that—so she figured—was to fight for his legal rights since it appeared he wasn't going to—he sincerely believed it wouldn't do any good. But she did.

Kate tightened the shawl around her shoulders against the wind, kicked up some dirt at the front of the land office as she wiped her feet of the place, and headed to the only other place in town she thought might be able to help her: the town's lone attorney.

Ronald Smith's eyes lit up when Kate stepped into the office. "May I speak with you for a minute, Mr. Smith?"

"Miss Donahue!" He rose from his chair, hurling it backward, and rushed to greet her with an outstretched hand. "It's so very good to see you." Shaking her hand, he asked, "What brings you out on this windy morning?"

"I presume you're aware of the friction that exists between the cattlemen and sheep farmer in the area?"

"Yes, of course," he said pulling out the chair in front of his desk for Kate to sit on. He practically jumped around to the other side of the desk and into his seat directly across from her. "And that is what you have braved the elements for today, to come and ask me this question?" A smile pulled up the corners of his usually stoic face.

"Of course not; there's more," Kate said, finding Ronald more animated than usual. Did he think she was here to see him? Personally?

Ronald stretched his arm across the desk with the palm of his hand up. "I've got no appointments for a while. Please, what's troubling you? I'd love to help if I can."

Kate gave a little background on the feud between the Circle J and Lucas McCurdy, and on the permit he'd obtained. "Is there any kind of legal action Mr. McCurdy can take?" she asked.

Ronald raised one of his near-invisible eyebrows as he looked at Kate. "Why is Mr. McCurdy sending you to ask me this question? Shouldn't he be doing this himself?" His voice for once rose and fell slightly from its usual monotone pitch.

"Uh . . ." Kate took in a big breath. She needed to distance herself from Lucas—for his sake. If there was even a hint that she was helping him other than just as his doctor, it might get back to Stanley and he could translate it as her having feelings for the man, and that could serve to fuel the battle rather than lend aid. "He was going to, but he needed to rush back to his place after I removed his cast yesterday—he's worried about his flock's safety. And rightfully so," Kate added with a touch of anger. She felt bad about stretching the truth, but desperate times required desperate measures. "I told him that I knew you well enough that I wouldn't mind seeking your advice for him, as I have plenty of time on my hands." She smiled at that truth. "I assured him that you were an honest, fair man who would help if you could because you didn't cower under the long arm of the local cattlemen," she continued, cringing inside all the while. This was so unlike her, but if it helped rally Ronald around her cause and gain his support in helping Lucas fight this unfair battle, it was worth it.

It seemed to be working. Ronald's face loosened further and his smile spread into his eyes. "There are things Mr. McCurdy can do to help him fight his case, or I could help fight his case."

"Wonderful!" Kate exclaimed. She rushed her hand to her mouth. That had been much too much excitement shown for someone who was supposed to be an uninvolved third party. "For Mr. McCurdy, that is. He will be glad to hear the good news."

"But that's only if he has proof of that permit," Ronald said, settling back into his monotone voice. "Do you know if he has a copy of his permit back at his ranch?"

"No." Kate felt her hopes sink.

"No, you don't know, or no, he doesn't have a copy?"

"No, he doesn't have a copy," Kate said, feeling the anger boil again inside her. "He said it was burned in a fire that destroyed his first home. And my guess was that the fire was no accident—more reason we need to help him with this."

"I remember hearing about that fire," Ronald said, hanging his head. "It sounded mighty suspicious to me at the time, but I didn't pay it much heed because I was new in town and I needed to establish my practice. I didn't want to get involved with something that didn't concern me."

"Oh." Kate felt her hopes fade further. "I understand," she said, not that she agreed. She understood that most everyone in this town didn't want to get involved in things that didn't concern them. That's why a helpless immigrant from Ireland was getting his house burned, his livestock killed, and his life threatened over something as petty as grazing rights upon land that was as stark as the surface of the moon, as far as Kate was concerned—though she knew the ranchers didn't see it as such.

"But that was then," Ronald said, straightening his back. "Now, if Mr. McCurdy is willing to pay the money, he can obtain another copy of his grazing permit. With that in hand, he could call upon the federal marshal to enforce the law and put the Circle J, or anyone else who may be grazing on his permitted portion of land, in their place. How they would do that, I don't know, but I do know the federal government is trying to implement stricter punishments against these old-time cattle ranchers who think they are above the law."

"How much money for the permit?" Kate asked, picturing the two ten-dollar gold pieces she now carried around her waist in her homemade version of a money belt. Most of the small change she'd had was already spent. "And how much for your services to help him obtain it?"

"I couldn't tell you about the permit. And I wouldn't charge Mr. McCurdy for obtaining a new copy, because I'm not going to do that for him." Ronald's face showed no signs of belligerence. So why had he said that?

She wanted to reach across that desk and slap the man's face for being like every other spineless man in the town. "But isn't that your job, if he pays you to do so?"

"If I agree to it, yes," Ronald said, his face like a statue. "But in this case I won't agree to it." He turned and opened a drawer while Kate felt her insides fume. He thumbed through some file folders, pulled out a paper, and placed it on his desk. "I don't want to take Mr. McCurdy's money." He pushed the paper across the desk toward Kate. "He doesn't have it to give. But this is something he can do by himself. I'll give you this information. You tell him he can file for the permit if he just follows these steps. The cost should be mentioned in there somewhere too." He pointed to the bottom of the paper with his pen, which he handed to her a second later. "Here. I'll get you a piece of paper and you can write down the information for him."

Kate wrote down the information, feeling much better than she had a few minutes earlier. She chided herself for thinking so poorly of Ronald. She stood, reached her arms across the desk, and shook his hand with both of hers. "Thank you, Ronald. You're a good man," she said, letting her emotions do the speaking. As she pulled her hands away, she could see a flush of pink on his cheeks.

He stood quickly and walked Kate to the door, fumbling with the corner of his suit coat. "Uh . . . I was wondering . . . if you might care to join me for supper one evening this week?"

Kate's first reaction was no. Then something clicked in her brain. It would be good for her to court. It could do the people of the town good to see her out with an eligible young man. Then another reason surfaced—an even better one. Word would hopefully get back to Stanley—he might even see them together. That could only serve to help ease the tension between Stanley and Lucas. Besides, it might help get her mind off Lucas in the area where it didn't belong: as a man who took her breath away each time she saw those golden curls at the nape of his neck or around the soft features of his face, and eyes as blue as the sky.

"Supper would be nice," Kate responded sincerely. "Sunny's place?"

"Where else?"

CHAPTER 21

Kate went directly home from the attorney's office. Climbing up the stairs, with each beat of her shoes against the wood, her determination increased. She didn't plan on giving this information to Lucas. She was going to file for the permit for him. Not only did she think it unwise to be seen going out to his place or having Logan fetch him to her, but she feared he'd not file for lack of funds. And she knew he'd never allow her to pull from what remained of her money to pay for it.

Once inside, she took an envelope and piece of paper from her small reserve atop the medical cabinet. She got out her fountain pen and bottle of ink and stepped into the kitchen. After clearing away any remnants of crumbs from her meager breakfast, she set to writing a letter. Halfway through, she misspelled a word, so she wadded the paper into a ball and tossed it into the stove along with a small log, saving the larger ones for nighttime. As she sat back down at the table, she glanced again at the dwindling woodpile and sighed. The cost to file for the permit, as stated in that form, popped into her thoughts. Ten dollars. *Can I afford to do this?*

No.

But even more so, Lucas could ill afford her not to do it.

In the second draft, Kate took extra care to pen the letter with less flourish in her handwriting, giving each letter a bolder presence on the page, hoping the letter looked more like a man had written it. When she signed the bottom, Lucas McCurdy, a twisting in her stomach made her grab the paper with the urge to wad it into a ball and throw it into the stove as well. She held back. This needed to be done. His address was the one she gave as to where the permit was to be sent. It wasn't like she was trying to gain a copy for her own greedy purposes. It was to save a man's rights, his land, and possibly his life. She hoped.

Once the ink had dried, she creased the letter into three even folds and placed it in the envelope. She didn't seal it, knowing it still required the needed fee. Ten dollars. That's what the information had said as she'd copied it down in Ronald's office. She set the open envelope on the table, lifted her skirt, and untied her money belt. Her fingers hesitated, pulling the gold piece away from its cozy pocket next to its twin sister—Kate's remaining funds to last her the winter.

You've got to do it; you've got to take the chance.

She snatched up one of the coins and clasped it close to her heart. This was a risk. There was no guarantee it would solve anything. But it was something she could do to help Lucas McCurdy. Tilting her head toward heaven, she offered a silent prayer. *Please don't let this be in vain.*

She slipped the remaining gold piece into her purse and out of habit, reattached her money belt to her waist. It was such a small amount to bother hiding away, especially when she'd be using half of it next week to pay her rent. November was but six days away. Then with a lift to her spirits, she remembered that cyst on Mr. Hoy's back had taken care of next month's rent. *See? You'll get more patients; you'll manage.*

Kate put on her coat, ready to slip out the door to head down to the makeshift post office in Decker's store. An idea prompted her to turn away from the door and head back into the kitchen. She grabbed another envelope and sheet of paper on her way. The pen still sat on the tabletop, full of ink. If only her idea came with the words she should write down. A letter to the federal marshal requesting his help to enforce the laws concerning grazing rights within the Yampa Valley would not be an easy one to write. It would have to be done just right to have the proper effect. She hoped she'd understood the laws correctly as Ronald had described them to her earlier. The last thing she needed was to sound like a whining, unintelligent woman demanding this marshal stop something he had no control over.

The letter took an hour to write.

She carefully placed it in an envelope and headed back to the door, hoping Mr. Decker had the address for the federal marshal serving this area of Colorado.

There was a definite chill in the air, more so than usual, as Kate walked to the mercantile. It saddened her to see fall turn to winter, but she knew it was inevitable. Her day brightened, however, when Mr. Decker, after she'd given him two pennies for two stamps, was able to convert her gold piece into a money order with no problems. And he hadn't pried into her reasoning for doing so.

But he did raise an eyebrow when she'd asked for the address to the federal marshal. He looked it up and then recited the Denver address with noticeable hesitancy in his voice.

Kate jotted it down on her envelope as he read. Once addressed, she placed stamps on each of her envelopes and shoved them into the slotted wooden box marked MAIL at the end of the counter.

Mr. Decker stood in the same spot as when he'd read from his thick book of government addresses, his eyes still on her. "Is there anything amiss, Miss Donahue? Anything I can help you with?"

"No, everything is fine," Kate lied, wishing there was some way Mr. Decker could actually help.

And then another idea formed.

Maybe there was something that could be done in addition to the letters she'd just mailed. She could ask for help from the townspeople, including Mr. Decker; ask them simply to stand up for what was right and not turn a blind eye when someone violated the law. Convince them that their town would become better if they did. It would be a tall order for a lot of the people. But for some, she knew it would merely be what they wanted to do. Maybe they just needed a little encouragement to stand up to the likes of Stanley Jones and his father; to be told that safety came in numbers, and if they all did it, they'd be okay.

Kate realized she'd been standing there by the mailbox longer than was normal. Mr. Decker was staring at her. She was about to put up a request for him to be the first to stand up to the Joneses, when she heard Lavender's infectious laughter ring through the wall. "Thank you for the offer, Mr. Decker," Kate said, knowing now whose help she needed to seek out first. "If you don't mind, I'm going to pay your dear wife a visit." She gave him a quick nod of the head and walked toward the back door that led to their home.

Lavender Decker stood over her kitchen table, kneading a large mound of dough. She looked up and smiled when Kate stepped into the room. "Afternoon, Kate."

"You're just the person I want to talk to." Kate pulled a chair out from the table and sat down.

"Really now?" Lavender pushed a wayward strand of hair from her eyes with the back of a floured hand.

"Yes. I need someone who is cheerful, kind-hearted, and whom everyone in town knows and loves," Kate said. "And I can't think of a person who fits that description better than you."

Lavender's eyes brightened even more than their usual cheery gray-blue. "Well, thank you. That's the kindest thing anyone's ever said to me."

"I only stated the truth." Kate picked up a stray piece of dough and tossed it into the mound being worked by Lavender's hands. "And look how good it made you feel. More people should be telling you those kinds of things."

Lavender batted a white hand at Kate. "Oh, come now. Other people don't think that."

"I believe they do. I can see it in their eyes when they greet you in the store. Or I hear it in their voices when they rant over your sweet rolls at Sunny's. The town thinks you're wonderful. But there's one problem with this town."

"What's that? No opera house?" Lavender said with a smirk.

Kate couldn't hold back. She grinned. "Besides that." She scooted away from the table as Lavender started rolling out the dough, pushing it to every corner of the table and forming a rectangle. "Seriously now," Kate said. "People don't speak up for what's true. They don't ever spread gossip like, 'Oh, that Lavender Decker is just the kindest lady. Did you hear how she made a whole batch of sweet rolls and gave them all to a stagecoach-load of homesteaders passing through town?' But neither do they say, 'Hey, that's just not true,' when Stanley Jones tells everyone in town vicious lies about a sheep farmer or, 'that was horrible,' when he runs over their pet cat because he 'just felt like it.' Or say, 'put that back,' when Stanley steals a pickle from that jar on your counter when you're not looking."

"This is all very nice," Lavender said as she sprinkled her dough with sugar and cinnamon. "Sounds like you don't care for Mr. Jones any more than I do, but heck if I can figure out what it all has to do with me being 'just the person you need.'"

"Something needs to be done about Stanley Jones and the way he bullies the people of this town into looking the other way instead of standing up to him. They all know he's in the wrong."

"You keep on talkin', but you still haven't told me what this has to do with me." Lavender added some chopped walnuts and then rolled the flattened dough on the table into what looked like a small, smooth log.

"People respect you—especially the women. I need your help to talk to them. I think the women of this town will listen to you more than me, and they'll follow your lead."

"What lead? Where on earth am I going to lead them to? I'm no Moses."

"You don't need to part the Red Sea here. We're just going to do something simple. Sometimes it's the small things that bring down the giant."

"Like David's little stone defeating Goliath?"

"Exactly." Kate loved the analogy. "If all the married women of this town would just whisper sweetly into their husbands' ears and encourage them to stand up to Stanley Jones and not look the other way when he breaks the law, then all those quiet whispers would add up to one big voice that could put Stanley Jones in his place."

"I hate to tell you this, honey, but very few women I know whisper sweet things into their men's ears. Now, if you had them threaten to not make supper . . . ." Lavender's grin turned mischievous. "Or withhold their wifely favors in the bedroom . . . then they'd have their menfolk more willing to do whatever they asked."

Kate felt herself blush for a second at Lavender's words.

"I was just jokin' with you, Kate."

"Whatever you think will work," Kate said. "But no manipulation—or intimidation. Stanley's done enough of that already. The men of this town just need encouragement." What had started out as a desperate reach for any help was materializing into something worthwhile.

"I like your idea." Lavender sliced the roll into one-inch pieces with a length of string. "I for one would like nothing more than to stop the man from parading into my store like he owns the place. Heck, we don't even own it, yet." She raised her chin high while a satisfied smile filled her face. "Thanks to my sweet rolls, that'll be sooner than later." Her expression grew serious. "But we're the ones paying for that piece of licorice he just takes from the jar, thinking his wink is as good as money. And that's nothing compared to the bargains he forces Sam to give him on his tobacco. My Sam's a nervous wreck after dealing with the man."

"Then you'll talk to all the women in town?"

"All of them I can," Lavender said. "There'll be some who won't care to join in."

"I realize that," Kate said. "Oh, and I think it's important that you don't mention my name at all. If word got back to Stanley that I had anything to do with this—well . . . ."

"Don't worry, I understand." Lavender waved a hand at Kate. "My Roselund will love this. She can't tolerate Stanley Jones. I only wish she had herself a husband so she could take part in our plan. Poor, mixed-up girl: wearing trousers, breaking horses like a man. What kind of fella is going to want her?" She shook her head.

"She'll find someone. You just watch; he'll be the best man in these parts." Kate patted Lavender's hand.

"You really think so?"

"Positive."

Lavender covered the pan full of rolls with a cloth. "Time for these sweet things to rise," she said and sat down next to Kate. "Now your turn to be honest." She looked Kate in the eye. "Why this sudden interest in reining in our notorious Mr. Stanley Jones?"

Kate shrugged her shoulders. She knew it was a pathetic response, but she was wary to tell even Lavender about her hope that the plan would help Lucas too.

"It couldn't be that our very same Mr. Jones is wagin' his own war on that poor sheep farmer, Lucas McCurdy, now could it?" Lavender's eyes seemed to twinkle with mischief.

Kate caught her breath.

"Girl, you can't hide it from me. I can see it in your eyes. You have feelings for Mr. McCurdy."

Kate shook her head. "No, I don't . . . I can't." She grabbed hold of Lavender's hand and squeezed as if it belonged to her mother—the mother she wished her own had been, one to confide in and go to for comfort. "If Stanley were to know I cared for Lucas, he'd only make things worse for him."

"Then it's time we put Stanley Jones in his place, isn't it?" Lavender said with a triumphant-looking smile.

CHAPTER 22

KATE FOLLOWED RONALD AS HE led her to what appeared to be the only empty table in the restaurant section at Sunny's. Passing booths on their way, Kate noticed they were filled with various townspeople she'd come to know. It did her heart good to see Sam Decker sitting across from Lavender in one of the booths, apparently enjoying the dinner and the company. She wondered if Lavender's whispering sweet things in his ear had done more than encourage him to stand up to Stanley. The thought made her smile.

"Thank you," Kate said to Ronald as he pulled the chair out from the table for her to sit down on.

"You're welcome." He dodged a couple of cowboys on the way to his seat on the other side of the table. He sat down and stared at Kate.

"Sunny's place is busy tonight," Kate said, trying to stimulate a conversation. She picked up the small menu and read through it, even though she basically knew it by heart from the numerous times she'd been here. "I'm glad the business is doing well for her."

Ronald nodded.

Sunny flittered across the busy floor in her bright-red dress, with a notepad in hand. "A big howdy to you, Kate, Mr. Smith," she said as she parked herself by their table. "Thanks for stoppin' by tonight. What can I get for the two of you?"

Kate glanced up at Sunny. "I'll have the chicken sandwich on rye bread. And a pickle on the side."

"And you, Mr. Smith?" Sunny wet the end of her fountain pen with her tongue.

Ronald looked at Kate with a floundering expression weighing down his eyes. "What do you suggest?"

"How about the roast beef dinner? I've been meaning to try it." Kate looked to Sunny. "It's fairly new, isn't it?"

"That it is," Sunny said, her face beaming. "First hot thing on the menu. I'm hoping it'll do good, and I'll add more like it."

When Ronald didn't respond, Kate pointed to the menu's poor description of the roast beef dinner. "What kinds of potatoes and vegetables come with it?" she asked, wishing Ronald would be more involved in this conversation.

"Tonight, mashed spuds and a helping of cooked carrots."

Kate nodded at Ronald, who simply stared back. "That sounds good. Why don't you try that? And while you're at it, why not add one of those delicious cinnamon rolls?" Kate thought she may as well help out Lavender as long as Ronald was basically letting her order for him. She glanced over at the Deckers' booth just a yard or two away.

Sam lifted a cinnamon roll to his mouth, about to take a bite. He hesitated, held it at arm's length, and stared at it. "I swear this looks just like somethin' you'd bake." He took a bite. "This is one of your sweet rolls! What's it doin' here bein' touted as Sunny's?"

Kate held her breath, remembering how adamant Lavender had been about Sam being against her selling her rolls at Sunny's. Was Kate's well-meaning encouragement about to blow up in everyone's faces?

"I've been sellin' them to Sunny going on four weeks now." Lavender pushed Sam's hand and sweet roll back toward his mouth. "And I've made nigh onto twenty bucks, you old coot. That's almost half of the down payment we need."

"Awe, you did that for me, woman?" Sam took a bite of his roll. With mouth full, he added, "I always knew I did good in marryin' you."

Kate let out her pent-up breath. She returned her attention to Sunny and Ronald, feeling the night had already turned out better than she'd hoped.

"I'll have what Miss Donahue suggested." Ronald handed Sunny his menu and returned his focus to Kate, silently staring at her.

"We'll get this right out to you." Sunny jotted something on her pad and then winked at Kate. "By the way, I like what you've got going," she said before heading to the kitchen.

Kate half-expected Ronald to respond to Sunny's last remark, with some sort of question at least. Even she herself was unsure what Sunny meant by that. Was it about her and Lavender's plan for the women of Craig to gently persuade their men to stand up to Stanley? Must be. The fact that Sunny had heard about it made Kate feel good. Maybe the plan might have a chance to work after all, at least to a small degree. The success of Lavender's cinnamon rolls, in all its aspects, gave her hope.

Kate met Ronald's stare, thinking about how he didn't have a woman to whisper to him to stand up to Stanley. That made her feel sad. He was probably lonely, living by himself so far away from his family and friends. However, Ronald didn't need encouragement to stand up to Stanley. Remembering that first day she'd gone to his office, she recalled Ronald's bland but firm voice tell Stanley he was the wrong person to help with a dispute over grazing rights. Yes, Ronald seemed to do fine in that arena. That was one thing she liked about him. But was that enough for her to continue seeing him like this? The way he looked across the table communicated that the attraction between them was very lopsided. Rosie's description, of drooling over someone, nailed it on the head. Kate felt like the lazy butcher's soup bone at the moment.

"Thank you for dinner tonight," Kate spoke up to break the staring and the silence. She moved her gaze to the floor. "I really do appreciate it." She sincerely meant that. Her noon meal had consisted of a cracker.

"We'll have to do it again." His eyes lit up, though his voice remained monotone. "How about next Tuesday night? And then the next Tuesday night after that?"

Oh, Ronald, so unexcited, organized, and orderly. That was not what Kate needed or wanted. If she were to break her vow of remaining single, it would be for a man whose voice sounded like music as it engaged her in stimulating conversation. She shook her head to dislodge the image of Lucas McCurdy that had filled her thoughts with his gentle Irish brogue, strawberry-blond curls, and zest for life.

Kate made a quick glance toward the kitchen. Relief lightened her shoulders when she saw Sunny headed toward their table with a tray of food in hand. "Wonderful, our meals are here," she said a little too quickly. The need to change the subject—like so many things lately—pushed her ladylike manners aside.

The sandwich Sunny placed in front of Kate looked delicious. So did the steaming plate of meat and potatoes she set before Ronald. "Thank you, it looks heavenly," she said before Sunny stepped away. Ronald dug into his food without a word. Kate desired to taste her sandwich more than carry the conversation at the moment, so she followed Ronald's lead and took a big bite. It tasted as good as it looked, with a hint of horseradish mixed in with the tang of barbeque sauce and the salty, tender sliced beef.

Neither of them said a word for several minutes. With a couple of bites of sandwich and half a pickle still to go, Kate heard Ronald clear his throat. She glanced at his emptied plate and then at his face. His eyes bore the look of one struggling to speak.

Compassion prompted her to help him proceed. "You appear as though you have something on your mind. Please, tell me what you're thinking. I'd love to hear."

"If Tuesdays are not good, how about Wednesdays?"

"Excuse me?" Kate could feel her forehead wrinkling with her confusion as she swallowed her last bite of sandwich.

"For supper. You did enjoy your meal, did you not? I know I did, and I would like to have you join me each week to do the same."

"Yes, I did enjoy my meal," Kate admitted. Dining with Ronald once a week would be very helpful.

"So, which evening would work best for you?"

Kate took in a deep breath. "Ronald, I enjoy your company." *When you talk.* She knew she couldn't lead this poor man on any further. "I think of you as a friend. And I hope you will always remain as such. But it would not be fair of me to lead you to believe that there could ever be anything more between us than just friendship." *There, I've said it; this is over.*

"May I ask why?"

Kate realized her jaw dropped. She hurried and closed her mouth, scrambling for an answer that would not hurt him and could maintain a certain level of truth. He deserved an answer after such an out-of-character, courageous question. "When I came out West, I was running away from a fiancé who had broken my heart. I am afraid, Mr. Smith, that my heart has not yet healed, and I am not ready to fall in love with another man."

"I am a patient person. We could set our next dinner date for a year from tonight if you wish."

"Thank you, but no. Let's not set any dinner dates for now or a year from now."

"Oh, okay." Ronald picked up his fork, running his thumb up and down its handle like he wished he had an excuse to still use it. He set it back down and stared at his emptied plate, his eyes not moving from it while Kate finished her meal.

"It sure is nice weather we've been having," she said after swallowing her last bite.

"Yes, it is." Ronald continued to stare at his plate.

Kate felt bad for him. Maybe she should agree to join him for dinner from time to time. "Ronald, I—" She wouldn't. That might still lead him on.

He lifted his head and looked at her. "Yes?" His voice sounded hopeful.

"Nothing, I'm sorry."

It appeared she wasn't as ready to court other men as she'd thought.

CHAPTER 23

THE HOMEMADE MONEY BELT NOW sat at the bottom of a dresser drawer. Kate wondered if she'd ever need it again. It being the first of November, she walked slowly down the wooden steps with her last gold piece clenched in her cold fist just in case that cyst she'd taken care of had not covered the entire rent. Plus she had groceries to purchase and she hoped that ten dollars would last longer than normal. Thankfully, Mr. Hoy and his brothers hauled her exam table up the steps to her apartment the other day without accepting any pay. She thought wistfully of the story in the Bible when Elijah made a widow's corn meal and bottle of oil to never run dry. She needed to tend to some more patients.

That was something she missed here in Craig—a church. Other people she'd met wanted a church too. There was talk of building one at the end of Yampa Avenue. She believed that, for the most part, the people of this town were good. Kate held on to that belief as she thought about Lavender and their discussion last week, and their plan. She wondered how Lavender's efforts were going. Were the women Lavender had managed to talk to so far brave enough to even stand up to their husbands? Kate thought about Mary Tucker over at the hotel, and her heart sank. The poor woman was intimidated by her husband—yet he was a nice man.

When Kate got to the bottom of the stairs, she discovered the saddle shop had not yet opened, so she decided to pay Mary a visit before she did anything else.

The moment Kate stepped into the hotel, the aroma of fresh pancakes delighted her nose and teased her stomach. "Good morning, Mr. Tucker," she said as she breezed past the front desk. "Do you mind if I drop in on your wife and wish her a good day?"

"If'n you want." Mr. Tucker's light-brown mustache twitched. "But I doubt it will do you or her much good," he mumbled.

There was no one in the dining room. *Good.* Mary was most likely making the pancakes to feed her girls. They'd be free to talk. And by the sound of her husband's remark, that was something Mary needed. The second Kate stepped into the kitchen, Mary caught her attention. She stood at the stove, tending to four bubbling rounds of batter needing to be flipped, yet her weary-looking eyes seemed to be a thousand miles away. "Mary!" Kate scurried to her side. "What's wrong?"

"Aw, nothing." Mary's attention snapped back to the pancakes and she gave them a flip.

"I think there is something," Kate stated simply. "Now, please, open up and tell me what's going on."

"Same thing as always." Mary gave the pancakes a moment or two and then scooped them onto a plate already heaped with the cakes and delivered them to the table and her four hungry-looking girls. "Only I s'pose it's gettin' to me." She plopped onto an empty chair and motioned with her chin for Kate to do the same. "Help yourself to some flapjacks if you want. Oh, you'll need to grab a plate first."

Kate stepped over to the cupboard and picked up a plate before she sat down. She slid into a chair next to Caroline and loaded two pancakes onto her plate. "Thank you for breakfast. I really appreciate it." She looked around as she ate. The kitchen appeared in order and the children well-mannered and taken care of. "If it'll help to talk, I'm here."

"Ah, Kate, I don't know if it will or not." Mary propped her elbow on the table and rested her chin in her palm. "That'd just be complaining. And I really have nothin' to complain about. The hotel's doin' fine."

The children finished their pancakes and ran outside to play.

"The hotel might be doing fine," Kate said once she and Mary had the kitchen to themselves. "But you're not. And that's just as—if not more—important. What's bothering you? Tell me, please."

"Oh, all right . . . I feel like all I do is cook and clean—oh, and care for kids. I don't even like to cook or clean."

"What do you like to do?" Kate reached over and lifted Mary's chin off her hand.

Mary glanced down at the apron she wore. "Doesn't matter. I don't have the time for such stuff."

Kate took notice of the apron. Strips of brightly colored fabric had been sewn together in such a way as to recreate a large rose on the front of the apron. She swept her hand down the front of the design. "This is beautiful! Did you make this?"

Mary gave a timid nod, yet her smile radiated a wealth of light. "I worked on it every night last week after I put the girls to bed. I had so much fun."

"It sounds to me like you need to make another one of these," Kate said.

Mary wagged her hand at Kate. "I don't need another apron."

"Then make yourself a dress—or your girls one. It sounds like you need a creative outlet. We all do, in some form or another, to be happy."

After another helping of pancakes and some more encouragement for Mary to follow her new passion, the two of them parted company, Kate feeling good having noticed that Mary seemed to have brightened. Kate then slipped away from the hotel and came back to the saddle shop before she headed to the mercantile.

A man and a woman carrying a baby stood at the counter when Kate stepped into Mr. Hoy's shop.

The woman turned and looked at Kate. Her eyes lit up. "Dr. Kate."

"Mrs. Castillo!" Kate's heart leaped with pleasure at the sight of her first—and only, so far—maternity patient in Craig.

"No, no, no, call me Maria."

"What a delight to see you and your family again, Maria." Kate hurried over to peer into the blanketed bundle and hug the baby's mother.

"Little Maria Katherine is such a joy." Maria smiled as wide as the stirrup her husband was showing to Mr. Hoy. "She's grown like a weed since you delivered her."

"Oh, she's beautiful." Kate gazed at the baby's face as Maria placed her in Kate's arms.

Kate and the new mother stepped off to one side and talked about the baby, letting the men discuss the damaged saddle. Kate unwrapped the baby and gave her a quick exam, making sure that she was growing normally and that the umbilical cord had fallen off and her navel was healing properly.

The sound of boots pounding up the steps turned Kate's head toward the outside wall.

Mr. Hoy's head turned too. "It sounds like you've got a patient, or at least a visitor."

"Oh!" Kate placed the baby back in her mother's arms and hurried over to the counter. "I came down to make sure that your office visit a couple of weeks ago covered this month's rent."

"Yep, we're more than even in my book." Mr. Hoy looked up at Kate and smiled.

"Thank you." Kate waved to Mr. and Mrs. Castillo, who now stood together at the other end of the counter. "It was nice to see you. Have a safe trip back to your place," she said before rushing out the door.

Kate saw the long coat and hat of a cowboy on the stairs as she rounded the corner of the shop. On further inspection, the cowboy looked considerably smaller than most. "Rosie!" Kate called out.

The person at the top of the stairs turned. "Kate!" Rosie ran down the stairs to meet her. "I'm so glad you're here." She offered a one-armed hug and turned to continue back up the stairs alongside Kate. "I got this nasty gash breakin' my last horse out at the Hoy place. I can't ignore it no more. I think it needs stitches."

"I'm glad I was here too." Kate unlocked the door and guided Rosie inside.

She set to work cleaning the four-inch cut in Rosie's forearm, keeping her patient distracted by talking about the horse that had gotten the best of Rosie, as she doused the laceration with carbolic acid. Rosie gritted her teeth and handled the pain better than most men Kate had treated, especially when she started stitching Rosie up. After wrapping the arm with clean gauze, Kate rolled Rosie's sleeve back down and gave her hand a squeeze. "There, that's done." She let go of the hand and wagged a finger at Rosie. "Now don't go and undo it by being rough with that arm. No more breaking horses until that cut has healed sufficiently. Come back and see me in about ten days, and I'll take those stitches out."

"I'll try." Rosie remained in the chair. "Oh, and for your payment, would it be okay if my pa gave you a credit at his store?" She shifted her weight but appeared not very anxious to leave.

"A credit will be fine." Kate was more than fine with it, picturing the near-empty pantry in her kitchen and the shopping she was about to do. "Is everything else okay?" Kate asked. "Any other bumps from that fall I should look at?"

"Naw." Rosie flipped her wrist at Kate. "I just wanted to stay a minute and talk." She glanced at the clock above the shelves and then at the door. "If that's okay? If you're not expecting another patient or something."

Kate let out a soft laugh. "No, not expecting a single soul. And I would love to talk." Shopping could wait.

They chatted for bit about Lavender's sweet roll business and how well it was doing. And then Rosie said, "Yeah, I was talking to Ma the other day while she was whipping up a batch of her rolls. She told me how you'd visited with her while she made a batch. Told me all about your idea. I love it. You're just what this town needs: a good doctor—one with a back bone and a prescription for each and every person in Craig to grow one.

"Ma's already got Pa tellin' Stanley to keep his hands out of the licorice jar and the pickle barrel. Sunny's convinced her bartender not to pour Stanley any more drinks until he pays up his bill. I haven't talked to anyone else to see what other things are happenin', but I did see Stanley walkin' across Yampa Avenue a minute ago with a lot less strut than usual in those big fancy boots of his."

"Really?" Kate wondered how many other people had stood up to him.

"I even talked to the ranch hands down at Hoy's place—before I fell off that darn horse—'cause I wanted to help. It's not like I have a husband so I can whisper sweet things in his ear," Rosie said with a smirk-like grin on her face.

"In any case, with that bunch of lugs, the only thing I could do was to ask real nice-like that they try to stand up to Stanley Jones 'cause everyone else in town was goin' to."

"What did they say to that?" Kate asked.

"Not much. But then most menfolk are not very good at expressin' how they feel. They keep their thoughts just bottled up inside 'em, and if you want to hear 'em, you have to pry 'em out with a crowbar. That's why I'm in no hurry to tie myself to a man. I want him to tell me how he feels about me, instead of me guessin'." Rosie rolled her eyes. "I just wish Ma would quit worryin' about me getting hitched."

"I know what you mean about"—Kate caught herself—"that." She finished her sentence so Rosie wouldn't suspect that something was wrong. Very wrong. She was about to base her observation on herself—and the men in her past. But Lucas McCurdy was different. She'd always sensed that. Perhaps that's what drew her to him like Lucy to a crystal-clear stream. He'd expressed his feelings for her with clarity. But what had she done in return? Tried to bury her feelings for him even further, and unlike Rosie or Lavender, she hadn't called things as she saw them.

Rosie glanced over to the clock above the medical shelves. "I promised Pa I'd help him at the store at three." She stood up. "I'd better be goin'. Thanks for the good company."

As soon as Rosie left, Kate ran and threw herself into the armchair. She'd been chastising the town for not standing up for truth, when she herself had withheld the truth from the very man she was trying to help. He'd expressed his feelings for her. It had probably taken a great amount of courage to do so, with the fear of rejection running high. And what had she done? She'd kept her feelings to herself and then refused to call them what they really were.

Why?

Because she was afraid.

Afraid of Stanley Jones.

Afraid to love again.

The feelings she'd been suppressing exploded in her chest. She could deny them no longer. An overwhelming sensation of love for Lucas McCurdy engulfed her, a cornucopia of emotion; the kind of love she had for a friend; the kind she had for a neighbor; even the kind she had for the downtrodden. But most importantly—and most intense—was the love a woman has for a man, one she desires to be her husband.

He deserved to know this. Then, together they would face the storm that would follow, whatever that may be.

Kate wanted to pull back that moment from time—the time when Lucas had kissed her—and relive it and do it right. She wanted with every fiber of her being to tell him how she felt. But was it too late? He'd probably gone back to his place that day, miles and miles away, undoubtedly feeling rejected. Did the poor man not have enough trials already to wade through? The idea made Kate cry.

⊰⊱

The tears had almost had time to dry. It had been nearly a good half hour since Rosie had left, and fifteen minutes since Kate had finally brought her emotions under control. She rose from the armchair, ready to clean up the mess left from Rosie's cut, when a timid knock sounded at the door.

Kate wiped her eyes for good measure and stepped over to answer it.

Susannah stood shivering on the landing. "Do you have a minute?"

"Certainly. Come in out of that cold." Kate opened the door wider.

Susannah hesitated. She looked down at the road, prompting Kate to glance down too. Logan sat on the bench of a wagon, reins in hand. He waved.

Kate returned the wave before leaning back into the warmth of her apartment. "Shouldn't we go get Logan? Have him come up?"

"It wouldn't be worth the climb for him. I'm only going to stay for a minute." Susannah stepped inside and closed the door behind her.

"You sure you two couldn't stay a little longer? Have a cup of coffee?" Kate asked, remembering she now had a small credit at Decker's store.

"No, we've got to get back to the ranch before sunset."

Kate's muscles tightened at the memory of the Jones men's reign over Susannah. "Ben and Stanley gone until then?"

"No, that's not it. Logan told me it gets way too cold to be out on the road after sundown." Susannah pinched her lips together in a timid-looking grin as she laid her hand on Kate's arm. "You'll be so proud of me. I came into town today without even asking their permission. I needed some more flour, and I thought a can of cinnamon would be nice, so I just told Logan to hitch up the wagon and we came."

"That's wonderful." Kate gave Susannah's hand a squeeze.

"I didn't worry about asking for no money but just figured I'd put it on Pa's bill at the store." The delight drained from Susannah's face. "That's what I need to talk to you about." She took in a deep breath before she continued. "When I asked Sam for credit, he told me my pa's account was way past due and I needed to tell him or Stanley to come in and pay it before he'd let us buy anything else. I must have looked disappointed, because he felt sorry for me and let us take our groceries, saying it wasn't me or Logan he was trying to punish. It was Stanley. He said the people of the town are trying to band together to stand up to him. Then he whispered to me that it was all your idea." She grabbed onto Kate's arms. "I can't say that I don't agree with what you're trying to do. Lord knows this town should have been doing this long before now. But I'm scared for you, Kate."

Lavender must have let Kate's name slip out as she'd explained their plan to her husband. How many other people knew Kate was behind this? How long until Stanley knew? "I'll be fine," Kate said, but inside, her fear forced its way into her heart and spread out.

"I hope so." Susannah squeezed Kate's arms tighter. "But watch your back every minute, just in case." She shut her eyes, opened them, and stared Kate in the eye. "Just yesterday at the dinner table, Stanley mentioned how the people of the town all needed their heads examined; that somehow they've all come up together with the notion that he's a bad guy. He appeared truly confused. I didn't know what he was talking about until I spoke with Sam at the store just now."

"Well, hopefully Sam won't mention my name to Stanley like he did to you, when he asks for payment from him. I had explained to Lavender that was very, very important."

"Oh, Sam didn't," Susannah said like she was trying to defend Mr. Decker. "It was Matilda Forbes."

The gossip! How could Kate have forgotten about her? "But how did—are you sure? Oh d—"

"I was there." Susannah let go of Kate's arms and leaned back. "Me and Logan were almost at the end of Yampa Avenue with our groceries when I realized I'd left my purse on the counter at the store, so we turned around. When I went back into the store, Stanley was there. He gave me a piercing look, but I shook it off and he moved on, trying to buy some tobacco. That's when Sam told him he couldn't give him any until he settled up with the twenty dollars he owed the store, and then he'd have to pay full price like everyone else for his tobacco. Stanley exploded, demanding Sam tell him where this all came from. I grabbed my purse and hurried toward the door when I noticed Mrs. Forbes slink out from behind the fabric shelves and say, 'Oh, that new lady doctor's the one who's set everyone in town against you. Of course, my lady friends and I don't cotton to her way of thinking.'"

"No!" Kate wanted to melt into the floor and disappear. What had she done? She felt Susannah's arms wrap around her, trying to soothe her, but comfort refused to come.

"I wish I could help—you know, maybe soften the wrath of my brother, convince him to go easy on you because Mrs. Forbes always stretches the truth, but . . ." Susannah wiped her eye. "Stanley never listens to me." She gave Kate another hug, released her, and stepped toward the door.

"Susannah!" Logan's voice reached up from below. "We've got to get going!"

Susannah opened the door and stepped onto the landing. "Be careful, Kate," she muttered before running down the steps.

Kate moved only enough to lean against the doorframe for support. Cold wind beat at her face and arms, hurling specks of sand to cut into her like knives. She welcomed the pain. It felt like fluffs of cotton compared to the pain tearing at her heart. Stanley wouldn't come after her. It would be Lucas.

Lucas might not survive this round.

And Lucas would never be able to hear Kate tell him she loved him.

CHAPTER 24

"Miss Kate! Miss Kate!"

The cries reached into Kate's dark dreams. They combined with a loud pounding and woke her from a fitful sleep.

"Miss Kate! Miss Kate!" The cries and pounding resumed. They came from the door.

"Logan, is that you?" Kate said as she pulled herself out of bed and put on her robe. She glanced at the clock as she rushed to the door, cinching her belt tight as she ran. It was almost noon—she couldn't believe she'd slept in that late.

"Yeah! I got important stuff to tell ya. Open the door."

Kate struggled to unlock the door. It had been well after three in the morning before she'd been able to fall asleep last night, tossing and turning, worrying about Lucas, chastising herself for the mess she'd made. Finally, the key managed to slip into its slot. She unlocked and opened the door.

Logan hobbled in.

"What's wrong?" Kate said, aware of the panic in her voice. She could sense he wasn't here to tell her "important" good news.

"I went out to the McCurdy place this morning to take Lucas the mail I collected for him yesterday when I was in town."

"Yes!" Kate wagged her hands as if she could pull the news from Logan even faster. "Is he okay?" A million horrible things popped into her head.

"He's beat-up pretty badly—mostly bruises and cuts." Logan ducked his head. "He told me not to say anything to you, not to worry you 'cause he'd be back up and around in a day or two."

"Was it your brother who beat him up?"

"No, Stanley never laid a finger on Lucas. Only his sheep." Logan swallowed hard. "Lucas got hurt trying to save his sheep from stampeding and running off the cliff into Hayden Gulch."

"Stanley caused the stampede?" Kate's voice rose with each word.

"I don't know for sure, 'cause I never seen him do it. But I seen him earlier on the edge of Lucas's land—him and three ranch hands from the Circle J. When I said howdy and asked him what he was doing out this way, he told me to mind my own business. Then he got that look on his face he has when he's up to no good." Logan sat down in the armchair. "I'm scared for Lucas. He seemed right upset when I left the mail with him. Hurting real bad-like, too. I know he said he didn't need no doctor, but I think he's wrong."

"Of course he's wrong." Kate raced across the room and grabbed her black leather bag from the shelf. She began filling it with every possible tool she might need.

"So you're going to go out to his place and fix him up?" Logan's face showed relief.

"Yes, I am." Kate reached for her coat and stopped. "But I need to change first into my riding skirt."

"You don't need to do that, Miss Kate. I can take you in my wagon." Logan stood and hobbled toward the door. "We can leave right now."

"Thank you, but I need to get dressed properly. Plus, I can get there faster by horseback," Kate said, not liking the thought of young Logan getting pulled into the middle of things. She'd blown up the bridges; she'd called the troops to action; now she needed to weather the consequences on her own. No more dragging others into her troubles.

"I s'pose you're right." Logan placed his hand on the doorknob. "How soon will you leave?" His concern for Lucas touched Kate.

"You like Mr. McCurdy, don't you?" she asked as she pulled her riding skirt from the dresser.

"Yeah, he's nice to me. I can tell he likes me." A peculiar-looking grin spread across his face. "But not as much as he likes you, Miss Kate. He talks about you more than his sheep."

"Really now?" Kate wanted to hear more. But she couldn't afford that pleasure—she needed to hurry. She already knew he cared for her; he'd already told her from his own mouth. It was her turn to do the same.

"Yes, really." Logan opened the door. "Hurry, Miss Kate. He needs you. You're going to be the best one to fix him up." The peculiar smile returned. "And help him feel better about losing so many of his sheep," he added before stepping outside and shutting the door behind him.

Kate immediately threw off her robe and got dressed. She looked down as she smoothed out the skirt. "What am I thinking?" She quickly pulled off her dress and stepped into her riding clothes, stuffing her petticoat down into the legs. There wasn't time to strip down to her chemise to take it off now. She put on her coat and grabbed her gloves, two scarfs, and her doctor's bag. She took off down the stairs and ran toward the livery stable, determined not to stop until she got to the McCurdy place.

The day felt unseasonably warm as she ran up Yampa Avenue—the opposite way she needed to go, but the livery stable was on the opposite end, east of town. A strong breeze blew in from the south, but it didn't chill her at all. She was tempted to stop back home and exchange her coat for a lighter one on her way out of town, but she knew she didn't have time. Besides, it was getting darker earlier in the evening and she'd be lucky to reach Lucas's place by sunset, when the temperature would surely cool off.

Winded, Kate quit running a block from the livery stable. The owner, Gus, was outside the stable, closing all the doors. Kate found that peculiar, knowing how smelly that place got on the cold, windy days when they had to keep the place battened down to keep the horses from getting riled up.

"Gus!" Kate yelled out, pushing herself into a fast walk, unable to manage anything more. "I need you to hurry and get Lucy ready for me."

Gus caught sight of her and nodded.

When Kate stepped inside, the smell of fresh manure had already started to gather within the closed-up stable. Gus had Lucy saddled and was just tightening the buckle beneath her belly.

"Where ya headed in such a hurry?" Gus straightened out a stirrup. "I see you've got your doctorin' bag. Someone sick?"

"Not sick, injured." Kate went around to the other side of Lucy and adjusted the stirrup on that side. "I'm heading out to the McCurdy place," she said as she climbed up into the saddle.

Gus grabbed onto Lucy's reins but didn't give them to Kate. "Oh, I wouldn't advise that, Miss Donahue. It's a long way out there."

"I've been there before. I'm fully aware of the distance." Kate reached out for the reins.

He kept hold of the reins, keeping Lucy's restless movements in check. "There's a storm brewing in that direction. A big one. The horses can sense it." He jerked his head toward three horses hoofing the ground in their stalls.

"I've been out in bad weather before." Kate patted Lucy's neck. "So has she." Kate reached down, grabbed the reins, and forcibly pulled them from Gus's hands. "So if you'll excuse us, we need to be going."

With obvious reluctance, Gus shuffled over to the end of the livery stable and pulled open the door. "Just look out there, why don't you. Now don't say I didn't warn you." He pointed to a darkened sky to the west where massive black-gray clouds rolled toward them in churning motions. "If you're going out to Lucas McCurdy's place, you'll be heading right into the heart of the storm."

"I know. But I've got to go." Kate secured her leather bag to the saddle, sunk her heels into Lucy, and took off.

⚜

The warm wind blew into Kate's face with uncomfortable force as Lucy transported her out of town at a full gallop. Kate slowed her down as the trail narrowed, knowing an even, steady pace would be best for them both. The black clouds rumbled with thunder in the distance, moving toward her with visible speed. It was like the wind had latched on to the storm and was pulling it toward town with a vengeance.

Lucy seemed skittish. It was with reluctance that she obeyed Kate and kept heading west. Should Kate have listened to Gus? To the horses in those stalls? She pulled on the reins and slowed Lucy down to a near crawl. Should she go back?

Visions of Lucas lying injured, alone in his tiny house, hurting physically and emotionally, tore at Kate's heart. The pain intensified as she imagined all those sheep, each one precious to Lucas, falling to their deaths over a cliff, knowing full well that even though she hadn't pushed them off, she had pushed the man who had.

"Come on, Lucy." Kate rubbed her horse's neck. "We've got to keep going. It shouldn't take us much more than an hour or so if we can keep up a good pace." She urged Lucy back into a trot, welcoming the wind in her face; she deserved every ounce of it. She owed this much to Lucas. No, she owed much, much more to him than just a doctor's visit. It might very well be too late to tell him now how she felt about him. He'd probably moved on, extinguished his feelings for her out of necessity. Maybe even out of anger. She wouldn't blame him if he had.

For the next hour, Kate beat on herself along with the wind. She'd had to slow down long ago. She and Lucy made marginal progress as far as the trail was concerned, but Kate spiraled into near panic with her thoughts. What if she'd hurt him so badly that he never forgave her, or he'd grown calloused to cover the hurt and thus would never allow her to spill the feelings from her overloaded heart?

She loved Lucas McCurdy. As she reflected back, she realized that she'd been attracted to him since that first day she'd arrived in Craig. He stood out from other men, the way he carried himself, the way he treated her and other people, and the way his eyes sparkled with light from within.

Oh why, oh why didn't I let myself love him back then?

Because she'd been running away from love. But not anymore! Darwin was in the past. The best way to run from love gone bad—she knew this now—was to run full force toward the love of a good man.

Those thoughts continued to burn deep inside her as the wind turned cold.

Kate guided Lucy off the trail and under an outcropping of rock for momentary refuge from the biting wind. She pulled out her scarfs and gloves, wrapping one scarf around her head and the other around her neck. Numb from the cold, her fingers fumbled with the buttons of her coat, buttoning it all the way to the top before putting on her gloves. "There, that feels better," she said to Lucy. "I should have done that sooner."

She should have done a lot of things sooner.

She clung to her burning desire for warmth and the hope that Lucas, being the good man that he was, would still have a sliver's space in his heart that he could offer to her and give her another chance.

Another mile or so down the road, even Kate's fired-up emotions failed to keep her warm. Rain joined the wind, pelting her face, soaking her scarfs and coat. The petticoat that earlier had been a nuisance to be endured was now a blessing. Kate's dry legs thanked her for that small bit of good fortune.

Within the next mile, the petticoat too became soaked, and cold seeped unmercifully into the flesh of her legs.

Kate held up her wet-gloved hand, shielding her eyes from the rain that was quickly turning to snow, and surveyed the road and surrounding terrain. She recognized the cluster of bare aspen trees at the base of a hill that Logan had pointed out to her. They were nearly there. The darkened landscape seemed to be growing darker, beyond the gloom inflicted by the raging storm. Could it be that night approached? Had they been moving that slowly? Kate's entire body tensed. She urged Lucy to go faster.

Large flakes of snow quickly covered the ground in a blanket of white. Kate appreciated the relief to her face. The fluffy flakes didn't cut into her skin as the pelting rain had. The wind had stopped, and the snow now fell from the sky to the ground without diversion, but it fell with such volume that Kate could only see a few hundred feet in front of her. The road had disappeared. She guided Lucy onward by steering her through the low, smooth sections of white, assuming the raised bumps in the snow hid sagebrush and the smooth hid road.

Kate didn't think it possible, but the snow began to fall thicker and faster. Her whole body shivered from the cold penetrating her wet clothing—and from fear. She could barely see a few feet past Lucy's nose. Poor Lucy kept shaking her head to keep the snow from encasing it in white.

"No!" Kate yelled, her voice swallowed up by the same monstrous mass of white that seemed to be swallowing her. This couldn't be happening. She needed to see. She needed to survive. She needed to get to Lucas.

Panic set in. The road became nonexistent; all sense of direction was gone. Should she and Lucy stop, hunker down in the snow, and await the total darkness of night to befall them before possibly freezing to death? Or should they keep going blindly ahead, hoping they were heading in the right direction, hoping they wouldn't walk off the cliff of a gulch?

Lucy whinnied and then stumbled.

Kate felt the saddle tilt and Lucy falling to the ground, taking Kate with her.

Pain shot through Kate's leg. She screamed out.

Lucy struggled to her feet, grinding her flanks into Kate's injured leg as she rose, intensifying Kate's pain and her cries. Once on her feet, the horse ran off, disappearing quickly into a wall of white.

They were so close—they could have made it. But now . . . to have this happen? Despair transformed Kate's cry of pain into sobs.

Gathering her wits, she reached down, pulled up her skirt, and felt her leg. The bump in the middle of her shin was unmistakable. The bone was broken. A yard or so away, she detected a rise in the snow. She dragged herself toward it hoping it could offer her something, anything. Intense pain shot through her leg. She continued toward the rise—she had to do something. As she inched closer, she saw a large snow-covered sagebrush growing out of what appeared to be an outcropping of rock, hanging over its face like an awning. She pulled herself underneath the meager cover and leaned against the stone to catch her breath.

Snow soon covered her body, as only her head was shielded by the sage-brush awning. She'd quit trying to brush it off after the first inch gathered, realizing that the blanket of snow was the closest thing to a real blanket she had out here. The pain in her leg lost its initial sharp sear, but it continued to throb, sending waves of nausea into her stomach and dizziness to her head.

As the remaining traces of daylight faded into darkness, Kate felt the desire to let the life fade from her body. Why fight it? She was tired of fighting; it only got her in trouble. Her fate was inevitable. Is this what death was like? She'd always wondered. The dizziness increased. So did the darkness. Was that because of night, or was she passing out? It didn't matter. Nothing mattered now. Kate gave in to the darkness that engulfed her.

CHAPTER 25

"Katherine!"

Her name reached into the darkness and pulled her into the light. It sounded like music, with that Irish flare that always set her heart beating faster. Was she dreaming? Or had she passed on to the other side?

"Katherine!" It came again.

Pain shot through her leg. Her eyes fluttered open. Sunlight poured down upon a world of white, crystals of snow sparkling like glitter on sagging branches of sage. Kate gasped at having made it through the night and then gasped from the pain.

"Katherine!"

Kate pulled herself up from her snowy bed and leaned on one elbow. "Lucas?" she cried out. Her voice came out crackly, barely above a whisper. She needed to yell louder. Could it truly be him? But why would he be out here? How could he have known she was here?

Reality told her it must be someone else.

No. No one else calls me by that name.

Infused with hope, Kate gathered her last remaining strength. "Lucas!" Her voice rang through the clear air.

"Katherine?" Lucas's voice sounded closer. "Thank God. Yer alive! Keep talking so I can find ye." His voice boomed strong, full of what Kate thought sounded like elation. It lent her strength.

"Over here," Kate cried. It came out weak and accompanied by tears. She struggled to sit, managing to pull herself up and lean against the rock. His voice sounded as if it were coming from behind her. She wanted so much to stand so she could see his face, so he could find her. But it had taken all her energy just to sit up. She wanted to keep talking, but her head felt light. A nauseating dizziness made her lean her head against the cold rock.

"Katherine!" There was panic in his voice. "Do not leave me now, lass. Hold on."

Kate had an odd sense she was slipping in and out of consciousness.

"Katherine!" His voice sounded like it was next to her ear.

She forced her eyes open and felt Lucas press his mouth to her cheek as he scooped her from the bank of snow. "Can't walk . . . leg broken," she mustered the words. They came from her lips sounding like a scratched whisper.

"I was not planning on making ye," Lucas said. His face looked serious.

Why wasn't he smiling? He always smiled around her. Was he angry at her foolishness? At everything else she'd done to bring misfortune upon him? She didn't blame him. "I'm so sorry . . ."

"I have ye. No need to talk now." He stroked her head, pulling it close to his as he carried her though the knee-deep snow toward his horse. "But I do need to get ye home fast. I just hope 'tis not . . . too late."

Kate blinked. And blinked some more. She wanted to stay conscious. He would need her to be awake to get her up on that horse. The idea of being draped over the back of the animal like a corpse did not set well with her. Nor would it with her leg. The pain continued to burn in her shin, begging her to lapse back into unconsciousness.

"I can lift ye partway," Lucas said, "but I need ye to put yer good leg over Dublin for me. You think ye can do it?"

Kate nodded, determined to do so.

She felt his strong arms lift her without struggle above his head. The saddle was right there. Rallying her strength, she managed to stretch her good leg over the horse and felt herself slip into the saddle.

"Ye've got to hold on by yourself for a wee bit while I mount. Can ye do that?"

She nodded again. A moment later, she felt Lucas nestle into the saddle behind her.

His arm went around her waist. Holding her steady, he reached around for something in his saddlebag. When he straightened back around, he had a blanket in hand which he draped over the front of Kate's body, letting it fall down on each side of the horse to cover her legs. He unbuttoned his coat and pulled Kate's back next to his chest, tightened his hold on her waist, and flicked the reins.

Kate relished the heat that radiated from his body, relished being close to him, wrapped in his arms. She just wished she felt good enough to enjoy the moment to its fullest. With the sun shining on the dark wool blanket, it soon added to the luscious warmth and gave her some strength. "How did you know . . ." She struggled to speak. "How did you find—"

"Shhh. Save yer strength," Lucas spoke softly into her ear, warming it with his breath. "Just sit there and rest, and I shall tell ye what I know."

Kate's mind slipped in and out of focus, trying to listen to Lucas tell of his surprise last night when he'd gone out to check on Dublin. He'd heard a strange-sounding whinny coming from the corral and found Lucy standing next to Dublin on the outside of the fence. Kate could have sworn he said he'd wanted to leave immediately to come looking for her, but that couldn't have been right. Even in her groggy state, the idea of Lucas heading into the blinding storm for her touched her heart and warmed her hope. Did he still care for her? Even after she'd responded so indifferently to his declaration of affection? Even though she'd pushed Stanley beyond what was wise? Pain throbbed in her leg. Maybe he didn't know yet that she was responsible for pushing Stanley. Her stomach felt queasy. But he would know soon enough; no more would she withhold the truth from him. Her head seemed to spin. How would he feel when she told him?

Kate's brain struggled to make sense of anything. She sensed Lucas talking. The words, "prayed all night" and "knee-deep snow" and "good thing . . . road . . . like the back of my hand" she heard, but the ones in between faded out. Soon they all faded into what sounded like the buzzing of bees and then went silent.

⚜

Intense pain shot through Kate's leg, and then she felt like she was falling. She could hear Lucas speaking. It wasn't frantic; it was calm. Her eyes opened. The sun stood directly behind Lucas, a halo of light illuminating his golden curls like it had that first day she'd seen him. Shadows darkened his face, so Kate couldn't read his expression. She could tell that she was no longer on the horse but cradled in Lucas's arms.

"Let me get ye inside and have a look at that leg," Lucas said in a voice laced with myriad emotions.

Kate couldn't tell if he was angry, scared, relieved, or something else. At the moment, she didn't care if he despised her. She soon would be lying in a warm bed, and the man she loved would be there at her side. Even if he did despise her, she knew he was the kind of man who would take care of her until she was able to ride out of here on her own.

She wanted to wrap her arms around Lucas as he carried her through the snow toward the house. It would be a natural thing. It sounded heavenly to

Kate, and it would help ease his burden. She lifted her arms, but they fell back into the cradle formed by his arms, too weak to move. "Sorry, I'm such a bother," she mustered the words. She wanted to tell him more, tell him how she felt. She wanted to pour out those feelings that had driven her into the storm in the first place, those feelings she should have told him long before, the ones he deserved to hear and she needed to tell. "Lucas . . . I need . . . to tell you . . ."

"Hush, now." He bent slightly, letting Kate tip a bit as he opened the door to his house. "Ye shall need all your strength for what comes next." He carried her directly to the bedroom and laid her on his bed. He turned to a set of drawers, pulled out what appeared to be a pair of men's long underwear and set it on the bed next to Kate. "Ye will need to take off all of your clothes."

"What?" Kate's mind whirled in a surreal frenzy.

"'Tis all soaking wet. Ye are apt to catch pneumonia—if ye have not already. I shall step into the other room while ye change. Holler when ye are done. Then we need to set that broken leg of yours." He stepped over to the door, turning back around as he placed his hand on the knob. "Sorry I do not have something more suitable for ye to wear. But I thought these'd be the most comfortable while ye are mending in bed anyway. Those frilly lady clothes look 'bout as comfortable as a scratching post," he said with his crooked smile curving his mouth into that grin Kate loved. "Oh, let me stoke this first for ye." He stepped over to the potbelly stove and inserted a couple of logs then left the room, closing the door behind him.

Kate pulled herself up to a sitting position, chiding herself for considering for even a moment that Lucas was in the same camp of men as Darwin and Stanley. He was a gentleman. He hadn't the money, the house, or the position of those men. But he had what she wanted: a kind heart and an open, pure mind. She just hoped he still wanted her. And hoped she'd be all right. Broken leg aside, she knew spending a night outside in a blizzard was not good for anyone's health. She could feel the effects setting in.

She struggled removing her wet clothing. The air chilled her bare skin. A glance over to the stove warmed her heart with appreciation even though her arms shivered. Pulling her riding skirt from her legs proved to be a much more difficult task than her blouse. Finally, stripped down to her bare skin, she pulled a blanket around her shoulders to keep warm as she examined her leg. It appeared to be a straightforward break, not a difficult one to set. But not from where she sat—she couldn't very well set her own leg—and especially not with the lack of strength that reminded her she was pretty much useless right now for anything. Taking off those clothes had exhausted her. She wanted nothing more than to drop back into that bed and never move. But she had to get the long johns on, not just for her own warmth and comfort, but because she couldn't stay in this room alone forever. She needed Lucas's help.

Kate let out a scream of pain as she pulled the long underwear onto her leg. She'd bumped it somehow in the process.

"Are you okay?" came Lucas's voice through the door.

Was he standing right outside it? Waiting? Listening? Kate was touched. "I'm all right." She bit back the pain, resting every other tug as she pulled the underwear onto the rest of her shivering body. Once on, and the front buttoned up to her neck, she slid down beneath the layers of quilts and let her body soak in the warmth. Her nose brushed across the sheet. It smelled clean and fresh. Had he changed them just for her? But how could he have known he'd find her and bring her back here? When had he done it? Last night? It certainly couldn't have been this morning while the sun shone. Knowing Lucas, he would have been up and out on the road searching the moment the snow stopped and there was sufficient light to see. That was Lucas. She knew it. She loved it.

And she loved him.

"I'm ready," Kate called out, wishing she were calling out to him under better circumstances. She couldn't think of anything more wonderful than having her strength back and calling out to Lucas to come to her in a home they shared as husband and wife.

The door swung open, interrupting Kate's daydream. Lucas stepped in, carrying two small boards and a leather strap in his hands. "Okay, let's get that leg set before it's too late." His face bore troubled expressions. It relaxed a bit, a smile forming as he gazed at Kate. "At least I'm going to have the best person in the world to tell me how to do this thing."

"Wait." She stared at a gash cut across his forehead she'd not noticed before now. "You're hurt. I need to tend—"

"'Tis nothing. Ye are who we should worry about."

He pulled the quilts up from the foot of her bed, placing them on her thighs and stomach. His hands, so warm and gentle, pushed the leg of the long johns up past her knee. She winced in pain. Then he ran his hand lightly down her leg. The smile on his lips quivered when he came to the bump in the middle of her shin. "'Tis going to hurt something terrible," he said, pinching his face into a grimace. "And I shall feel mighty awful inflicting such hurt."

"Wait!" Kate's mind cleared slightly at the anticipation of the pain. "By chance, was my doctor's bag still attached to Lucy when you found her?"

"As a matter of fact, 'twas." Lucas's eyes lit up. "Is there something inside that will help ye with the pain?"

Kate nodded. Talking took such effort.

"'Tis in the other room." Lucas darted off and was back in seconds, holding Kate's black leather bag out. He opened it for her to look inside.

Kate located her bottle of laudanum, pulled the cork with her teeth, and took a swig, guessing, hoping it was a proper dosage. She replaced the bottle, and Lucas set her bag down.

Placing his hand on her ankle, Lucas caressing the bare skin as if it were fine silk. He looked into her eyes. The blue within his seemed so intense, as if determination heightened the color. "What do I do first?"

"Wait." Kate held up a shaky hand. "The laudanum needs time to take effect. I'll tell you when."

He grabbed hold of her hand and then moved to the side of the bed. Gathering her other hand in his, he squeezed them both. "Can I hold yer hand while we wait, while ye tell me what I'm s'posed to be doing?"

Kate responded with a weak nod, wishing he would just hold her entire body and make her all better.

Fortunately, she had determined it was a stable fracture and would heal quickly once set and immobilized. She explained the process of setting a leg the best she could with her head swimming, her leg throbbing, and her entire body aching now.

"I think I've got it." Lucas assured her. "I am ready when ye are."

"Give me another minute." Kate could feel the laudanum taking effect, but not before she'd noticed a tightening in her chest and a wave of chills. The room was plenty warm, so it wasn't that. She'd witnessed the signs many times. She knew pneumonia could be setting in. She glanced down at her toes to confirm another fear. Each toe appeared a creamy shade of white. They stung horribly, but the burning in her leg had muffled their scream of pain. Frostbite.

Even if Lucas were to set her leg properly, there was a chance she might not survive the illness she felt coming on. She couldn't let Lucas slip from her again, not without telling him how she felt about him.

"Lucas," she spoke his name like it was a gift from heaven, though barely above a whisper.

"Yes, Katherine." He said her name with the same hint of feeling but stronger volume.

"Please, I must tell you something." She took in a breath, stinging her lungs. "Something very important."

"Can't it wait, lass?"

"No. I can't risk you not hearing this. Not again."

"Do not talk like this. I shall hear anything ye want to say, everything ye want to say, once ye are better."

"I might not make it."

"Yes, ye will. Where is that fight, that stubborn determination I saw the first day I met ye—and have admired ever since?"

Kate shook her head. She didn't feel like fighting anymore. The medicine was reaching through her body, relaxing every muscle and clouding her brain. She had to get her feelings out. She had to tell him now before it was too late. "I . . . love you," she said simply. It was all she could say, though her heart yearned to spiel a lengthy sonnet to express the full expanse of her feelings. Her eyelids refused to remain open any longer.

"And I love you." Lucas's lips touched her ear as he whispered. They moved down to brushed across her lips. "I think ye are as ready as ye will ever be," his voice came to Kate with more volume.

She sensed him move away. No! She wanted him to stay there and linger on her lips forever. "Hold on now," she heard his voice say and felt him lift her arms above her head and wrap her fingers around the metal bars of the bed frame. She sensed his hands on her ankle, and then she felt him pull.

Scorching pain ripped into her leg and shot up through her body. She screamed out. The cry robbed her body of all strength, her head of all clarity. Everything went black.

CHAPTER 26

WARMTH ENGULFED KATE. IT INTENSIFIED, growing hotter and hotter until she felt she'd suffocate from the heat. Her eyes opened, and the pain in her leg and chest grounded her, reminding her where she was and of her dire situation.

"Here," Lucas said, lifting her head and holding a cup to her lips. "You need to drink some water."

Kate sipped in the cool liquid without argument, grateful for each drop. "I've got a fever," she said. It came out a mere whisper.

"I know. Ye had it all night," Lucas said. "I've been worried sick. I thought ye'd never come to." He wrung out a rag into a bowl of water next to the bed and placed it on Kate's forehead. "Please, tell me there is something else I can do to bring down a fever besides a cool cloth?"

"My bag," she said. Each word took such effort. She forced more out. "Bring me my bag."

Lucas had her bag to her side in an instant. "What am I to look for?"

"Brown bottle . . . with . . . white pills." Kate had ordered them after she'd told Lucas to try the willow bark for his arm. She'd not had an opportunity to try them out on a patient. It was just as well—she'd only read about the speculative use of acetylsalicylic acid. It would be best if she tried it on herself first.

Lucas poured some of the little white pills into his hand. "How many?"

"Two . . . or three." Kate's mind couldn't think straight let alone remember all she'd read.

"Let us try three." Lucas picked out three pills and put the rest back in the bottle. "Open your mouth," he said.

Kate obeyed, tasting a salty-sour flavor as the pills touched her tongue. She felt the lift of Lucas's gentle hand raise her up to where she could drink again from the cup he offered.

After she'd swallowed the pills, he laid her back down. "Would ye like a bit o' food?" he asked. His voice sounded nervous.

"No . . . thank you." Kate didn't feel like doing anything. "Just sleep." She closed her eyes, longing to rest, longing to slip back into the relief of unconsciousness. She felt his large calloused hands wrap around one of hers. They were cool and comforting. "Lucas," she spoke his name softly. "You . . . are . . . an angel." She wanted to say more, to tell him he was the best nurse any ill person could ever wish to have, but the heat was letting up and sleep begged to take over.

When she awoke, Lucas was sitting next to her bedside on a chair he'd pulled in from the kitchen. "Is there anything I can do or get for ye?" He spoke in tones so tender Kate wanted to cry.

"A drink," she whispered.

Lucas lifted her back and put the cup of cool water to her mouth. "Anything else?" he asked as he lowered her back down.

Kate was about to say no when she felt a pressure in her bladder. It begged for release. "Help me up." She reached out her hand. "Out of bed."

"I do not think ye are strong enough to get out o' bed yet." He lifted her back up to a sitting position, but no farther.

"Do you have a bedpan then?"

"Oh," Lucas said. A slight flush of pink formed on his cheeks. "I'm so sorry, I don't. Just a pot." He pointed to a white porcelain-lined chamber pot sitting in the corner of the room.

"A pot will be fine." Kate pulled away the covers and noticed a splint that immobilized her bad leg. It had been implemented exactly as she had instructed. "Well done . . . on the splint."

"Thank you." Lucas offered a quick smile, and a look of concern returned to his expression.

With her hands, Kate swung her bad leg over the side of the bed, letting her feet touch the ground. Pain surged through her leg. She'd momentarily forgotten about one little detail—squatting over a pot on her own would be impossible.

"Ye will be needing me help." Lucas looked into her face. Not an ounce of awkwardness shown in those blue eyes. Only an intense determination to help her.

Kate's initial reaction was embarrassment. Here was this man, whom she only knew a little but desired with all her heart to know fully, willing to assist her while she relieved herself. *Is this how patients feel when I require them to disrobe?* She chewed on her lip to suppress her discomfort and let him help her. She had no other choice.

Lucas never even flinched. When she was finished, he helped her back into bed. She snuggled down into the quilts, feeling somewhat better. "Thank you," she said, but desired to say more, to express her feelings more fully. "I'm very grateful—"

Lucas held his hand out. "Hold on for a wee bit." He picked the pot up by its handle and held it out to one side. "I shall just dump this outside and be right back."

As Kate watched Lucas leave, she could feel her fever breaking. She gazed at him with new appreciation. Through these difficult first moments of Kate's recovery, Lucas had never made her feel like he was disgusted or wanted to be somewhere else. Quite the contrary. The only way she could describe his actions was love. He truly loved her. She felt it. She knew it. The feelings she had felt for him when she'd headed into that storm were like a sprinkle of rain compared to the kind of love she had for him now.

Succumbing to her sleepiness, she let her eyes close, basking in the most heavenly of feelings.

❦

"Now, keep warm," Lucas told her as he pulled the quilt up to her chin one afternoon. "And I shall be back in an hour or so to put more wood on the fire."

"I will be fine," Kate assured him, her cough having settled down to an occasional outbreak now and then, and the pain in her leg having grown into an endurable ache. For the past few days, Lucas had waited on her every spare moment he had. "Thank you, I appreciate your care immensely, but you need to tend to your ranch as well."

"I am grateful ye are getting better, and I wish for things to stay that way."

"And what about you?" She pointed to a nasty scrape on his lower arm that had begun to scab over and then to a bandage on his forehead. "The reason I came out here was to tend to the nasty fall I'd heard you had taken." She chewed on her lip. "But it appears you've been forced to tend to both of us."

"Oh, this?" He flicked his hand at his head and arm. "'Tis nothing." He looked her in the eye and with a hint of teasing—or was it worry—in his voice, said, "'Tis the only reason you came? As a doctor?"

"No—o." She stretched out the word, unsure how much to divulge.

"Who told ye I had taken a fall?"

"Logan."

A smile lit Lucas's face. "Ah, Logan. The lad always seems to know what is going on. He told me I needed some doctoring. Specifically from ye, Miss Katherine. 'Twas quite insistent, in fact."

"As he was adamant about me coming out to tend to your injuries." Kate pointed to his bandage. She moved her hand to cover her mouth, and a light laugh escaped from her. "I daresay we might have a thirteen-year-old matchmaker on our hands."

"Aye." Lucas chuckled. His smile softened into a look of appreciation. "A heart o' gold the lad has."

⁂

Three days later, Kate requested to go into the kitchen for a while. It was lighter in the big room, and she could sit in the rocking chair and watch Lucas as he made supper.

"Now that the swelling has gone down, I wish I could put a cast on my leg. It would be better—and it would allow me to put some weight on it sooner."

"Why can't ye?" He lifted his arm that had born a cast not more than a month ago. "Ye did a fine job on me arm."

"I didn't pack enough gauze and plaster of Paris in my bag to cast a leg." She rubbed her leg through the splint—something she wouldn't be able to do wearing a cast. "The splint is just fine. I'll be all right. You did a wonderful job with it."

Obvious delight sparked Lucas's eyes as he gathered her in his arms. "You do not need to put weight on yer leg. I will gladly carry you where're ye need to go." He picked her up as easily as if she were a rag doll and carried her from one end of the room to the other. "Is there anywhere else ye want to go?"

"Back to the rocking chair will be just fine," she said with a light-hearted tone to match his. She gave him a playful punch to the arm. "Now go check on the mutton before you burn it."

When he set her down, his hands brushed across hers slowly, as if he wanted to let them linger a moment or two. The sensation of his skin against hers sent tingles all the way up her arms.

That evening they sat around the fire that crackled beneath the beautiful hearth Lucas had carved. Kate read one of the three books that Lucas owned while he whittled a long piece of wood.

The next day, while Lucas was out checking on his sheep and tending to the needs of his ranch, Kate remained indoors. Hating being alone, she softened the edge of the loneliness by mending clothes. Luckily the frostbite had been minimal and only on a few toes, and her pneumonia had been nipped in the bud, so the cough that lingered didn't prevent her from doing such menial tasks. Helping Lucas out in this very small way brought her a measure of joy.

The next few evenings and days passed in pretty much the same way, but each day, Kate felt a little stronger.

Kate sat in the rocking chair on a sunny morning, finishing up the last bit of mending. She bit the thread to cut it and looked around the living room and kitchen, searching for something else she could do to help Lucas. The place looked rather tidy for a single man's house. There was a pot in the sink, still soaking from the overcooked oatmeal from breakfast. It had been a week and a half since she'd set out in that storm. She was finally feeling somewhat normal—except for the limited use of her leg. She really wished she could have created a walking cast. Perhaps she could try hopping on her good leg to go over and wash the pan out.

She stood on her good leg, holding onto the arm of the rocking chair for balance. Taking the first hop made her a little dizzy. She stopped for a second to let her head clear. If she had to sit around the rest of the day with nothing to do, she was going to go crazy. Besides, she wanted to be of service to Lucas. She took another hop and then one more. Her head really started swimming. She reached out for something to grab. There was nothing close. She felt herself tipping, struggling for balance as the front door swung open.

"What are ye doing?" Lucas ran in, leaving the door wide open and the cold air rushing in. He swooped Kate up into his arms and carried her back over to where he could kick the door shut with his snowy boot. He carried her back over to the rocking chair and set her down. "What in the world are ye trying to do, lass, break the other leg?"

Though he smiled, Kate could read the concern in his eyes. She loved it; it warmed her heart, and she wanted to stand back up, wrap her arms around his neck, and release the feelings mounting inside her. She lifted her leg and rested it on the footstool instead, reminding herself to act like a lady. "I'm sorry," she said, trying to look apologetic as she gazed into his eyes. "I was done with the mending, and I wanted to be of some use. I thought I'd finish up the breakfast dishes."

Lucas rolled his shoulders as if a load had been taken from them. "Aye, does this mean ye are feeling better?"

"I am. Thanks to you." Kate felt a burn of tears swell in her eyes.

Lucas wagged a hand at her. "I did nothing; ye are a strong lass." He turned away from her and stepped over to where he'd rested his whittling project against the hearth. As he turned back around, he said, "Ye shall need this if ye insist on getting around by yerself. 'Tis not quite finished, but the important part is."

He rested the narrow end of the wood he'd been carving on the floor next to Kate. It looked like an ordinary stick at the bottom, being about two inches in diameter, whittled clean of its bark. Three feet up from the floor the ordinary transformed into the extraordinary. A handle of sorts extended straight out from the stick at that point, and the remainder of the wood had been carved with intricate detail into leafy vines and roses in various stages of bloom. At the top, the stick jutted out on each side, forming a T, only it sagged in the middle like a saddle. That part was smooth. Kate envisioned it fitting under her arm comfortably.

"'Tis a crutch." Lucas sounded like a child giving a homemade gift at Christmastime. His eyes glimmered like a child's as well.

"I can see that." Kate stood and slipped it under her arm. It fit nicely. "It's wonderful. I love it. Just like I love the necklace you carved for me." She used the crutch to help her take a few steps and then turned around and came back to where Lucas stood.

"I noticed ye were wearing it when ye changed your clothes the first day," he said, beaming.

"And I'm wearing it now." Kate pulled it out from beneath the shirt Lucas had lent her. She found his clothes much more comfortable and conducive to recovery than any of hers would have been. "They are both beautiful—the necklace and the crutch. You're very talented." She wiggled the crutch. "It's just the right size. How did you do that?"

His forehead, with the bandage now gone, wrinkled into a sheepish wince. "I measured ye while ye slept. But I suppose I could have done it without me measuring stick." His expression relaxed. He moved closer to her, their bodies just inches apart. "I know ye by heart—how tall ye stand next to me and the length of your untiring arms, always anxious to help others. How could I forget their length as they wrapped around me that day in your office?"

Kate felt her face flush with warmth—good warmth, not fever. She could feel her heart pounding in her chest, beating faster and faster.

Ever since she'd left Craig, she'd been meaning to tell Lucas about Stanley— that it was her fault that Lucas had lost half his sheep. There were no more excuses. She had to tell him now, before she stole his affection only to have him take it back. He needed to know the truth so he could decide whether or not he could still love her.

Using her crutch, Kate took a step back. She maintained her gaze on his face. "Lucas, I've got to tell you something; I've been meaning to since I arrived. You deserve to know this, and I won't blame you if you choose to terminate your association with me hereafter."

The light in his eyes faded as his face sagged. "Tell me what?"

"Your sheep, all those you lost . . ." Kate swallowed the lump forming in her throat. "I was responsible for that."

"Impossible!" Lucas's face grimaced into an expression Kate had never seen before. It scared her.

"I drove Stanley to it."

"What do you mean?" Lucas's disbelief softened to confusion.

"I set the entire town of Craig against him," Kate's words came out as sobs. "I rallied their fear of Stanley Jones, used it against him, and with Lavender's help convinced them to stand up to the man. He found out I was behind it, and he took it out on you. I was just trying to help, but it backfired horribly." She broke down and cried like a child—she truly wasn't as strong as she'd once believed. Now that she thought about it, her need to fix other people's problems was more of a weakness. Strength did not equate to one's ability to come up with creative or quick-fix solutions—not even close.

She felt his arms wrap around her.

"You did that for me?" Lucas said so gently that Kate's tears ceased to flow. He lifted a hand to her face, and with the back of it wiped the remaining tears from her cheek.

"You're not upset?"

"No." He drew out the word in a soft tone that melted her fears. Blinking his eyes, he continued. "And I am more than a wee bit relieved. The way ye were talking, I feared ye were going to tell me something horrible. But this . . ." He shook his head. "'Tis wonderful."

"But you've lost half your sheep!"

"I still have the other half. And most importantly, I have you!" he said with a lift in his pitch. He picked her up, and she let the crutch fall to the floor. "Is it true?" His voice softened and came out a tender plea. "What ye said the other night? That ye love me?"

Kate felt her insides swell with a pleasant pressure. "Yes, very true."

She leaned her face toward his, drawn to him by an unstoppable, wonderful feeling. His arms embraced her with tender force as his lips met hers. His mouth opened, begging hers to follow. She never knew kisses could be so enjoyable—not before she'd kissed Lucas. *Is this what it feels like to be truly in love?* Kate marveled at the intense yet tender feelings filling every part of her. She didn't want to stop the kiss. And didn't, leaning into him as she returned his kiss with intensity.

A knock came at the door.

Kate could sense Lucas's reluctance as he pulled away from her and glanced out the front window. She too looked outside.

A horse stood tied to the outside of the corral. The knee-deep snow between the horse and the trough-like trail Lucas had shoveled to the house looked as if it had been dragged along rather than stepped in.

"It's Logan," Kate said.

"I wonder what brings him out here?" Lucas placed Kate down in the rocking chair. "He normally does not bother with me mail unless the road is clear." He headed for the door.

"I hope everything's okay," Kate said, sensing Lucas's unease as she battled her own.

A gust of wind blew in with the swing of the door. "Come in, lad." Lucas motioned for Logan to hurry inside, sweeping his hand quickly through the cold air.

Logan's eyes met Kate's. A noticeable sense of relief washed over his face. "Miss Kate! You're all right!"

Kate lifted her splinted leg and smiled. "Except for a broken leg."

"I was worried something awful after that storm set in." Logan hobbled over toward the kitchen table. "'specially when you didn't show up back in town for so long. After all, it was me that told you Mr. Lucas needed you."

"So ye did not come out here on your own accord?" Lucas shot Kate a teasing glance.

"Oh, she didn't need no encouragement," Logan said, making Kate feel a blush rise in her cheeks. "Once I told her, she wouldn't accept nothin' else but to ride out here herself and tend to you."

"Really?" Lucas's crooked smile appeared.

"I appreciate your concern." Kate pulled a blanket over herself and propped up her leg. "But you didn't come all the way out here in that snow just to check on me, did you?"

Logan sat down at the table. "Well, that was part of it." He reached inside his coat and pulled out two envelopes. "And I wanted to bring Mr. Lucas these. One's from Boston. The other's from the government. They both looked important." He held them out for Lucas.

Lucas took them and opened the one from Boston first. His hands trembled slightly as he extracted the single sheet of paper it held. He read it with a serious expression furrowing his brow. Then his face relaxed.

"Is it about your daughter?" Kate asked.

"Aye." Lucas's eyes took on a faraway gaze as he continued to read. "The lass's grandmother has reconsidered. Me letter made her think maybe 'twould be good for wee Celeste to be with her pa." He looked at Kate and smiled, his eyes brimming with gratitude. "Thanks for helping me to write it."

Kate clapped her hands together. "Oh, Lucas, how marvelous!" *At least he'll have his daughter eventually.*

"She has stipulations though." His smile faded. "She insists on making sure I can provide well for the child and that Celeste will be safe out here in the 'wild West,' as she put it."

Kate's heart sank. This was no place for a little girl—not right now. Lucas too knew that as soon as the snow from this storm melted, there would be more scandalizing, terrorizing, and whatever else Stanley Jones could dream up to throw their way. "What's in the other letter?" she asked to distract Lucas from the bittersweet news.

Lucas sat down at the table and pulled the other envelope from Logan's hands. He opened it and read, staring at it as if confused. "Where did . . . how did . . . wow . . . 'tis great!"

"What is it, Mr. Lucas?"

"A copy of me grazing permit." Lucas slapped the paper with his hand. "Proof that me sheep—not Circle J cattle—have the right to feed on that government land." He offered Logan a timid grin. "Uh . . . sorry."

"Don't feel bad for me," Logan said. "I think it's great news. The Circle J ain't mine. Never will be. But you, Mr. Lucas—you're my friend. You're the only rancher who treats me like an equal, like a man."

"Thank you, lad." Lucas wrapped his arm around Logan. "That's because you are one."

Kate couldn't hold back her delight. "It came so quickly." She rushed her hand to her mouth.

Lucas stared at her with an expression that vacillated from disbelief to disapproval to appreciation. "Ye sent away for the permit, didn't ye?"

Kate offered a timid nod.

"You nay have the money any more than I." Lucas's grin appeared more crooked than ever. "I should tan yer hide. After I kiss ye first."

"Yep, things look like they're goin' just fine here." Logan wore a big grin as he pushed his chair back and stood. "I better be getting back now." He held out his hand, palm up. "Wait, I forgot. I wanted to tell you some other good news."

"Other good news?" Lucas lifted an eyebrow at Logan.

"Yeah, really good news for you, Mr. Lucas." Logan grinned. "But not so good for my brother."

"Tell me more." Lucas put his feet up on Logan's vacated chair.

"There's a federal marshal in town," Logan said with eyes wide. "The people in Denver sent him our way for some reason. Henry Walker is his name. I met him. He's a right nice fellow. Said he's going to stay a while. At least until the cattlemen can get along with sheep ranchers."

"That could be a long time," Lucas said with a comical twist to his mouth.

"That's wonderful!" Kate felt relief. Hope surfaced. Maybe things could become safe sooner rather than later.

Logan looked at Kate. "How much longer do you figure you're needin' to stay here before you can ride out?"

"I can't really say at this point." Kate bit her lip, not wanting to think about leaving but knowing the longer she stayed away the more her struggling medical practice would suffer. "It might be quite a while. Legs can be tricky things to heal sometimes," she said and immediately thought of Logan. She swore the boy had grown since she'd last seen him.

Logan hobbled to the door. He turned and faced Kate as he placed his hand on the knob. "Well, I'll make sure I tell everyone about your leg and the poor road and that you'll be a while mending so no more of that gossip gets put out there."

"Thank you, Logan," Kate said, wondering what people were thinking back in town. Then she caught herself. She didn't care a bit if there was gossip—because if there was, it would come from either Stanley or Mrs. Forbes. And neither of those persons was worthy of listening to. Kate felt the townspeople knew that now, and that brought a smile to her lips.

"What are ye smiling at?" Lucas said as Logan shut the door on his way out.

"You." Kate was smiling at him now.

Lucas stood, sauntered over, and scooped her back into his arms, cradling her against his chest. "Is that because ye like me?" he asked, his extra-crooked grin returning.

"Yeah." Kate wrapped her arms around his neck. "Just like Logan," she said with a bit of teasing in her voice. "You treat me like an equal. And I like that."

"I am so glad, 'cause I must ask ye a big, big favor now." His voice was lighthearted, but his eyes were serious.

"Favor?" Kate wondered where he was going with this.

"I didn't tell ye all that was in that letter—the one from Celeste's grandma."

"There was more?"

Lucas nodded. "The woman insisted she would only let her granddaughter come out West and stay here if I remarried. She said the girl needed a mother, not just a father to raise her. I totally agree with the woman." He grew silent for a moment. When his voice resumed, it sounded shaky. "I was planning on asking ye this long before I got the letter—but me courage waned." He glanced out the window. "Today, though . . . brought me courage." Lucas now looked at Kate with eyes that begged, caressed, and rejoiced in the same glance. "I need you, Katherine. Not just for me daughter. For me. I was like rangeland in winter—ready to die. But ye came along, full of life, and gave me hope. Now I feel like the Yampa Valley in springtime. I have always longed for spring to last forever." He closed his eyes momentarily and with a sniffle said, "I love you, Katherine. Marry me."

Every care and worry slipped away for the moment. Only love for this man consumed her now. "Oh, Lucas, yes! I will."

"Yippee!" Lucas spun Kate around and together they lowered into the big rocking chair, laughing. "So you like that I think you're me equal, do ye?"

"Yes, I do."

Lucas shifted his eyes, gazing from her face to the shirt she'd borrowed from him to wear. "Oh, you're more than equal. But you're not a man."

But she could be as forward as one. Kate pulled Lucas closer and put her mouth to his. This kiss was going to be even better than the last one.

If that was even possible.

CHAPTER 27

THAT EVENING, CRADLED IN LUCAS'S lap, Kate rocked back and forth with him in the big rocking chair as they shared stories of their pasts and plans for their future together.

"I hope Celeste will like me." Kate felt a crack pierce the storybook magic that had engulfed her the entire day. Was she prepared to be a stepmother? A mother? A wife?

"What's not to like? She shall adore ye, like her daddy does." Lucas kissed Kate lightly on the lips. He looked up at the rafters of the cabin as if in thought. Then he stood. With Kate still in his arms, he carried her toward the bedroom. "I think 'tis best we call it a night."

"What, so soon? The night is still young."

"Aye, 'tis that." Lucas kept walking. "But I think I shall take a trip into town tomorrow, so I need to get up at the crack o' dawn to get to me chores before I leave."

"But—"

"Don't ye worry. If Logan made it through the snow, so can I." He lowered her onto the bed. "And if ye will sit tight and not hop around, nor do things ye should not, ye shall be fine. I shall hurry in, visit with the U.S. marshal for a wee bit, and hurry back."

"Oh, the new marshal," Kate muttered, Lucas's sudden desire to go into town making sense now. "Yes, it would be a good thing to contact him."

"Aye. The sooner me homestead is safe," he said with a faraway look in his eyes, "the better . . . for Celeste . . . and for you, Katherine."

"Stanley!" Kate clutched a pillow to her chest to calm her cough—and her fear. Since her accident, she'd forgotten about him. "Do you dare leave?" *Do I dare stay?*

"Aye, 'tis a risk I believe must be taken." Lucas left her on the bed and headed for the door. He turned and looked at her before he stepped into the main room. "But do not worry," he said as a knowing grin pulled up the corners of his mouth. "Our infamous Mr. Jones is a fair-weather villain. He no more likes to traipse through deep snow than be kind to his neighbors. I doubt we shall see the likes of him 'til the roads are clear."

Kate's eyes remained on Lucas as he ran into the other room, brought back her crutch, and then pulled the door shut. She got ready for bed, hoping he was right about Stanley. Reflecting on the events of the day, she slid beneath the covers, determined not to let mere thoughts of Mr. Jones taint the end of one of the most beautiful days of her life.

❧

With the first rays of sunlight poking through the bedroom window, Kate pulled herself up into a sitting position in bed. She listened for the scrape of chair legs across the floor or the clank of a pot being set on the stove. The silence told her Lucas must be out doing his chores. She crawled out of bed, got dressed, and hobbled into the kitchen with her crutch, wanting to make breakfast for Lucas before he left for town.

Just grabbing a log from the woodpile and stoking the fire gave her cause to sit down for a moment to rest. The same need arose after she stepped outside in the cold to fetch some water in a pot and then placed it on the stove. But with lots of sitting down and the promise of a nap later on, she managed to get a pot of mush on to cook.

It had come to a boil when Lucas opened the door and hurried inside. He looked at her, took a deep breath, and stopped, his crooked grin barely noticeable in the gray light of the early morning. "Are ye making breakfast for me?"

"Yes, I am," Kate responded with a new blend of excitement and affection.

His face grew serious. "But what of yer leg?"

"If I rest often, I'm fine." She pointed her spoon at him as he approached her. "Besides, I was afraid you'd take off to town without eating something first. As your doctor, I don't think that would be wise."

"Ye are speaking only as me doctor, aye?" He wrapped his arm around her waist and pulled her close, his face just inches from hers.

Kate's heart beat faster as the air between them charged with delectable energy. "Well . . . no." His mouth brushed one corner of hers. "As . . . your . . ." She couldn't resist; she let their lips connect for a quick kiss. ". . . fiancée too," she breathlessly finished her sentence as he pulled away. She definitely could get used to this every morning.

"Ye are a sharp lass." He glanced into the pot. "I had no plans of eating before I headed out—but I can see fit to eat a spot of breakfast now that ye mention it." He let go of Kate, stepped over to the cupboard, and grabbed two bowls and two spoons. "I only came back here because of me idea. 'Tis a grand one," he said as he set the dishes on the table.

"Tell me, please." She stirred the mush with extra vigor.

"If ye give me the key to yer place, I shall fetch the plaster and gauze ye need to make a proper-like cast for yer leg."

"That's a wonderful idea!"

"I knew ye would like it." Lucas gave her a quick kiss before he sat down at the table.

After their simple breakfast of oatmeal and milk, and another kiss goodbye, Lucas darted outside. Kate stood by the window, leaning on her crutch, watching as he rode away. Part of her didn't want him to go, but a bigger part of her did—it was imperative that Lucas contact the marshal.

When Lucas totally slipped from her view, she made her way over to the rocking chair and propped her leg up, trying hard not to dwell on the loneliness filling her insides. She kept telling herself he'd not be gone very long—only long enough to ride into town, talk to the marshal, grab some more plaster of Paris, and ride back. Three or four hours, that was all.

That felt like forever.

Would it feel the same to Lucas if the tables were turned? If he had to watch her ride away in less than ideal road conditions to go into town to tend to a patient?

She'd been so caught up in the magic of exploring her love for Lucas, she hadn't thought about her other love: that of being a doctor.

All morning and into the afternoon until Lucas returned home, Kate's thoughts churned. How could a woman be a good wife and mother and a dedicated physician at the same time? One or the other would surely suffer. She came up with idea after idea, trying to find a solution that would allow her to do both. Nothing satisfactory came.

A week and a half later, Kate gazed out the window again with a mixture of anticipation and dread. The sun's warmth lit the clear sky with brilliant blue for the third day in a row. Combined with the rain that had fallen two days after Lucas had proposed, the snow banks had melted into mere bumps, and portions of the brown yard and road peeked through the white. She could make it into town without too much trouble now. But was she ready to leave physically? Emotionally? For the past ten days since their engagement, her head and her heart had been dancing in the clouds—sparkling ones spun of dreams. Yet at times, mostly when Lucas was out doing chores and couldn't see her, she let those clouds morph into black ones brimming with doubt that she could be both a good wife and a good doctor.

Her leg felt somewhat better. Now that the road had cleared—and one never knew when another snowstorm might hit—she acknowledged it was time she return to town.

Reaching down, she felt the cast Lucas had helped her apply to her leg the evening after he'd visited with the marshal. Lucas had told her that meeting Henry Walker had brought him hope, but he knew a resolution would take time. The cast had helped her gain reassurance she was ready to get her life somewhat back to normal. The cast did an amazing job at immobilizing her fractured tibia while allowing her to put weight on her leg and walk fairly easily now with her crutch—at times even without it, though somewhat clumsily. With a little help, she imagined she could even mount Lucy.

Lucas stepped behind her. "'Twill only be until this dang land dispute is settled." He wrapped his arms around her waist and pulled her to him. "Then I shall marry ye the very next minute, lass, and never let ye go."

"Oh, you will, will you?" She turned to face him, the teasing words curling up the corners of her mouth. "The very next minute, huh? I'm sorry, but weddings take time to plan."

Memories came to her mind of the stained-glass windows and ornate architecture of the church she and Darwin had reserved for their wedding ceremony. Then of the elaborate dinner menu and enormous guest list her mother had labored for weeks to prepare. Between Darwin's family and her parents' acquaintances, they would have needed that massive cathedral to fit them all. Once Craig's new church was built, it wouldn't matter that the modest little chapel could never fit even a fraction of Kate's one-time guest list. Only a few people would be in attendance: Susannah and Rosie—and Logan, of course. But the church barely had its foundation formed and wouldn't be completed until next spring. Would Lucas be willing to wait until then? Was she willing to wait? Then two disturbing questions arose. What if the land dispute was not resolved before then? And what if her personal disputes were not resolved by then? She had yet to tell Lucas about her inner doubts of being both a good wife and a good doctor. She felt the smile fade from her face.

"What's there to plan? I fetch the justice o' the peace, he performs the ceremony, and . . ." Lucas's voice trailed off. "Uh, sorry, lass, how thickheaded

I have been. I can see it in your eyes: ye want a right proper wedding. An' heaven knows ye deserve it." He covered his face with his hand, dragging it down then clutching his chin.

"I don't need anything fancy," she said, trying to hide the real reason for her long face. "But it would be nice to get married somewhere other than city hall." The image of the mayor's tiny office he shared with the sheriff and two jail cells left a sour taste in her mouth. There might be room enough, barely, for her three wedding guests, but she might have some unwanted guests standing behind those bars watching her and Lucas on their most cherished of days. "The new church would be lovely. But what if it's not finished by Easter like the new pastor hopes?"

"Easter?" Light drained from Lucas's face as if he'd have to wait five years instead of five months to be married. "Oh, Katherine, 'tis so far away."

"I'll tell you what: let's not worry about the location or the date until things get cleared up between you and Stanley Jones." And between Kate Donahue and Dr. Donahue.

His eyes did not perk up as Kate had hoped. "What if the new marshal is unable to stop the harassment? I cannot wait forever to marry ye, Katherine." He hung his head momentarily. "But neither can I have ye live here while 'tis so dangerous." His head came up, and he released his hold on her, stepping over to gaze again out the window. "All the more reason for me to hurry and get ye back into town. If ye and Lucy are able to make the trip, as sure as rain in spring, Stanley and his horse will be up to it as well."

"You?" Kate would have stomped her foot if her legs were more in a position to do so. "There's no need for you to come with me. It wouldn't be wise to leave your place unattended. If you'll help me mount Lucy, she and I can make it into town just fine by ourselves."

"And how, lass, do you propose to get down from Lucy once you have arrived? Resort to a bit o' shouting as you ride up Yampa Avenue: 'Whom of you dear townsfolk can I impose upon to help this damsel down from her horse?'"

"Okay, you're right," she admitted, holding in her mirth.

For the next half hour, Kate got dressed in her own clothes and gathered her things as Lucas prepared the horses. She took one last look at the rustic haven that had been her place of convalescence for almost a month—and would soon be her permanent home. She laughed inside. If her parents were to see this cabin and know that their daughter would give birth and raise their only grandchildren in a log structure that their horse stables back on Long Island could put to shame, surely they would protest more than they had at her desires to be a physician.

Should she tell them? When Lucas had first proposed, she'd wanted to share her good news. It'd been the first time since she'd arrived in Craig that she'd truly had the desire to write to her mother. Maybe a short letter after the ceremony would be best. She'd simply state she'd married the man of her dreams and she was completely happy. Or perhaps it would be easier to continue to remain silent about her life and her whereabouts—especially since she didn't know if she would be completely happy.

Lucas stuck his head inside the door. "Horses are ready."

The ride into town proved difficult. With many a mud puddle to avoid, the journey was anything but smooth.

"Don't worry." Lucas tried to sound chipper when he'd realized her leg had begun to ache several miles into their journey. "The road . . . 'tis usually not so rough. On a good day, I can make it to town in an hour or so—if I keep Dublin at a good speed. And once your leg is mended, 'twill be better. Ye shall still be able to tend to the needs of your patients just dandy."

"Oh, yes, perhaps so," Kate responded as her mind recalled the few times they had discussed this issue. The fact that he was totally supportive of her following her dream of being a doctor was wonderful. Unfortunately, they hadn't thought out the logistics. But with his mention of her continuing to see patients, it brought up a whole other issue to add to those that plagued her. What about the practicality of living more than an hour or so outside of town? That most certainly could hinder her medical practice.

It seemed her heart ached worse than her leg as she rode into town. Bittersweet solace came, however, from the fact that no one really depended on her services in Craig—there wasn't much of a decision to be made.

She and Lucas pulled their horses to a stop in front of Mr. Hoy's shop. As Lucas helped her down from the saddle, his eyes met hers with a look of concern. "Ye've said nary a word for the last mile or two. What's wrong, lass?"

"I've just got lots on my mind . . . thinking about you having to go back to your place all alone. And Stanley. And thinking about how everything will play out."

"I shall be fine, lass. 'Tis you I worry about." Lucas glanced at the stairs. "Would you like me to carry ye up to your place?"

"Thank you. You're so sweet, but no." She placed her hand on his cheek. Oh, how she loved this man and was determined to make this marriage—that some would deem an odd match—work. "I've got to learn to take them sooner or later. I don't plan on being holed up there until this cast comes off."

"May I give you me arm then to hold onto as ye climb?"

"No, you need to hurry and head back to the ranch. I've already taken you away too long. Besides, I need to stop in and speak with Mr. Hoy before I go up. I should let him know where I've been for so long," she said, adding a demure smile. She hoped it covered the angst growing in the pit of her stomach. She also needed to talk with her landlord about the possibility of trading more medical services for rent.

"My, ye are a stubborn lass. But 'tis why I love you." He pulled her close and kissed her, firm and quick. "At least let me carry your bag upstairs and take Lucy to the livery stable," he said with a wink.

"Thank you. That would be lovely."

"Aye." Lucas released her. "And I shall be waiting like a wooly sheep for the shears of spring 'til I can be done with this messy business of land and wed me sweetheart. Goodbye, lass." He grabbed her bag and ran up the steps.

Kate took a deep breath to slow her pulse before she stepped into the saddle shop.

Mr. Hoy looked up from the stirrup he repaired and caught her eyes. "Miss Kate! You're back! So good to have you home."

"Why, thank you." Kate was taken aback by his noticeable delight at her return. "I would like to speak with you about working something out for my upcoming rent payment."

"Oh, no need to pay me for December." Mr. Hoy waved a hand at her as she approached the counter. "You haven't used my place upstairs for nearly a month."

Kate swallowed hard, overcome by his generosity. "Thank you. Are you certain? That is so very kind of you."

"It's nothing. Besides, I heard about you getting caught in that big snowstorm." He nodded at her noticeable limp. "And your broken leg. It's good to see you're on the mend and it's not keeping you down."

"No, no, I'm not going to let it slow me down."

"The townsfolk will be glad to hear that. Your absence was definitely felt."

"Whatever do you mean?"

"I had a whole passel of folks come in here, asking me if I knew when you'd be back, or telling me about their ailments—wanting me to pass on their whining to you, I suppose. Got mighty tiresome, so I rigged something up for you. It's at the top of the steps, next to your door. I'm hoping it'll help for the next time you're away, or if you just have to run to the mercantile for a spell."

"Well, thank you, Mr. Hoy." Kate gave him a nod goodbye and headed for the stairs. Curiosity quickened her awkward gait. She found ascending the stairs slow and tiresome, stepping up with her good leg and pulling her cast up one step at a time. As she approached the top of the stairs, she noticed what looked to be a box attached with nails to the railing of the landing.

Her thoughts raced, trying to figure out how a wooden box could help her while her mind attempted to comprehend the possibility that a "whole passel of folks" had stopped by. Once she reached the landing, she ran her fingers along the smooth wooden surface of the bread-loaf-sized box and the hand-painted lettering that read, *Leave a message if the doc is out.* She opened the hinged lid and peered inside. A pencil and a small notebook rested at the bottom. She pulled out the book and opened its cover. A variety of handwriting jumped from not just one page but three. Fumbling with her key, she hurried and opened the door, anxious to settle into her chair to read the notes people had left for her.

On the first page, in scrolling handwriting, Lavender Decker stated her rheumatism was acting up and Sam had a nasty cough. She'd written, *We miss you* in parentheses beneath their ailments. Below that, a Mrs. Baxter mentioned she was due to have a baby soon and wanted to meet "the new woman doctor" before she delivered. Also that her sister was due to have a baby shortly thereafter and she too wanted to meet Kate; she hoped Kate would stop by as soon as she got back. The second and third pages held mention of ailments ranging from ingrown toenails to a child's broken arm—the child's mother mentioned she was sorry Kate wasn't in and would now have to stop by Doc Greene's and have him set her boy's arm.

Kate set the notebook aside, overwhelmed yet thrilled at this apparent need for her services. Her name was finally getting out there; her patience rewarded. True, every one of those notes had been left by women, but even if she were to treat only the women and children of this area, she'd have plenty of work to keep her busy. Excitement swelled inside her, leaving her with an intense feeling of satisfaction.

But the excitement quickly vanished. In its place rushed overwhelming feelings of confliction. So strong were her desires to serve these women who had sought her help—and others who would surely follow—that her heart ached with near-unbearable pressure. Yet that same heart yearned, beyond anything she'd ever imagined, to be with Lucas—to marry him, to bear his children.

She doubted her ability to do them both and do them well.

CHAPTER 28

KATE OFFERED A SINCERE THANK you and goodbye to Logan, extremely grateful he'd taken her on her rounds in his wagon. Trudging through the muddy streets had proven difficult at best. Yesterday, after she'd returned to town and taken a short nap to give her leg a rest, she'd gone out and visited as many of the women as possible who had left messages in the wooden box. Today, with Logan's help, she'd managed to visit and attend to the remainder of those who'd written in her notebook.

Exhausted, and her leg sore from walking with her cast, she dragged herself up the stairs, the light and warmth of day fading fast with the early setting sun of late November. The day had been tiring, but nonetheless very rewarding. She looked forward to tomorrow, now having caught up on her visits. If someone were in need of her services, they would hopefully come to her office or send Logan to fetch her.

After unlocking her door, she lifted the lid of the wooden box to see if anyone had stopped by while she had been out. A new, lengthy message had been scribed in the notebook. She grabbed it and stepped inside to get off her leg. As she settled into the chair, she noticed the note was from Lucas. A wave of sadness engulfed her at having missed his visit. A second, stronger surge hit her as she contemplated the disappointment he must have felt. She let out a frustrated breath and read.

My Dearest Katherine,

I've waited here on your doorstep as long as I dare. I had so longed to see you today—

A full line had been erased. Smiling, Kate could imagine the deleted words, knowing what she longed for herself. She would have erased them too.

but alas, our meeting is not to be. I need to head back before dark. I shan't be able to visit you tomorrow. I shall be at the Circle J. The marshal will be with me. Pray that all will go well, for then I will visit you and stay all day. And forever.

Love, Lucas

P.S. I have high hopes, so start planning our wedding.

P.P.S. I cannot bear to wait until Easter. Please, I beg of you, choose an earlier date. May I suggest this Saturday or next?

Kate grinned at his last line. Oh, how she loved that man—and would definitely pray for all to go well out at the Circle J.

She also loved being a doctor.

Sleep refused to come that night. Kate tossed about in her bed. Though her body lay there exhausted, her brain refused to quit churning. One moment she was wondering if she should call off the wedding and the next she was shuddering beneath her covers at the thought of breaking Lucas's heart. And her own.

By the time the sun rose, she'd managed to get a few hours of sleep. She pulled herself out of bed, got dressed, and set to the task of cooking herself a bowl of mush.

A rapid knock sounded through her door.

Kate hobbled toward it with concern. She opened the door to see Mary Tucker holding her little Caroline in her arms, a cloth with bright-red blood seeping through lying across the child's forehead.

"Kate, I'm so glad you're here." Mary rushed inside. "I'd heard you've been gone for quite a spell."

"What happened?" Kate ushered Mary to the exam table and motioned for her to sit the girl upon it.

"She stood on her chair after breakfast. I told her to sit down, but she held out her hands instead, like she does when she wants me to catch her in my arms. She loves that game, but I wasn't ready. She jumped. I couldn't catch her, and she hit her head on the corner of the table. I feel just awful. What kind of mother am I?" Mary let out a sob.

The whimpering four-year-old on the exam table followed suit. From the redness of her eyes and the tear-streaked little face, Kate surmised the child had done plenty of crying since the incident. But other than that, she appeared to be all right.

"It's going to be okay," Kate assured the little girl as she carefully laid her down on the table. "I'm going to take care of you," she said calmly and removed the blood-stained rag from her forehead. She turned to Mary. "Pull up a chair, sit down, and try to relax. Everything is going to be just fine. Caroline is going to need a few stitches, that's all." She placed a hand on Mary's trembling arm. "And you're not a bad mother. You're one who plays with her children and obviously loves them immensely."

After having her hands batted away and the child refusing to lie still despite her mother holding her down, Kate knew she had to try something else. "I'm going to have to give her something to anesthetize her for a little while."

"Ann-what?" Mary's eyes opened wide.

"Put her to sleep while I stitch up that nasty laceration. Hold on to her while I get what I need."

Kate went to her medical cabinet and returned with a drip inhaler and a bottle of chloroform. She'd never used this on such a small patient, but she knew there was no other choice. The cut ran deep and would be painful to stitch properly. She placed the mask over the girl's mouth and nose and carefully dropped a small amount of the chemical onto its porous surface. In less than a minute, the little body relaxed, and Kate was able to tend to her wound.

When Kate had finished, she had Mary carry her child to the overstuffed chair and hold her close. "I'd like you to stay here until Caroline wakes up fully." Kate sat down next to her on a kitchen chair. "So just sit and relax for a while and tell me how you and your family have been doing."

Mary chatted about her children, how she was expecting another one and looked forward to Kate delivering it rather than old Mrs. Watson, who'd served as a midwife in Craig since it'd been settled. The old woman had been going blind for the past year and had told everyone she was giving up midwifery.

Kate's spirits slumped. It must have shone in her eyes, because Mary stopped and gazed into her face.

"What's wrong, Kate? You look as though someone's just knocked the wind right out of you."

"It's nothing. At least nothing I can't handle." Kate knew it was a lie the moment it fell from her lips.

"You don't sound very convincing. And it's not at all fair coming from the person who told me to open up and share my woes with her." Mary reached out her free arm and took Kate's hand. "It does help to talk about it. Promise."

Kate told Mary about the time she'd spent out at the McCurdy place, how Lucas had proposed, and about their plans for marriage as soon as conflicts with the Circle J were resolved. She found it therapeutic to open up. Continuing, she poured out her heart concerning her desire and need to be a physician.

"Those are two wonderful stories." Mary shifted the groggy child on her lap. "I must be missing something though, 'cause I'm yet to understand the reason for your long face."

"You don't see the problem?" Kate stared at Mary.

Mary shook her head.

"I can't give my whole heart to Lucas if I insist on putting it into my practice. On the other hand, I can't give my all to being a doctor if I want to give Lucas the attention he deserves—and that I want to give him."

"Who says?" Mary's words came out boldly.

Kate felt as though truth had just slapped her in the face.

"I know you, Kate. You're one who could do both—and do them just fine!"

It sounded like encouragement Kate would have rendered the day she'd stepped off that stagecoach, determined to succeed in her dreams no matter what—and help others succeed in theirs. "You really think so?" Though she could feel the cogs of determination stripping away the rust, she thirsted for the affirmation.

"Absolutely. You've just got to learn to balance and juggle. I did that after you challenged me to pursue my dreams. I love my kids, but I love to sew and decorate, and I realized I did need a creative outlet. So I started sprucing up the hotel with my homemade decorations. Then I started myself a little sewing business. I found I could do both—as long as I was organized and set limits. And now I'm a better mother and a better seamstress. Campbell's happier and letting me have more input with the running of the hotel, and I'm a whole lot happier."

Little Caroline awoke, but Kate and Mary continued talking. For the next hour, they discussed plans of how Kate could come into the office twice a week— as long as the weather permitted—and see to patients whose ailments could wait a day or two. If there was an emergency when Kate was home tending to her home and family, Doc Greene was still here. They both agreed that where Kate was really needed was in taking on Hazel Watson's role as the town midwife. With all the young families flocking to the area, there would be more babies born than ever before and a need for someone with more training in that area to deliver them. Kate wouldn't be busy every day delivering babies or taking care of women's health problems, but it would be enough to satisfy her desire to serve as a physician while giving her plenty of time to be a good wife. And mother. When she and Lucas were blessed with children, Mary had volunteered to babysit them the days Kate came into her office. She'd also offered to sew Kate's wedding dress if Kate brought her the fabric.

By the time Mary left, Caroline was ready to dance around the room and get back to being a little girl. Kate too was tempted to dance around the room. She was ready to get back to being a girl in love. There was white fabric to buy and a wedding to plan. She grabbed her coat and purse and followed Mary down the steps and then headed to Decker's store, hoping Lavender could help her do more than pick out lace.

CHAPTER 29

KATE PLACED THE BOLT OF white satin and spool of lace on the cutting table. "I need four yards of lace and eight of this fabric," she said to Lavender.

Lavender stared at Kate, her eyes opening wide. "Are you—" She appeared to be at a loss for words.

Kate nodded. "Making a wedding dress—or should I say, Mary Tucker is making it for me."

"You and Lucas McCurdy?" Lavender shouted, nodding her head as if it would tumble from her shoulders at any minute.

"Yes, we're getting married." Kate grabbed Lavender by the shoulders to calm her down.

The bell above the door jingled. Rosie stepped inside. "What's all the fuss about? I can hear you two clear outside."

"Kate's gettin' married!"

"You don't say." Rosie sauntered over to the cutting table. "Lucas McCurdy the lucky man?"

Kate nodded. "More like I'm the lucky woman."

"Well, congratulations." Rosie punched Kate in the arm and then watched her mother roll out the satin.

"I'm going to give you ten yards. Eight might not be enough." Lavender's smile stretched from ear to ear as she measured the yardage. Kate doubted the woman could be any more excited than if she was measuring out fabric for Rosie's wedding dress. "And I think you'll want at least six yards of trim. That's some right pretty lace you picked out to go with this satin. Don't you think so, Rosie?" She nudged her daughter.

Rosie hunched her shoulders. "All lace looks the same to me—scratchy."

"Someday, I'll be measuring out satin for your wedding dress." Lavender gave Rosie a hopeful look.

"Aw, Ma, even if I were to get hitched, I certainly wouldn't want to wear no frilly dress that wastes ten yards of cloth to make it. Why, a good heavy shirt takes less than three. Give me one of those and a new pair of denim trousers, and I'll be happy—you can even make the shirt white if you want." Rosie turned to Kate. "So where you gettin' married?"

Kate grimaced. "We don't know yet. Any suggestions?"

"Well, if'n I ever get hitched, I want it to be out on the range under the stars on a warm summer night."

Kate grinned. "Unfortunately, I don't think that will work for us. If all goes well with a bit of business Lucas is taking care of today, the wedding will likely take place as soon as Mary finishes my dress." She blew out a breath of frustration. "And we find a suitable location. And find someone to perform the ceremony. And send out invitations—not that we have many acquaintances to invite." She latched onto Lavender and Rosie at the same time, worried this special day could turn out disappointing for Lucas. "You two will come, won't you?"

"Wild horses couldn't keep me away," Rosie said.

"Of course I will!" Lavender straightened out the fabric, ready to cut. She laid down her scissors and stepped around the cutting table. It was her turn to take Kate by the shoulders. "And I'll do more than that. You leave the entire weddin' up to me." The excitement in her voice sounded near that of a giddy schoolgirl. "I'll plan everything. I can even make your cake—I have more tasty recipes up my sleeve than just those darn cinnamon rolls."

Kate straightened her back, ready to protest transferring such a heavy burden onto such a short-time friend. Then she saw the yearning in Lavender's eyes. This dear, sweet woman knew as well as Kate did that she'd most likely never have the chance of planning a traditional wedding for her only daughter. Kate's could perhaps help fill that need. "That would be wonderful." Kate gave Lavender a tender hug.

Later, when she was on her way home from delivering the satin and lace to Mary Tucker, Logan pulled his wagon up alongside Kate.

"Do you need a ride to an appointment?"

"No, I'm headed home, thank you. But I'd appreciate a lift that far."

"Sure thing!" Logan stopped the wagon and held the horse extra still while Kate pulled herself aboard and maneuvered her cast into place. "I'm glad I could give you a ride home, Miss Kate."

"That's awfully sweet of you, Logan."

"It weren't sweet. It's selfish."

Kate lifted an eyebrow.

"I been itchin' to tell you somethin'. Been driving 'round town looking for you."

"Is that so?" Kate's curiosity piqued. All day, she'd been thinking about Lucas being out at the Circle J. Did Logan have some insight on what had happened or was happening? "Please, share with me what you're 'itchin' to tell.'"

"Well, I've been doin' those exercises, just like you told me, Miss Kate."

"I'm glad to hear that. You keep it up." Kate's shoulders slumped. "Is that all you wanted to tell me?"

"Nope, there's more." He flicked the reins. "Lucas paid Stanley and my pa a visit today. The marshal came with him."

"Yes?"

Logan's smile grew. "The marshal told Pa about all the nasty things that had been done to Lucas and his sheep and his land. And that he had evidence it was Stanley who'd done it. Then he told Pa they could both go to prison if the destruction of Mr. McCurdy's property didn't stop. Pa blew up at Stanley. I wouldn't be surprised if my brother's gotta sleep in the bunkhouse for a month."

"That's wonderful!" Kate hugged Logan.

"Shucks, I didn't do nothin', Miss Kate. I mostly stayed to the background."

"But you came all this way to tell me the good news."

"Now you and Lucas can get married." Logan grinned as if he were as happy as Kate.

"How did you—"

The grin still lit his face. "Lucas told me. I'm so happy for the both of you."

"Is he still there, at your ranch?" Kate wanted to see Lucas, to wrap her arms around him and feel his arms around her. And celebrate. Not a thing stood in the way of their union now.

"Could be. They were signing lots of papers when I left. I don't know how long that'd take. Or he could be headed out to his place. He said he needed to tend to some things before nightfall." Logan pulled up on the reins. "You want me to take you out there and look for him?"

As much as Kate wanted to be with Lucas, she felt such an attempt unwise. They could cross paths and miss each other. Even if she did catch Lucas at home, at this late hour she'd have no choice but to spend the night at his cabin. Very unwise. There would be no three-foot drifts or broken leg to justify her stay. The gossip could be intense—and likely true the way Kate felt at the moment. "No, take me home. I'll patiently await a visit from him tomorrow."

Once home, Kate made herself a sandwich and settled onto her overstuffed chair with a book to try and pass the evening quickly. Morning could not come soon enough.

Three pages into the story, a knock at the door interrupted her reading. "Coming!" She hurried to the door, wondering what kind of ailment had brought someone by at this late hour.

She opened it. Her heart ignited with warmth. Lucas stood on the doorstep.

His face beamed. "Katherine, good news!" He stepped inside and scooped her into his arms.

"I know, Logan told me." She threw her arms around his neck and hung on while he spun her around. An immense sense of relief swelled inside her at having met with Mary this morning. This moment would have been tainted horribly if she were weighed down by second thoughts. "We can get married now."

"How about tonight?" His crooked smile emerged. He dropped her onto the overstuffed chair. "I'll go wake the justice of the peace right now."

Kate laughed at his honesty, even sharing a bit of that sentiment, but she really did want to have a traditional wedding—at least as close to one as was possible here in the high desert of Colorado. "We've got to wait at least as long as it takes to make a wedding dress."

He pulled her out of the chair, sat in her place, and patted his knee for her to sit down. She settled onto his lap and relayed the events of her day. He spoke of his dealings with the Joneses. Acutely aware of his body next to hers, the smell of his freshly laundered shirt next to her nose and his clean skin beneath, and the thought that he'd stopped home and bathed for her before he'd come set her heart racing.

After she'd explained every aspect of her busy day, silence befell her. And him. Their eyes locked. The brush of his hand against her wrist sent electrifying tingles up her arm and filled the air between them. She struggled to find her voice. "We could have discussed these things tomorrow—you should have never come into town so late."

"Aye." Lucas let out a breath of guilt. "But I could not wait 'til then to see you."

"It will be dangerous traveling back to your—"

Lucas pressed two fingers to her lips. "Hush, I am staying in town tonight."

Kate gulped.

"Do not worry, lass. My friend Ronald Smith has bought himself a new house, and I have arranged to stay in his extra bedroom." He flashed his crooked grin. "But I shall be staying here until you kick me out."

"It's absolutely gorgeous, thank you!" Kate pulled Mary into an embrace while admiring her stunning wedding dress hanging in the doorway of the hotel kitchen.

Mary carefully wrapped a sheet around the dress and handed it to Kate. "You best be hurrying along now. The ceremony starts at two o'clock, and you've still got plenty to do. I've gotta get myself ready too."

Kate gave Mary one more squeeze. "Thanks for being willing to come."

"Pish." Mary waved toward the door. "You make it sound like it's a task to come to a friend's wedding. Get going now."

A light snow had begun to fall. Soft flakes kissed Kate's face as she stepped outside. Lifting her skirt with one hand, holding fast to her wedding dress with the other, and grateful she'd finally shed her cast, she navigated the muddy wooden sidewalk, scurrying down to the end of the block to Sunny's place. Her mother would surely faint if she knew her only daughter was getting married in a saloon. That's why Kate had yet to write her. She hadn't decided how—or if—she should share the details of this totally foreign lifestyle she'd embraced.

Sunny had insisted that Kate come through the saloon doors and walk straight up to her apartment when she arrived. Kate would have preferred entering through the restaurant side but wanted to comply with her friend's wishes. After all, Sunny had graciously offered to host the wedding at her place. And she wouldn't accept a dime—her gift to Kate and Lucas, she'd insisted.

Kate had to open one of the heavy full-length doors of the saloon to enter—the pint-sized swinging doors had been replaced for the winter. The smell of pine delighted her nose as she stepped inside. Not even a trace of beer lingered. She noticed garlands of pine boughs tied with red bows hanging above the mirror behind the bar. The festive decorations appeared to extend into the restaurant's arm of the building. Though she couldn't see around the corner, she envisioned the location of the ceremony trimmed nicely as well. It brought a smile of appreciation to her lips, especially as she realized Sunny had closed for business this entire day.

"Don't just stand there gawkin', get up here." Sunny stood at the top of the stairs, motioning for Kate to come.

Kate hurried up the stairs and followed Sunny into her bedroom.

Lavender stood next to a dressing table inlaid with brass that shone like gold. One hand rested on the top of a short-backed chair upholstered in plush pink fabric; the other held a brush. "Sit down," she said in place of a greeting.

Kate complied, settling onto the soft chair and gazing into the brass-trimmed mirror attached to the dressing table.

Lavender pulled the pins from Kate's hair and let the dark-brown locks tumble to her shoulders. "It's damp," she complained with the first stroke of her brush.

Kate reached up and felt it. "Sorry, I tried to towel it off the best I could last night after I bathed and washed it." She'd spent the evening alone, as she had the previous two evenings. Lavender had insisted. She'd said the groom shouldn't see his bride for three full days before they were to be wed—it made the moment he'd see her walk down the aisle all the more special.

"Darn winter weather." Lavender resumed brushing. "I've never known a girl besides you who wanted a December wedding." She glanced at Sunny. "Throw another log in that stove. Let's see if we can get this hair dried out so this girl don't freeze when she walks down the aisle."

"Kate's unique." Sunny gave Kate's shoulder a squeeze. "That's why we all love her."

"Thank you." Kate felt her face blush and could see the pink rise in her cheeks. In her mind, she gladly added Sunny to the mental picture she'd formed of those attending her ceremony, thrilled to see the growth of its small gathering of guests.

In her mind, Kate relived the days since she'd come to Craig as Lavender curled and pinned her hair into place and Sunny highlighted her lips and cheeks with a touch of rouge. Some might deem her situation as a whirlwind romance. Others might criticize her for not waiting until spring and the completion of the chapel. True, when she'd been engaged to Darwin she'd never considered anything less than a big, June wedding, though he had wanted a quiet affair at the Long Island Social Club building. Her life had changed dramatically over the last five months. She wanted what Lucas wanted. And she knew Lucas felt the same way toward her. What a wonderful feeling, to be as one.

With her hair all pinned neatly into place, Lavender and Sunny helped Kate into her dress.

"Now twirl and let us see our handiwork." Lavender motioned for Kate to spin around.

Sunny laid a hand to her cheek. "My, what a beautiful bride. Our Lucas McCurdy won't know what hit him when he sees you walking down that aisle."

Lavender sat Kate back down on the pink chair. "You sit tight now until you're fetched. Me and Sunny got some last-minute preparations to tend to, and we don't want you comin' down until it's time."

Minutes later, the scraping of table legs and chairs across the wooden floor below set Kate's curiosity to churn. What were they doing down there? Myriad voices soon took the place of moving furniture. Then the sound of a piano filtered through the door and the floorboards. The tune was unmistakably that of Mendelssohn's "Wedding March," but with a tinny, burlesque flair—and slightly off-key.

A timid knock rapped at the door. Kate opened it. Dressed in her Sunday best and holding two bouquets of holly and pine, Mary's oldest daughter, Bethany, stared up at her. *Bless her heart—has Mary brought her entire family?*

"They sent me to fetch you, Miss Kate." The young girl handed Kate the largest bouquet and bid her to follow.

Kate fell in sync with the Tucker girl, taking each step in rhythm to the music. As she descended, Kate noticed every chair and barstool had been taken from the saloon. The round tables of the restaurant now filled the portion of the room farthest from the restaurant. A quick glance at the piano player revealed Sunny plinking away at the keys with a smile on her face. Blocking her view into the restaurant, Sam Decker stood with back erect and elbow extended. *He's playing the role of my father, and Bethany Tucker my flower girl.*

Kate smiled and looped her arm through his. *Lavender's thought of everything.* She realized that thought had been an understatement as she, Bethany, and Mr. Decker turned the corner and emerged into the restaurant portion of the building.

On both sides of the aisle, formed by every chair of the restaurant and saloon, plus more, sat a wealth of cheerful-faced people dressed in their Sunday best. Seeing Rosie in an aisle seat, wearing a skirt, though her cowboy boots poked out beneath its hem, brought a lump to Kate's throat. The lump grew as she recognized more and more of the wedding guests. In the back row, Doc Greene removed his hat as she passed by, his white mustache appearing as if it had been combed for once. Ronald Smith sat next to him, wearing an expensive suite and a gracious smile. Young Mr. Hoy and his family sat in front of them. And then the two sisters whose babies she'd soon deliver. On the other side of the aisle, Susannah gazed at Kate with joy brimming as she reached across her pa and Logan to grab Kate's hand for a quick squeeze. She spotted Gus from the livery stable; John Mills, the stagecoach driver; Hazel Watson, the retiring midwife. And the mayor, the undertaker, and the gunsmith and their wives, whom she hardly knew. The new marshal sat amongst them—she surmised as much from the gold star on his coat. She wondered why he was here. Then she looked down the aisle to the man with the broad shoulders in a crisp black suit standing in front of the new pastor, and she knew.

Lucas! The man who warmed the heart of all he met.

Almost all. Stanley Jones was nowhere to be seen.

Lucas jerked when he caught sight of her. His eyes widened and spoke volumes. Kate had never felt so beautiful in all her life—his gaze communicated so clearly his thoughts. His eyes moistened, and hers did too. Everything felt so beautiful—it was more than she could have hoped for. And it could have never happened without the help of all these people.

In that moment, she knew her old notion that strength meant standing alone had been wrong. Strength came from standing together, united with the people she loved. She could write to her mother now. No qualms. No fear of being pulled back to New York. This was her home. These were her friends. She belonged here.

Everyone else in the room faded into a haze. It was only her and Lucas now. A few more steps and she would be there, standing beside him, basking in the ardor she could feel emanating from her-soon-to-be husband, her love. The man who viewed her not just as an equal, but more.

EPILOGUE

Ten Months Later

KATE STOOD ON THE WOODEN sidewalk in front of the town hall, awaiting the stagecoach, feeling the urge to pace. Instead, she adjusted the blankets to protect baby Lucas from the October cold and shuffled closer to his papa. Kate hoped her new son's stepsister could grow to love him as much as she and Lucas already did. It seemed like ages ago that she'd arrived in Craig on the stagecoach. Yet at times, it felt like it had been just days ago that she'd been a bundle of suppressed nerves, having left everything behind and journeyed west to start a new life. Little Celeste had to be feeling some of those same anxieties right now. Most likely more—the poor child was not quite even six years old. It would be hard enough for a little girl to lose her mother. But added to that pain was having to travel far away from her grandmother to live with a father she hadn't seen in years and, hardest of all, having to adjust to a new mother.

Kate swallowed hard, struggling to admit that the biggest fear she had for Celeste was more accurately her own fear. Would Celeste accept her? Would Kate be able to handle her? Or would their personalities be at odds? She'd heard all sorts of horrible stories about stepchildren and stepparents never connecting. Add to that that Lucas hadn't seen his daughter since she was toddler. She'd barely started to talk when Tempest had taken her away from Craig—though "Papa" had been her favorite word. Standing next to Lucas, his arm tightly wrapped around Kate and their baby, she could sense his anxiety too.

Lucas pulled out his watch and looked at it for the umpteenth time. "Stage must be running a tad late."

"No, there it is!" Relieved, Kate's heart raced as she spotted the stagecoach coming over the hill in the distance. The battle to get Celeste's grandmother to relinquish custody to Lucas had gone on for nearly a year now. Lucas couldn't have taken much more delay.

Kicking up a cloud of dust in its wake, the stagecoach barreled toward town. The horses slowed down by the time they reached the first house on the east end of town. Minutes later, John Mills pulled the stagecoach to a stop in front of the town hall. Kate took a deep breath and stepped forward to meet the passengers.

A youngish man in an expensive suit stepped out before Mr. Mills could put the wooden box in place that served as a step. He reached back inside, grabbed the hand of a handsome woman in a well-tailored traveling suit, and helped her climb down.

"Mr. and Mrs. Cleon Johnson, I presume?" Kate asked. Only children remained in the coach. She and Lucas had indeed been fortunate to discover the manager of Craig's new bank had a daughter who lived in Boston and that this daughter had plans to bring her child on an "adventure" to visit her grandparents in the Wild West. Mrs. Johnson had willingly accepted the role of traveling companion for Celeste. The woman had said that she saw it as a blessing for her six-year-old daughter. The long trip would be much easier for the girl to have a playmate.

Kate hoped her mother could find such a suitable companion for her journey to Craig next month to see her new grandson. The thought of her mother riding in a stagecoach brought a smile to her lips.

"Yes, we are the Johnsons," responded the woman. She accepted Kate's hand and shook it. "And you must be Mr. and Mrs. McCurdy."

"That we are." Lucas shook both Mr. and Mrs. Johnson's hands. "I hope me daughter was not too big a handful."

"Not at all." Mrs. Johnson motioned for the children to climb out of the coach. "I must admit, she's quite a precocious child." She pinched her lips into a straight line as a little girl with golden-red curls hopped onto the box and then onto the ground. Behind her, a girl with long dark braids eased her way out of the coach. "But nonetheless delightful in her own way. She not only kept our Sarah company, but she kept my husband and I in stitches." She ruffled the hair of the girl with the golden curls, only to have her hand batted away.

"I am not a poodle," the girl said clearly and succinctly.

Kate knew in an instant this was her stepdaughter.

"Aye, that's me daughter all right." Lucas stepped forward. Bending down he gave her a hug. "You'll never know, lass, how long I have waited for this moment." He let go and backed off, indicating with an outstretched hand for Kate to greet the girl.

Kate handed Lucas the baby and crouched down to bring her face even with the child's. "You must be Celeste. And I'm—"

"I already know who you are." Celeste looked at Lucas with a smug smile. "You're my father." And then to Kate. "You're Kate. My new mother."

Lucas nodded. "Then ye should call her Mother, not Kate. That is not right."

"But it is right. You just agreed her name was Kate." Celeste puckered her lips and closed them tight.

"He meant that's not proper," Kate said.

"I don't want to call you Mother." Celeste's eyebrows wrinkled.

Kate's fear was becoming real: the fear she'd had for the past month, ever since she and Lucas had received word from the grandmother that her health was not up to coming out West, Celeste was getting to be too much to handle, and she was finally willing to send her to her father. "But I want you to be my daughter," Kate said, her heart and words heavy with sincerity.

Celeste's eyebrows relaxed, but her face took on a serious look. "Mother sounds too stuffy. I'll call you Ma."

"Ma would be wonderful." Kate cautiously gathered Celeste into a quick hug. Celeste didn't reciprocate, but neither did she wiggle free. That gave Kate hope.

After a quick travelogue and several more exchanges of gratitude, Kate and Lucas waved their goodbyes to the Johnsons, climbed aboard their wagon, and headed west, out of town. Celeste sat between Kate and Lucas, her little legs bundled in a blanket to ward off the brisk October breeze. She had insisted that Kate wrap her doll in a blanket too.

Celeste looked up at Kate, her arms clenched tightly around her bundle. "See, I can take good care of my baby too."

"Yes, you can," Kate agreed.

"My baby doesn't cry and hurt my ears like your baby does." Celeste spoke like a bragging housewife.

"That is true." Kate peered into the bundle of blankets that held Little Lucas. He'd just eaten and was happy now. His eyes no longer held the blurry dark-blue look of a newborn, but with light-blue irises, he gazed at Kate with his own form of a smile. "Did you know that my baby is also your baby brother?"

Celeste's green eyes opened wide. "Really?"

Kate nodded. "Really."

"I always told my other mommy that I wanted a baby brother or sister. She said I couldn't have one." Celeste ducked her head. "She said lots of mean things."

"Really now?" Lucas joined their conversation with a note of concern in his voice. "What kinds of mean things?"

Kate held out her hand toward Lucas. "Let her open up when she's ready."

"You are right." Lucas patted Celeste's bundled doll. "Well, now ye and yer baby have the best little brother in the world. And who knows?" he said with a wink to Kate. "Next year ye might have a wee sister too. Do ye think ye could handle that?"

"Yes!" Celeste smiled the biggest smile Kate had seen yet. She leaned toward Kate and peered into the blankets at Little Lucas. "He's cute when he's not crying."

"A sharp little lass, ye are," Lucas responded.

Celeste looked up at Kate. "I can help you take care of my baby brother."

"I would like that," Kate said.

"I know how to shush my baby and I can teach you."

"Oh, really?" Kate had a hard time holding back the urge to laugh.

"I'm really glad I came out here to the Wild West now. I can see my baby brother needs me." Celeste tipped her head up and caught Lucas's gaze. "And so do you, Pa." She turned and stared at Kate. "You're gonna need me too, Kate—I mean, Ma."

Kate wanted to scoop that little girl into her arms and hug her tight. She settled for a pat on Celeste's leg. According to the grandma, Celeste didn't like physical affection. Kate would have to ease into that slowly—but she was determined that hugs would come sooner rather than later. "You are correct. And I look forward to your help," she said.

Kate also looked forward to getting to know her new daughter better. The little girl wiggling next to her on the wagon's bench reminded her of another girl who came to Craig, Colorado, about a year and a half ago. Though twenty years apart in age, they both came equipped with strong wills and big hopes. And Kate was going to do everything in her power to see that this little girl found the same happiness she had found.

LAVENDER'S CINNAMON ROLLS

Modern, easier version of her recipe

3 cups warm water
½ cup honey
½ cup vegetable oil or melted shortening
2 teaspoons salt
1 tablespoon + 1 teaspoon of instant yeast
1 tablespoon dough conditioner
¼ cup vital wheat gluten
8–9 cups of whole-wheat flour (Freshly ground white wheat is best. If you don't have access to white wheat, you can substitute half of the wheat flour with white flour.)

Place all ingredients into a bread mixer and knead on medium speed for 8 minutes. Initially add only 8 cups of flour and gradually add the remaining cup as needed. Stop the bread maker from time to time during the first two minutes of kneading to make sure the dough is not too sticky. If it sticks to your fingers when you pull them away, add more flour.

Roll the kneaded bread out onto a flat, greased surface, forming a rectangle. Spread with the following ingredients:

6 tablespoons of softened butter
¾ cup brown sugar
3 tablespoons cinnamon
1 ½ cups chopped walnuts

Form the dough into a log, rolling up the wide direction of the rectangle to make a long, skinny log rather than a short, fat one. Cut the dough into 36 even slices using a piece of string or unflavored dental floss. Place in a greased baking dish and let rise for one hour, or until double the original size. Bake at 350 degrees for 30 to 40 minutes, until the edges barely begin to turn brown.

When the rolls have cooled, spread with sour cream frosting.

Sour Cream Frosting

    ¾ cup soft butter
    ¾ cup sour cream
    6 cups powdered sugar
    1 tablespoon pure vanilla extract
    ⅛–¼ teaspoon salt (to taste)

Mix together until smooth.

Makes 3 dozen cinnamon rolls. You may choose to divide the dough into thirds and make 1 dozen rolls and two loaves of bread, or 2 dozen rolls and 1 loaf of bread. Divide the butter, sugar, cinnamon, nuts, and frosting accordingly.

For Lavender's old-fashioned version, make the following changes:

In place of instant yeast, put the water and honey in the bowl first, add regular yeast, and let it become frothy before adding the next five ingredients. In place of the tablespoon of dough conditioner, use a tablespoon of powdered whey. In place of the vital wheat gluten, omit 4 cups of the wheat flour. Add 4 cups of white flour and mix with a beater or whisk until smooth. Then slowly add the remaining 4 to 5 cups of the wheat flour until workable. Knead by hand for 8 minutes on a flat surface. Let the dough rest and rise until almost double. Roll out and finish according to the recipe above.